Printed in the United States

Library of Congress Catalog Number: 2012938932
ISBN: 978-0-9848694-2-8

Published by:
Mystic Hippo Media Publishing
P.O. Box 350
Cottleville, MO 63338-0350
(636) 922-3593

Email: lois@mystichippo.com
Web: http://www.mystichippo.com

Cover designed by Kimberly Killion of Hot Damn Designs

1900OLD-LADYs
The Lost Art of Making Lefse

"Life is too short as it is,
without me having to complicate
it with a lot of extra bullshit."

– Marge Severtsen-Carter

L. Lee Starr

This book is dedicated to the two most colorful sisters-in-law that any lucky woman could have—Sheryl and Jean. You are the true inspiration behind my heroines.

Thank you, Sheryl, for allowing me to steal your idea for this novel. Thank you also for having the foresight to pen Grandma Olive Severtsen-Prettyman's lefse recipe "before her brain went kaput." I cherish the times you, I, and Joe communed together in your tiny kitchen to preserve this family tradition.

Thank you, Jean, for helping me research the many details of this novel for authentication. I love you two with all my heart. Please don't sue me!

I would also like to thank the eight Canadian night crawlers who unknowingly sacrificed themselves for accuracy in the writing of this book: Jackson, Paul, Vincent, Marc, Pablo, Henri, Georges, Georgia, and Claude. Know this: You have not died in vain.

Chapter 1

"De secret to great lefse is dat you have to use de right potatoes—Idaho White Russet. Not'ing else will do. Begin with no less den a ten pound bag. A family dis size will polish off what ten pounds of potatoes yields in four days, tops."
SIGRID SEVERTSEN

Ellie Peters wrapped herself tightly in her favorite pastel pink handmade sweater, before venturing outside to her mailbox. It was the second week of October. The weather had been unusually warm the previous week, but now the North Dakota winds had picked up substantially over the past few days. As she walked the quarter mile driveway down to check her rural mailbox, the early evening air chilled her. She had always been thin, frail, and somewhat intolerant of the cold. Her teeth chattered as she flipped opened her mailbox.

She checked the mail every day. As a matter of fact, she was probably more faithful at checking the mail than the postman was at delivering it. For many years, she had trekked through relentless blizzards, blinding dust storms, and hot summers in order to discover a rare and long-awaited bit of correspondence from a loved one abroad. Usually, she would only find bills. But today, she gasped in excitement to discover a letter from her daughter-in-law, Rosa Peters, who lived with her only son and new grandchild in Tucson, Arizona. She raised her outdated reading glasses to her nose, which had been suspended from a chain about her neck. She needed to get a better look at the letter.

The envelope was addressed to Ellen Severtsen-Peters. She opened the envelope and grinned broadly. Enclosed was a picture of her son, Stanley Peters Junior, her daughter-in-law, Rosa, and their new arrival—Ellie's grandson—Little Robert. The child was barely three days old in the photograph. He was dressed in blue and was clearly not very happy. His small knitted cap covered most of his tiny head. Squinty little eyes peered out from beneath the rim, and his complexion was still blotchy and very red. Nonetheless, Ellie decided that he was the most beautiful grandchild ever born anywhere. His parents displayed him proudly from behind, obviously beaming with pride.

"Land sake's! Isn't he just the most precious thing?" She whispered this to herself as she caressed the photograph. Then she turned it over to read the inscription on the back, written in her daughter-in-law's hand. *October 5, 1992. Missing you. Wish you could be here. Love, Stanley, Rosa, and Little Robert.*

Ellie gazed at the photograph in her hand for several minutes and wiped a small tear of regret from the outer edge of her right eye. Then she sniffled, gathered up the rest of the bills, scrunched up the opening of her unbuttoned sweater, and crouched to shield herself from the dust while she walked the long walk back to her dilapidated farmhouse.

It seemed the walk *back* from the mailbox was always a bit longer than the walk *to* the mailbox. Her heart always seemed a bit heavier as she ventured back toward the house. Perhaps the anticipation of not knowing what lay in the box motivated her to walk a little faster. Usually, when she discovered only bills or some sad correspondence regarding a recently deceased family member, the burden of bad news seemed to weigh her down on the trip back, always making the trip seem longer.

In reality, the news of her new grandson was not bad news at all for Ellie. But she suddenly remembered how she desperately missed her son Stanley Junior and his wife. She only met Rosa once, when they came to the farm to visit two years ago. But Ellie found her be a sweet match for her beloved son. If it were not for having to care for Ellie's husband Stanley Senior, she might have considered abandoning the farm and moving to Tucson with them. She had never left the state of North Dakota during her lifetime, but maybe she would in a few years, she thought, *if Stanley ever passes away.*

Stanley Peters Senior was Ellie's husband. He was twenty-one years older than she was. Next month, they would celebrate their twenty-seventh wedding anniversary. Not that they would do anything special for it. Last year, Stanley celebrated by himself at the local bar, where he had run up a tab during his career as the town drunk. But Ellie spent the evening at home, sewing an anniversary quilt. She was an accomplished knitter, sewer of quilts, ex-schoolteacher, and maker of lefse.

As a young woman, Ellie had been commissioned by her Norwegian grandmother to preserve the family tradition of baking lefse, a popular Norwegian flatbread made from potatoes. The practice of making lefse was fast becoming a lost art, even in North Dakota, a state inhabited by numerous citizens of Norwegian ancestry. In addition, the making of lefse was also very time consuming. Most housewives nowadays simply didn't have the time to make it, if they even possessed the expertise. But many residents in Ellie's home town of Himmel still enjoyed partaking of the delicious flatbread. Some, like Ellie, would spread home churned butter on the bread, which somewhat resembled a Scandinavian tortilla. Other more affluent consumers would coat the bread with sugar, honey, or jam for sweetening. For those who had grown up in these predominantly Norwegian North Dakota communities and homes, lefse was still a satisfying comfort food.

As Ellen returned to the old farmhouse, she opened the storm door to enter. *This door is just about to fall off its hinge*, she noted again. She had begged her husband to repair the door on several occasions. Of course, he always ignored her repeated requests to perform any household task. Stanley Peters had never been handy at anything.

She carefully opened and closed the door behind her and made her way to the ice box. She pulled out a stack of lefse she had rolled into wax paper and stored in a plastic bag. It was suppertime, but she wasn't very hungry.

Ellie was not usually very hungry. She was very small and frail in stature and almost anorexic. She was a very plain looking, typical North Dakota woman. She had medium-length, blonde hair, which had grayed substantially since her son left home nine years ago and which she usually wore tied back into a plain, schoolmarm bun. She was only fifty-four, but she looked at least ten years older. Her Scandinavian family heritage was evident in most of her facial features, which were not very remarkable. She had a broad nose, blue eyes, and a pointed but slightly dimpled chin—a feature she had inherited from her Grandmother Severtsen. Perhaps she might have been more remarkable if she had worn makeup, but she hadn't really worn makeup since before she married Stanley.

Ellie warmed up a can of soup on the gas stove as she unrolled a few slices of flatbread and placed them on a plate. Then she smeared some fresh butter on them and carefully rolled them back up into small cigars. She poured the hot soup in a bowl, placed the bowl on the plate, stuck a large soup spoon on top of the lefse, and walked into the living room to deliver the meal to her husband.

Stanley Peters was dozing and snoring on his favorite arm chair, which was badly worn and taped at the seams with a mass of duct tape. He had worn a butt print into the seat, so it sagged comfortably on one side, where he tended to lean. Of course, it wasn't comfortable for others to sit there, and no one who knew Stanley would have the audacity to try to sit in his beloved chair if he was ever present in the room. But for the most part, he and Ellie never entertained guests. First, Stanley didn't have any friends. Secondly, Ellie was much too embarrassed to invite people over to see how cluttered their house had become. Most evenings, Ellie sat next to Stanley in the wing chair beside him, knitting or hand-stitching something as he lazed around watching TV.

They had one television with a twelve-inch screen in their very small living room. With their tower aerial antenna attached to the house, they could still only receive two U.S. stations and one Canadian one. But it was sufficiently large enough for the two of them to enjoy watching the tube in this small room. Regardless of what was on, Stanley usually kept the tube blaring non-stop as he ate, slept, or heckled the news commentator from his favorite armchair.

Stanley was a tall man, who was grossly overweight due to years of physical inactivity. He was now seventy-five years old and mostly bald. He had blue eyes and a very stern and almost evil look about him. His brow was broad, but his bushy eyebrows seemed to sweep up at the outer edges. For the last 40 years, he sported a long, mangled-looking mustache, which added an even more villainous appearance to his already demonic eyebrows. He had been injured in his right leg and buttock on D-Day, after he was drafted during World War II. Most of the shrapnel still lay embedded in his badly deformed leg, so he had limped with the aid of a cane ever since. Ellie theorized that he might have suffered from lead poisoning due to the still imbedded shrapnel. This was because he often seemed irrational and violent. But Stanley's older son Robert (a son by his first marriage) assured Ellie that Stanley had been insane and hateful his entire life.

Ellie gently moved Stanley's cane, which sat next to his easy chair. She quietly nudged him awake to give him the plate of soup and lefse she had prepared. He took the plate from her and placed it on his lap. He picked up the soup spoon and slurped some of the soup from the bowl.

Enraged, he spit out the soup.

"Shit, woman! This soup is fuckin' cold!" He picked up a rolled-up lefse and threw it against the wall. "And what the hell is this—shoe leather? You know I hate this shit!" He picked up the plate of soup from his lap and tossed the entire contents against the wall to the right of the television set, which sat only five feet in front of him. "You're trying to poison me again, woman?"

Ellie cringed.

"Give me my cane!" he ordered.

She handed Stanley his walking cane, which was one of his many prized possessions—an antique English walking stick carved of red chestnut with an ornate sterling silver cobra handle. Ellie reluctantly handed the cane to Stanley as he angrily used it to propel himself off his recliner. In reality, she was a little afraid that he might strike her with it.

As he rose, he pushed her out of his way, in the direction of the soupy mess he had created. She knelt down to pick up the plate which had shattered against the wall, now in shards on the floor.

"That's right. Clean this shit up!" He walked past her into the kitchen, grumbling, "I'm going out for a drink." He opened the front door and turned back to her, still kneeling down, retrieving the pieces of plate and the discarded lefse. "And don't touch any of my stuff, or I'll fuckin' kill you, bitch!"

Stanley Peters Senior left angrily through the kitchen door, but not without slamming and loosening the front storm door almost completely from its upper hinge. As he hobbled with his cane to make his way to the barn, he cursed an endless stream of obscenities and insults directed at his poor, frail wife. He marched to his dilapidated barn doors, unlocking the combination padlock blocking public access. He pulled open the massive doors, and made his way to a worn work bench. Under the work bench was a small heap of straw. He pushed away the straw to reveal a tin Folgers coffee can hidden under the straw. From there, he pulled out a thick roll of twenty dollar bills, which was secured tightly with a sticky rubber band. He removed five bills, replaced the remaining rolled bills back into the can, and hid the can back in the straw. Then he closed and locked the barn door and hobbled to his red Chevy pickup truck. Still cursing, he slammed the door and drove off.

Ellen mopped up the soup he had angrily tossed against the wall, which now had dripped onto the floor. She rose, as she looked out the living room window to witness her furious husband drive off.

After twenty-seven years, Ellen was accustomed to her husband's outbursts. Despite the abuse he had piled on her and her young son over the course of the last twenty-seven years, she now almost seemed unmoved by his histrionics. She never lost her temper, and she never cursed at him. And she would never permit herself or anyone in her presence to utter the obvious truth about her husband's character.

That truth was this: **Stanley Peters Senior was a mean, despicable son of a bitch, who hadn't one redeeming quality about him and who truly deserved to die.**

Ellen turned from the window to study the mess surrounding her in the living room. In her head, she recalled Stanley's parting words: *"And don't touch any of my stuff, or I'll fuckin' kill you, bitch!"*

She surveyed the living room around her: the duct taped recliner, the television set with piles of old *TV Guides* stacked on top, stacks of *National Enquirer* magazine piled on the floor dating several years back, empty pistachio nut shells that he had dropped next to his chair, and collections of useless tools, knick knacks, and memorabilia which remained stacked in heaps for Stanley to look at and admire but never actually touch or fondle.

Stanley had collected and hoarded possessions he acquired over the course of the last twenty-seven years, which had now consumed the entire living room. Ellie was somewhat of a neat freak herself. But throughout the years, she allowed herself to eventually become buried under the mire that was Stanley's life.

At first, the clutter was confined to the barn. But then after about ten years of marriage, the collections of old car skeletons spread throughout the front yard. Five years later, the smaller items made their way to the house, simply taking over all their available living space. *Yes, Stanley is a chronic hoarder*, Ellie thought. *There's no bones about that.*

Not only was Stanley a hoarder, but he was also the laziest person who had ever lived. Ever since he was wounded during World War II, he managed to discover ways to earn a living doing virtually nothing. When Ellie was younger, she supported him with her modest school teacher's salary. Later, he was paid by the government not to farm, while he collected her even more modest pension checks. This worked out well for him, because ever since Ellie first knew him, he was nothing but a lazy drunk. Aside from achieving an almost continual state of inebriation over the course of the last twenty-seven years, he had not accomplished or completed one single task he had ever set out to do.

He was, however, in charge of the family's finances, and he used the household income to fund his bar tab. The few times when he was sober, he took his wad of cash and attended local auctions. There he acquired more stuff and simply stored as much of it as he could out in the barn. He never shared any of this wealth with Ellie. Resentfully, she considered the pair of underwear she was now wearing, which was currently being held together at the seams by two safety pins. *I can't even get him to give me five dollars for a new pair of panties,* she thought to herself.

Stanley collected a lot of tools—tools that he would never, ever use. This was mostly because he was just too lazy to *do* anything with them. He considered them an investment—like the antique gun collection on the far wall, which he kept in a locked gun rack. He often recounted to the interested men of the town how much his collection was worth and what items were included. He constantly bragged that, as long as he was alive, he would never sell them. One would need to "pry the guns from his cold, dead hands" in order to get them. In addition, he often threatened to shoot Ellie and others with one of these guns, particularly if they had somehow managed to piss him off. Needless to say, these threats occurred quite regularly—mostly because Stanley had a hot temper and a helluva lot of enemies.

Once Ellie had cleared away the soupy mess and the broken plate, she decided that she was a little hungry. She ate two lefse and a can of kippers she had discovered in the kitchen cupboard. She then sat down in her wing chair while she watched an episode of *Seinfeld*. She picked up her knitting basket and needles and continued knitting a sweater that she was making for her oldest sister, Marge.

The yarn she had selected for Margie's sweater was hot pink. Margie was six years older than Ellie, but they spent a great deal of time together as children, in spite of their six year age difference. Both Ellie and Margie loved pink, but aside from the fact they had the same parents and grew up in the same home, their similarities ended there. The two had completely polar personalities. And even though they both loved pink, Ellie was fond of a particular shade of muted pastel pink. Margie was more of a hot pink personality.

It was quite ironic that Ellie had decided to knit Margie a sweater. That was because, ever since Margie was nineteen, she had moved away from North Dakota to live in warmer climates with her husband, John Carter. For the last thirty years, they had lived in Homestead, Florida in a very roomy four bedroom home. That was until Hurricane Andrew swept through their neighborhood last summer and destroyed everything in its wake, including their pretty home and their entire subdivision. At least Ellie *thought* the home was pretty in pictures. She had never actually *been* there.

Now Margie was living in a trailer park in Wauchula, Florida, waiting for her home in South Florida to be rebuilt. It was about a four-hour drive north of South Florida, but Ellie wasn't sure it was ever cold enough for a sweater. *Oh well*, Ellen decided. *It's the thought that counts. Besides, she only cares that it's pink. Margie loves anything pink.*

So, deserted by her family and with nothing better to do, Ellen Severtsen-Peters spent the entire evening in her dilapidated, crowded North Dakota farmhouse alone— knitting a hot pink sweater for her sister in Florida, watching a rerun of *Seinfeld*, and waiting for her husband Stanley to eventually stumble home—drunk, as usual.

Chapter 2

> "You start by scrubbing de potatoes in de sink wit' a brush and clean water. Get all dat dirt and manure off dem before you t'row dem in de stock pot. Den, you fill de pot wit' water and boil. Keep an eye on dem, and don't let de ones on de bottom burn. And don't peel dem before. You just boil de dickens out of dem until dey are good and soft." SIGRID SEVERTSEN

Stanley Peters drove his rusty Chevrolet pickup truck to The Trading Post Bar and Grill, hobbling through the front door and up to the bar. He let out one long grunt as he sat down on his favorite barstool.

Doris Baker, a slightly plump but attractive Native American woman in her mid-thirties, stood behind the bar wiping dish spots off some highball glasses with a rag, before suspending them from a rack above the bar. She peered out of the corner of her eye to see Stanley perched on his seat, but she refused to acknowledge him with a greeting. She took off one of her freshly wiped mugs and squirted some Miller draft beer into the mug. She then shuffled the beer down to William Knutson who was seated four stools down from Stanley at the other end of the bar.

"Thank ya, Doris. Yer an angel," William complimented.

Doris smiled at William. Then she looked back at Stanley, sneered, and turned her back to him.

William Knutson was the Himmel Postmaster. He had held that position for the past twenty-six years. He was a former classmate of Ellen's and had grown up and lived in the town of Himmel all his life. He began working for the U.S. Post Office part-time during high school and continued on with them as a full-time postal deliveryman ever since he and Ellie graduated. After ten years of service as a rural carrier, he was promoted to Postmaster, but he still continued to make rural deliveries to the present day. The town was small, and so too was the post office. Currently, it only took two people to run the entire postal operations and delivery for the town.

William, like Stanley, was a regular fixture at The Trading Post. But unlike Stanley, everyone in town *liked* William. Like most of the town's residents, he had descended from Norwegian immigrant farmers who helped establish the town before the turn of the century. He knew everyone in town, not only because he lived there all his life, but because of the nature of his work. He knew about everyone's comings and goings. He was, however, the perfect person to be postmaster, because he was very good at keeping secrets and he didn't meddle in other people's affairs.

He was a tall man with a farmer's build. Like Ellie, he was now fifty-four. What was left of his hair at his temples was still auburn, dotted with spurts of gray. He had transparent blue eyes, and he usually sported a wide grin. He had a friendly face. He often wore coveralls after working at the post office, because they made him feel more comfortable.

Although he was friendly and polite, William Knutson had never married. As far as anyone ever knew, he never had a lady love. Rumor was that he carried with him a spark of unrequited love for some woman in the town, who was already spoken for. But William had also always been very discreet and shy about his feelings. He never confessed to a living soul the true identity of his love interest, and she remained a mystery woman.

Stanley let out another grunt, hoping to gain someone's attention. Disgusted at the realization that he was being ignored, he cried out to Doris, "Hey, bar keep! What's a guy gotta do to get a drink around here?"

Doris glared up at Stanley. "Pay their bar tab. Yours capped out at a hundred dollars."

"Aw, come on. Just one drink," Stanley demanded.

Doris pulled a beer mug off the rack above her head and squirted water into the glass, serving it to Stanley.

Stanley pushed the glass aside. "Fine!" He pulled the five twenties out of his pocket, which he had retrieved from his coffee can stash earlier. He slapped the wad down on the bar and pushed it toward her.

Doris picked up a clean old fashioned glass from behind the bar. Then she grabbed a fifth of Jack Daniels and poured the glass for Stanley, setting the fifth back in front of the bar mirror. She apathetically dropped the glass on the bar with her right hand as she scooped up Stanley's wad of bills with the left.

"Bitch..." Stanley whispered under his breath.

"What's that?" Doris asked, putting her hand to her ear.

"Nothin'," Stanley replied.

Stanley was a hateful person, who was hated by everybody in town, but William Knutson never really carried much of a grudge. He moved one stool over, attempting to make pleasant conversation with his fellow barfly.

"Looks like it's goin' ta get a little nippy again—eh, Stan?"

Stanley grunted again, as he gulped down the entire glass of bourbon. He slammed the glass down on the bar, squinted, and smacked his lips. He motioned for Doris to pour him another.

"It's too damn cold in this place!" he answered.

William laughed. "It's just gettin' cold, Stan. After all, this is Nor' Dakota. Pretty much it's cold all the time, except for two weeks in the summer. What ya goin' ta do?" As William posed his rhetorical question, he held up his beer in toast and then took a swig.

"I need to move outta this shithole," Stanley replied.

Doris poured him another glass of bourbon, which he again swilled down, almost as if he had swigged down the plain glass of water.

"Ya and Miss Ellie goin' ta move?" William inquired.

"I'm thinkin' about movin' in with Stan Junior in Tucson," Stanley commented.

"That should be an adventure fer Miss Ellie. She's never been ote of the state, has she?"

"I'm going alone." Stanley seemed kind of annoyed at William's questions.

Doris took a sudden interest in the conversation and chimed in. "—And leave poor Miss Ellie behind?"

"She can rot here, for all I care!" He swigged down his second glass of bourbon and motioned for another. "That bitch has been trying to poison me ever since I married her. She can fuckin' freeze up here, as far as I'm concerned!"

Doris looked at Stanley as she hesitantly poured him another drink. "I don't know how Miss Ellie has stayed with you all these years. Everybody in town loves her. She was my favorite teacher. Paul's, too."

Doris Baker was a woman of Native American heritage. Her father was primarily of German ancestry, but her mother descended from the Lakota Tribe. She had an older brother, named Frank. Both Doris and Frank were named after Doris Day and Frank Sinatra by her mother, after she had seen the first and only movie she ever saw during her lifetime. That was the 1954 movie *Young at Heart*.

Doris' mother died when she was five from what Doris's father dramatically called a "broken heart". Her father often told Doris that her mother was devastated, when her reservation had been reclaimed in 1948 after the government decided to flood fertile reservation lands in order to build a dam. Ever since the tribes were relocated to New Town, leaving Doris's mother behind, her mother's health began to deteriorate. In retrospect, Doris figured that her mother had probably died of complications from undiagnosed Type II diabetes, a condition from which she now suffered.

Having lost her mother at a very young age, and having to grow up in North Dakota biracial, Doris found it very hard to get along in school. Ellie had taught for many years at Doris's school, a one-room elementary schoolhouse for grades 1-8. Doris felt a special connection with "Miss Ellie", as she and most of the younger townsfolk fondly called her.

□□□□□□□

She recalled one morning, when she took the school bus on the way to the school. She was in the 2nd grade. She always kept to herself, since the other students on the small bus were primarily white. One morning, Erik and John Dickinson decided that they would tease poor Doris. Erik and John were in the third and fourth grades respectively. They were scrawny and had curly red hair and freckles. They started calling Doris names.

"Little fat Doris squaw-shit!" Erik teased.

"Shut-up!" Doris warned. "If you don't shut-up, I'm gonna beat you with my lunch box!"

Seeing that she was clearly upset seemed to encourage the two brothers to provoke her even more. Pretty soon, the two boys were chanting, "Squaw-shit! Squaw-shit!" over and over.

So, an upset Doris grabbed hold of her brand new, prized Mary Poppins metal lunchbox and whacked Erik Dickinson repeatedly on the nose until it bled profusely. With tears streaming from her eyes, she demanded, "You take that back! Take it back!"

Erik screamed in pain, and his older brother John yelled at Doris to stop. But she kept demanding that Erik take his racist comments back as she continued to mercilessly wail him. The combined sounds of childish screams and banging metal forced the bus driver to look back into her rear view mirror in order to survey the situation.

"Okay, okay!" Erik blubbered. "I take it back! Now stop!"

By this time, Edna Krauss, the school bus driver, had stopped the bus to intervene on Erik's behalf. She pushed Doris back into her seat, as Erik sobbed uncontrollably, tending to his bloody nostrils. The rest of the students sat flabbergasted, after witnessing Doris's outburst. Doris, overcome by rage, sat also sobbing in her seat, alone and staring down at her dented and bloodied lunch box.

When the bus arrived at the schoolhouse, a visibly upset Edna confronted Ellie, who waited inside, and related to her the details of the encounter. Erik and John attempted to elicit sympathy from Ellie as they informed her about Doris's violent fit of rage.

Ellie took one look at Erik's bloody and possibly broken nose and commented, "I'm sure ya probably had it all coming ta ya. Now go ta the basin and wash off yer face."

Doris sat outside on the steps of the old one-room schoolhouse, still in tears. Ellie sat down beside her and tried to comfort her.

"I know, hon'. Boys can be cruel sometimes. Don't let them get the best of ya."

Doris looked up at Ellie with tear-filled eyes, as she wiped them.

"Don't ruin those beautiful little eyes by clouding them up with those big alligator tears."

Doris let out a sniffle and a half-hearted smile.

"Ya know, my momma died when I was little, just like yers. And she was part Indian, too. My grandmother never liked her very much because of that. I'm not even sure she liked any of us kids, ya know?"

Ellie stood up. "Wait here, hon'. I've got somethin' I want ta give ya."

She went into the school house and found a book she had hidden in her desk and brought it back out to Doris. The book was entitled, *The Sneetches* by Dr. Seuss. She sat down next to Doris and opened it.

"This is fer you, hon'. It's a funny book abote how foolish people try ta judge you by who you are on the oteside. But really, we are all just the same on the inside. Stupid people don't know any better. The smart ones do." She handed the book to Doris. "Keep it, hon'. Now, let's go inside."

Ellie and Doris rose to their feet, while Ellie examined the dented Mary Poppins lunch box. "Land sakes! Ya sure did a number on that lunch pail, didn't ya?" She walked Doris back into the schoolhouse and put her arm around her shoulder, pulling her closer. "And between you and me," she whispered, "I think ya did a number on poor Erik, too." Ellie chuckled.

Doris chuckled along with her.

"I don't think he's ever goin' ta bother ya again, sweetheart," Ellen assured her.

After that episode, Doris felt that she and Miss Ellie had a special connection. For the next seven years, she strove daily to please her teacher in the classroom. She was an exemplary student—probably the best student Ellie ever had. And Doris's husband, Paul Baker, the town Sheriff, also loved Miss Ellie. He continued to call her "Miss Severtsen", even though she had been married to Stanley for almost twenty-seven years.

Somewhere, buried deep in her bedroom closet, Doris kept two mementos of that day—a dented Mary Poppins lunchbox, and a worn copy of her favorite book by Dr. Seuss entitled, *The Sneetches*.

It was just more than Doris could bear to—once again—be forced to listen to old Stanley Peters sit at the bar and heap more insults on poor Miss Ellie's character. That is why she chose to come to her former teacher's defense. But on this evening, seated at the bar, Stanley seemed particularly unrelenting with his criticisms of his ever-devoted wife.

"I'm telling you," Stanley continued, "That bitch is trying to poison me by giving me that shit shoe leather she's always making!"

"Ya mean, lefse? Everybody loves Miss Ellie's lefse," William commented. "Ya know, Stanley, Ellie's a good woman. Especially ta have ta deal with yer sorry ass all these years. She has always deserved way better than ya, fer sure!"

"Who asked you, you son of a bitch?" Stanley now slurred his words. "I'll bet you've been having wet dreams about that bitch since you were twelve, huh?" Stanley stumbled to his feet and walked over to William Knutson's stool and threatened him, "Why, I oughtta…"

He sloppily took a right hook to William Knutson's jaw. William fell off his stool and started to move backward. By this time, Stanley was so drunk, it was almost as if he was moving in slow motion. As William evaded Stanley's successive drunken punches, Doris picked up the phone to call her husband Paul, who was on duty across the street at the jailhouse.

Her husband answered the phone, and she declared, "He's back!" Then she hung up the phone.

This scuffle continued for a few minutes and consisted mostly of William Knutson maneuvering around Stanley's drunken strikes at the air. Twice, William dodged Stanley's attempt to butt heads with him. He veered to the left, and Stanley collided with the far wall. Then Sheriff Paul Baker stormed his way into The Trading Post to break up the brawl. Stanley aimed one final punch at William, missing him completely and instead knocking the Sheriff's hat off his head. The Sheriff grabbed Stanley by the shoulders, led him out the front door, and pushed him to the ground, face down.

"Ya need to go sleep this off in yer truck!" the Sheriff commanded.

Stanley grunted again. He lifted his head to spit out the dirt in his mouth, as Doris threw his cane out the front door and struck him on the head.

"But it's cold out here," Stanley commented, defeated.

"Ya shoulda thought abote that before ya started suckin' down yer whiskey and lookin' fer a fight, eh?" William Knutson added. "Heck, ya got enough bourbon in ya ta keep ya warm 'til mornin' at least!"

"And don't cha dare try to drive like that—or I'll gladly throw ya in jail! There's not one living soul in this town who'll bail ya ote!" The Sheriff warned. Then the Sheriff, his wife Doris, and William Knutson went back into the bar, slamming the door behind them.

After about twenty minutes of lying with his face in the dirt, Stanley Peters stumbled to his feet, picked up his favorite cane, and walked back to sleep off his inebriation in his red Chevy pickup truck. It was bitterly cold, and Stanley passed out in the driver's seat, shivering and angry.

Although Ellie Peters had retired from teaching over six years ago, she was still an early riser. When she taught school, she rose at 5 A.M. in order to feed breakfast to Stanley Junior and prepare for school. As a child, she rose with her father and grandmother, who kept farmer's hours. She was used to waking an hour or two before sunrise, which, in North Dakota in early October, could be as late as 7:45 A.M.

Now that she was retired, she still woke early and tried to immerse herself in projects. Sometimes she baked, being especially careful not to bang any pots and pans at the risk of waking Stanley from his slumber. The later he woke, the better. He would become especially irate if awakened prematurely.

But this day, Stanley had not yet returned home from his night at the bar. And Ellen decided that she should boil some potatoes to make more lefse for the following day's preparation.

Making lefse could be a two-day process for just one woman. In her grandmother's day, troupes of townswomen went from house to house, making batches of flatbread before moving on to the next home. There they commenced the bread making ritual, communed, and gossiped about their families and townsfolk. They did all this while they mixed, rolled, and baked this Norwegian staple in sufficient batches to sustain a large farm family for a sufficient amount of time. This practice was the North Dakota equivalent to the modern day progressive dinner party.

Now Ellie had no neighbors to help shoulder the household burden and perpetuate the family tradition. Her older sisters had moved away long ago. She baked all by herself most of the time, reflecting and reminiscing while she worked. It was always a grueling day for her. As the years grew on, it became more stressful on her back to have to lean over, continually kneading and rolling. But often, as the long day ended, Ellen would finally permit herself the luxury of savoring the fruits of her labor. She would hold the warm flatbread up to her nostrils and take in the aroma of her day's work. She would then smear a dollop of home-churned butter on her lefse, roll it up, and bite it. She spent the day reminiscing about her Norwegian family history while she engaged in the work of baking. But she was reminded of the satisfaction of having a belly full of starches and being surrounded by the warmth of hearth and home when she ate the bread. This was the joy Ellie derived from making (and consuming) Grandmother's lefse.

She scrubbed the five pound bag of Idaho Russet potatoes in the sink. After rinsing the unpeeled potatoes, she placed each one in a large stock pot, filled it with water, and lifted the pot onto the gas range. She set the stove to boil. She also decided that the trash needed to be taken out, so she patted down and tied up the kitchen trash bag, donned her favorite pink sweater, and ventured outside to add this bag to the accumulating pile of trash scheduled for her weekly incineration.

This time, as Ellie opened the storm door, she completely knocked the upper hinge plate off its jamb. She set her trash bag down on the front porch while she surveyed the damages. She bent down to retrieve two lost screws which had fallen onto the porch.

"Land sakes!" She was unsure of what to do next. Now, it seemed, she had no choice but to attempt a repair on her own.

Ellie recalled Stanley's orders from yesterday, instructing her not to mess with his tools. She decided that she would have to find one of his screwdrivers in order to properly attach the hinge plate back to the door jamb. After all, Stanley wasn't about to fix it. She figured, if she stole one out of the barn quickly and hurried to fix the door, she could replace the tool before Stanley ever noticed it missing.

She picked up the trash bag, walked out to the heap in the backyard, and tossed it on the trash pile to be burned. Then she walked over to the barn, opened the combination padlock, and pulled open the creaking barn doors. She stepped over to Stanley's work bench and opened the drawer to reveal an assortment of screwdrivers—all much too big for the current task. After a lengthy search, she discovered a Phillips-head screwdriver, which was still too large to appropriately fit the screws she held in her hand. But it would have to do.

There was nothing remarkable about this screwdriver—or any of the tools which Stanley had hoarded over the years. This was a standard Phillips-head with a hard, transparent, yellow handle and twelve inch shaft. One could buy this at any hardware store, gas station, or drug store. This one was also definitely more screwdriver than Ellie's job required, but it seemed to be the smallest one that Stanley owned. As she made her way out to the house to repair the storm door, she wondered how on earth Stanley could have fostered such an attachment for a bunch of meaningless tools—such as this screwdriver she now carried in her right hand.

The task of repairing the storm door hinge took five times longer than it needed to, simply because Ellie's choice of tools was inadequate. Several times, she managed to let out a "for heaven's sake" and a "gosh darn". Her grip slipped once, and she cut her left index finger with the screwdriver. She uttered an almost irreverent "my goodness" as she stopped to examine and bleed her wound. That was as far as Ellie's expletives ever went.

But soon the hinge plate was reattached, and she proudly stood back to admire her accomplishment. She fixed the storm door by using the wrong tool for the job and without the help of Stanley. Her father encouraged her to be self-reliant. She smiled and quietly thought to herself, *Father would be so proud!*

Regrettably, it was at that moment that Stanley Peters decided to return home. He drove up to the house to discover his wife, standing on the front porch, holding his prized screwdriver. He didn't notice that she had used it to repair the storm door hinge. It was likely that if he *did* notice, he wouldn't have cared.

He parked his truck and hobbled with his cane up to the front porch step. He was extremely hung over and obviously furious.

"What the fuck, woman? Didn't I just tell you yesterday to leave my tools alone???" He angrily snatched the tool from Ellie's hand. At first, she cowered as he raised his hand, fearing again he might strike her. He pushed his way past her and entered the house, slamming the newly repaired storm door behind him.

Good, she thought to herself, as she examined the door hinge. *That'll do me for another year's worth of abuse.* She again smiled and then quickly followed her husband inside.

Stanley slammed the screwdriver down on the modest kitchen table and sat down at the far end of the dinette. He noticed the stack of bills, which Ellie had brought in the day before.

"Would ya like some breakfast, dear?" Ellie inquired cheerfully.

"Hell no, woman! Just make me some coffee for this hangover," he demanded.

"Certainly, dear."

As Ellen put the kettle on for coffee, Stanley flipped through the bills. He opened a few marked "Past Due" by tearing the short end of the letter, holding the torn end to his face, and blowing it open. Then he reached two fingers in to yank out the bill, unfolded it, and read it.

Ellen observed the manner in which Stanley reviewed the mail. *That was the way Stanley opened every letter and bill he had ever gotten during his lifetime.* Each letter was violently ripped at the side and its contents fiercely extracted like a hunted animal being butchered. *Perhaps it's Stanley's way of "conquering" the mail,* she comically thought to herself. Once he had extricated the notice from its hiding place and read it, he never took the time to put it back in the envelope. He just tossed the bill aside and moved on to the next.

He read the phone bill, while he let out a loud grunt. He frowned as he skipped over a few expected bills. Then he discovered the photograph mailed from his son's wife, which Ellie had removed from the envelope originally addressed to her.

Examining the photograph, Stanley smirked. "Hmm. Kid came out pretty white, in spite of Junior's taco-bending."

Ellie tried to ignore Stanley's bigoted comment. "Isn't he just precious?" she asked.

Stanley turned the photograph over to read Rosa's invitation. *Wish you could be here.* He contemplated the photograph, while his wife prepared the morning coffee. She filled his favorite mug with hot water from the kettle, added a spoonful of Taster's Choice instant coffee granules, and walked over to the fridge to get some fresh, unpasteurized cream. She handed the mug to Stanley.

He continued to study the photo as a he lifted the mug to his mouth for a sip of coffee. His expression soured as he reluctantly gulped down the brew and slammed the mug down on the table.

"What the—Where's the sugar?" he demanded. Stanley always required at least two heaping teaspoons of sugar in his morning coffee.

Ellie took the cup. "Oh, dear. I'm sorry. I must've forgot. I'll fix—"

"—Forget it!" Stanley stood up and grabbed his cane. "What's wrong with you? You're a fucking moron!" Stanley left the room, once again angry. He shuffled past the living room into his first floor bedroom, pounded his cane, and screamed another endless stream of obscenities.

His frail wife stood in the kitchen, still able to hear his curses at the far end of the house. The potatoes boiled over into an uncontrolled foam, which flooded out of the stock pot and dripped onto the stove top. She turned down the heat and followed him to his bedroom.

Stanley pulled out a worn Samsonite suitcase from his closet. He opened and slammed drawers and pulled out piles of clean clothes from his bureau and night stand. He piled clean jeans, underwear, and socks, which Ellie had previously laundered and folded, into a careless heap at the center of his suitcase. He packed as many items as he could manage into the Samsonite.

"Where are ya goin', dear?" Ellie inquired innocently.

"I'm leaving you and this God-forsaken iceberg to go live with my son in Tucson!"

Ellie was shocked. After all, Stanley had threatened to leave for the past eight years, since Stan Junior originally moved to Arizona. But she never actually *believed* that he would really leave. He threatened everyone constantly, but he seldom lived up to those threats. Ellie had just sort of accepted that he was a mean, miserable, hot bag of wind. That was Stanley, and that was what Stanley had always been about. Once he cooled off, he usually forgot his threats—at least temporarily—until the next time somebody pissed him off. She was speechless to discover that this time, Stanley was serious.

For a man who had a difficult time getting around, it really didn't take Stanley Peters long at all to pack. Ellie stood in a stupor, watching him as he threw every bit of clothing he owned into his small Samsonite. He closed the lid and threw himself on top of the suitcase, smashing down its contents until he had secured both latches shut.

Within minutes, and without uttering an additional word to Ellie, Stanley was out the front door. In moments, he had unlocked the barn and retrieved the entire contents of his Folgers coffee can. Stanley was moving so fast that Ellie didn't have enough time to process what was really happening.

He threw his suitcase in the back of his truck and opened the driver's side door. Ellie ran out to meet him. She tried to speak, but the words seemed to stick in the back of her throat.

He turned to her, before jumping in the driver's seat of his truck. "I'm telling you one last time—Don't screw with any of my stuff! I'm coming back after winter is over with a big UHaul, and I'm going to pick up all of my things. If I find you—or anybody else for that matter—has been messing with my things, I will fucking kill you. Don't even think about going out in the barn!" Stanley pointed his index finger harshly at Ellen. "I'm not kidding!"

Stanley slammed the door and sped away.

Ellie stood in the driveway, motionless for about ten minutes. Then she decisively turned to go back inside her dilapidated farmhouse. In the kitchen, her potatoes were now cooked. She turned off the heat, drained the hot water in the sink, and sat down at the kitchen table and waited for them to cool.

While she waited, she sipped Stanley's rejected cup of cold coffee, into which she had failed to add sugar. *Just the way I like it,* she thought. *Fresh cream, no sugar. Could be warmer, but this'll do fine.*

Chapter 3

It had been fourteen days since Stanley Peters left his poor wife Ellen to waste away in their dilapidated North Dakota farmhouse. He left her without warning, penniless, and alone. After he packed his suitcase, he had cleaned out the entire contents of his Folgers coffee tin stash and headed for Tucson, Arizona, with the intention of living there with his son, Stanley Junior.

Ellie was used to doing without. She grew up a farmer's daughter—the fifth child of seven children. Her mother died after giving birth to her twin brothers Lars and Gunnar. She was primarily raised by her father's mother, Grandmother Sigrid Severtsen.

Ellie's oldest siblings, Margot, Morton, Normann, and Inga, were born during the height of the Dust Bowl, at the beginning of the Great Depression in 1931, 1932, 1933, and 1934, respectively. By the time Ellie was born in 1937, the family's fortunes began to reverse. Still, by the time Ellie's mother died in 1941, Good Fortune was measured by the fact that one simply didn't have go to sleep hungry every night.

There were plenty of times, especially after the dust storms of '33, '34, and '35, where even Father considered packing everything up and simply abandoning the family farm. Ellen surmised that her mother's influence had more to do with her father's decision to ride out the bad times. She passed away when Ellen was just four, and Ellie hardly remembered anything about her, but she understood from stories told by her older sister, Margie, that her mother, Marguerite, had descended from French Canadian fur traders. Her mother's mother was a Native American from the Mandan Tribe. Ellie's mother was crafty, highly intelligent, resourceful, and reportedly very hard-headed. It was easy to see how a soft-spoken guy like her father could fall for such a dynamic woman. Ellen concluded that Margie was probably a lot like Mother was.

Ellen's father was pure Norwegian stock, born and raised in North Dakota. Grandfather Severtsen's parents had barely settled here in 1879 from Norway, when he was born. Grandmother Severtsen's family, however, moved to the state much later, a little after the turn of the century. That was after the railroad had begun setting up land offices in parts of Scandinavia and Germany, enticing farmers to emigrate to North Dakota. Grandfather Severtsen spoke English with a typical Midwestern accent. Grandmother Severtsen still had a very distinct Norwegian accent. She was ten years old when she moved to North Dakota with her parents. She met Grandfather Severtsen as a young girl. When they were old enough, they married and started a family of their own.

Later in life, after Grandmother Severtsen had passed on and Stanley Junior was small, Ellie would watch reruns of old movies on television. She loved Ingrid Bergman pictures, because the actress's voice and accent reminded her of times she spent with her grandmother. Sometimes she wouldn't watch the movie at all. She would simply lie back, close her eyes, and imagine her grandmother there in the room with her, talking to her.

Grandmother Severtsen was a smart and practical woman. She was extremely frugal, as was her son and Ellie's father, Anders. Father was a plain man of few words. He worked on the farm, rising often before the sun did and often coming home extremely late, after the sun had set. His philosophy was that one should work hard until one simply collapsed from exhaustion. Then one rested a few short hours, before getting up to do it all over again. Her father never had to say much to get his point across. He was very strict, but Ellie really only recalled a few occasions where Father actually lost his temper. Usually it was always for good reason, and if he chose to administer discipline to one of her misbehaving siblings, they most certainly deserved whatever they had coming.

Neither Father nor Grandmother Severtsen were very emotional people. It was often instilled upon the children that it was essential to keep one's feelings to oneself. But Ellie did recall the night her mother gave birth to the twins and subsequently died. Ellie was four years old, and she recalled watching her father—for the first and only time ever—sitting at the kitchen table with his face in his hands, outwardly weeping for the loss of his wife. Even though Grandmother Severtsen never seemed to grant Ellie's mother one ounce of respect for being—as she called her—"a red-skinned savage", her father always seemed to regard Ellen's mother with genuine respect and love. He was never the same man after Mother died. And, until Father passed away in 1957, he never found another wife to replace the one he had so tragically lost.

Ellen was hungry. She was penniless, cold, and her cupboards were bare. She had to think up something to do to get enough food, wood, and cash for the winter. It was obvious that Stanley wasn't coming back, and she needed to be the woman Grandmother Severtsen had trained her be. She needed to be resourceful.

Ellie dug through her kitchen drawer to find the latest number she had for her sister Margie in Wauchula, Florida. Then she dialed Margie's number on her rotary wall phone.

Margie's husband, John Carter, answered the ringing line. At that moment he happened to be standing next to the cordless handset, which was plugged into the kitchen wall socket of their small trailer house.

"Well hello, Ellie dear!" John greeted. "How the heck are you, honey?" John Carter was always fond of his sister-in-law. "Sure, doll. I'll get her for you." He placed his hand over the receiver and handed the phone to his wife. He mouthed the words "your sister". Margie smiled and spoke into the handset.

"Hello, dahlink. What's up?" she inquired.

Ellen recounted the events of the past few weeks to Margie in detail, informing her that Stanley had left her to move to Tucson.

"That friggin' dickhead! Well, dear, it's for the best. I've always told you, you should've dumped his sorry ass a long time ago. You're much better off. If only his son Robert hadn't died in 'Nam. I've always thought that you two would've made the perfect couple."

Margie Carter was never one to mince words. She always told it like it was. In addition, she was always uninhibited about sex or most anything that would have embarrassed ordinary people. She talked boldly, candidly, and as frequently as she could about anything sexual in nature. If someone stated anything with mixed messages, she always interpreted its meaning in the filthiest way possible.

As a young girl, she was a tomboy. Unlike her sisters and most girls her age, she chose to wear boy's overalls. Of course, she had to wear dresses to school. But she took any other opportunity outside of the schoolroom to wear pants, which were less restrictive than dresses. She loved to get dirty, and she wasn't squeamish about anything unpleasant.

The name Margie was actually a nickname for Margot. But nobody called her that, unless her grandmother, father, or sister Inga were angry at her. Otherwise, she was simply known to friends and family as Marge or Margie. Marge, like her two oldest brothers—Morton and Normann—was slightly darker in complexion than the four youngest children—Inga, Ellen, Lars and Gunnar. The older children favored their mother Marguerite. Margie's face had strong Aryan features and mysterious green eyes, but her complexion was darker, and her natural hair color was a medium ash brown. Her Native American and French heritage was evident in her looks, as well as the looks of her brothers Morton and Normann.

Because Margie, Morton, and Normann had significantly darker complexions and coloring than their younger brothers and sisters, Grandmother Severtsen often told the children and family that the three oldest children were not fathered by Anders Severtsen. Instead, she accused "the French whore" (Sigrid's nickname for her daughter-in-law) of philandering with other not-so-white men of the town. She believed that

Anders married Marguerite to "make a respectable woman out of her", because she was pregnant with Margie when they wed. But she was adamant throughout her lifetime that Margie and her two oldest brothers were not Ander's children. The youngest four children, who all possessed perfect Scandinavian features, were clearly worthy of their father's name.

Although Sigrid Severtsen told the children quite boldly that they were or were not fathered by Anders (depending on which child they were), she never repeated her suspicions to Anders himself. The truth was that, although Margie, Morton, and Normann didn't favor their father as much as they resembled their mother, they were just as much his as the younger siblings were. But Grandmother Severtsen's failure to recognize Margie, Morton, and Normann as true Severtsen descendants did not sit well with any of the children and caused a great deal of deep-seated resentment and prejudice among them.

□□□□□□□

One day in the summer of 1947, shortly after the twins Lars and Gunnar had turned six, the two approached Margie and Morton, who sat reclining on a stump, sucking the nectar out of some white clover. Margie and Morton were sixteen and fifteen respectively. Inga, who was thirteen, and Ellen, who was ten, also sat with them. Often, the children didn't have much time to just sit and loiter, because they were usually performing chores on the farm. Normann was out in the field assisting Father.

Lars sneered at Margie. "Grandmother Sigrid says yer not Dad's kids."

Margie, who had been leaning back on her elbows, leaned forward to spit out of a piece of straw upon which she had been gnawing. Then she grabbed Lars and drew his pale little face toward hers, holding his chin about two inches from her own.

"What did ya say?" She lifted her brow in a threatening manner, while speaking to her youngest brother.

"Grandmother says you and Morton and Normann aren't white. She says yer not our dad's!" Gunnar repeated, standing behind his twin brother, unafraid.

Margie knew that Grandmother Severtsen didn't regard the three oldest children as belonging to her son. And she knew that her twin brothers were simply repeating what they had heard their grandmother tell them their entire lives. But she wasn't going to let the little imps get away with smearing her mother's good name, simply because her grandmother was a racist.

Margie motioned at Morton and pointed to Gunnar. "Grab his feet. Let's go." With one fell swoop, Margie jumped to her feet, reached over, and grabbed Lars by the ankles, flipping him upside-down. Morton did the same with Gunnar. The two oldest siblings walked the twins the fifty steps to the dual-holed outhouse, located behind the barn.

"It looks like some little snobs need to be taught a lesson!" Margie cried.

By this time, each of the twins yelled, "Put us down, Margie!"

Inga and Ellie followed behind. Margie opened the latrine door and entered, suspending Lars upside down above one of the two holes of the privy. Morton did the same with Gunnar at the other hole. All the while, the twins screamed hysterically. The blood rushed to their heads, and their faces were now bright red—partly also because they were mad and crying.

Ellie and Inga watched the entire episode. Ellie begged her oldest sister sympathetically, "Don't Margie! Please…"

Inga, who was the family tattletale, warned, "I'm going ta tell Grandmother!"

"Go right ahead, ya little snitch! I'll get *you* later," Margie threatened.

Inga ran off to search for Sigrid.

The twins continued to scream, as Margie and Morton kept them suspended upside-down above the holes of the latrine. Ellie held her nose and tried not to sniff in the unpleasant odor of human excrement which pervaded the air.

Margie calmly instructed the screaming twins. "I'll let ya down, if ya say the magic words. Now what do ya say?"

Lars hesitated. Margie dropped him five inches closer to the latrine hole opening, before stopping herself. "Feel like takin' a swim? Now what do ya say?"

"I'm sorry!" Lars resigned.

"Me too!" Gunnar also gave in.

Ellie begged Margie once more and tapped her on the arm. With tearful eyes, she pleaded, "Please, Margie. Put them down."

Margie relented. She and Morton released the twins, dropping them carefully on their heads, before they darted away screaming and sobbing. They met up with Grandmother Severtsen on her way out to the shithouse. She was followed by Inga, who had dutifully reported everything that went on. Sigrid confronted Margie and Morton, who still stood standing in front of the privy.

"What is happening in der? What is going on?" Sigrid inquired of her granddaughter. She hugged the twins, who were still sobbing. Inga devilishly peered out from behind her grandmother's apron.

Margie brushed herself off and exchanged a look of collusion with her oldest brother and fellow cohort in crime. Then she gazed at her grandmother with an impertinent grin and answered, "Nothing, Grandmother. Just a tiny misunderstanding. Everything's fine." Margie then walked back to the house, past her suspicious grandmother, while Morton followed. She plucked off another piece of straw and resumed her gnawing. As she strutted off, she hummed to herself. Ellie, still a little shaken and teary, chased after her big sister.

As Margie grew older, she became aware of her own unique combination of overt sexuality and innate beauty. There was something exotic about her that people couldn't quite place. Mandan tribesmen were significantly lighter in complexion than other native tribes prevalent in North Dakota. But her combination of green eyes, Aryan bone structure and long dark hair, made her striking and unlike her fairer brothers and sisters. She wasn't quite Scandinavian, but she wasn't exactly full-blooded Indian. Early in her life, she was often insulted and hurt by her grandmother's repeated comments regarding her alleged illegitimacy. But as Marge grew older, she learned to laugh off Sigrid's comments for what they were—simple ignorance.

As Margie became a young woman, she realized that she was regarded as one of the most desirable young women in town. She consequently decided that she would use her good looks to her advantage by finding a way out of the state. She first moved to Rapid City, South Dakota and initially got herself a job waiting tables at a local diner. She met her future husband, John, while attending a party at the Ellsworth Air Force Base. After John was deployed to Korea, she joined the USO as a dancer in one of their overseas shows. As fate would have it, she and John met again in Tokyo and quickly married there during one of his R&Rs.

After the war, John continued to serve in the Air Force for four more years. He was stationed in Jacksonville, Florida when Margie gave birth to their first and second sons, Eugene and Joseph. After John's time in the Air Force, the family moved to South Florida where John worked speculating in real estate. Margie had two more daughters, Penny and Caroline. For thirty years they lived in a cozy neighborhood in Homestead. That was until hurricane Andrew swept through South Florida last summer and destroyed their home and almost the entire city of Homestead in its wake.

All Margie's children had since gone on to jobs or college and had moved away. When the hurricane annihilated Margie's home and all its contents, Margie and John decided to take the few possessions that remained and move to Wauchula until the insurance company could rebuild their home. A lot of homes had been destroyed, and it would take years to restore the devastated town.

□□□□□□□

Ellen quizzed Margie on the phone about her life in Wauchula. She lived in a tiny rusted trailer, probably built in the early '70s. The kitchen shelving was avocado green, and the carpeting throughout was a multi-colored orange shag. Each trailer had exactly twelve feet of open space between it and each of the neighboring trailers in the park. And Margie wasn't sure that some of the other park residents weren't all members of one single inbred family. She was still trying to wrap her head around their exact relationship. Ultimately, for people like Margie and John who had grown up in a Plains State with lots of wide open spaces, this "little crampy trailer park of inbred crackers" was almost suffocating. But they managed to keep their spirits up, because they considered their present living situation only a temporary one. And despite everything they had lost, Margie still had John.

"I feel like a friggin' sardine here," Margie confided in Ellie over the phone.

Ellie quizzed her about the progress of the construction of her home in Homestead.

"Well, it seems we owe twice as much on the house as it will be worth when we replace it….It's a long story, but John and I are very pissed about that. We don't know what we're gonna do right now. John's doctor seems to think he needs a stress test and other stuff we really can't afford. He's retired, but he's not eligible for Medicare for another three years, so everything is out of pocket…….No, the hospital here in Wauchula is closed because of that whole baby swapping thing, so we have to drive all the way to Avon Park to see his doctor…..John took our last one hundred thousand dollars in savings and found a guy who was selling offshore investments in the Turks and Caicos, and he sank every last penny into that. So all of our funds are tied up right now."

Margie decided to find out more about Ellie's condition. "Really, honey. How are you doing? Did Stanley take everything with? He didn't even leave you a dime?"

Ellie confirmed that Stanley had left her destitute.

"Oh, honey. I wish I had something to send you. I used the last five hundred dollars on my credit card to buy some 900 numbers that John wanted me to buy....I don't know! It was some motivational home-based business seminar we went to in Tampa. Can you believe he wants me to start a sex chat line to make extra money? He says I have a sexy voice."

She laughed. "I tell you, Ellie—That man is so nuts. He's been into almost every hair-brained scheme ever concocted. He lost his shirt when the Broward Savings and Loan went defunct."

Margie sighed. "Things haven't been good for us financially, either. And in the bedroom—well, let me tell you. I have officially traded in my organ for an accordion. John needs like three months of foreplay before he can get it up anymore!"

John sat listening to Margie's end of the phone conversation. She grinned at her husband while continuing her frank discussion with Ellie. "Yeah, if he wasn't so damned sexy, I would have to leave him for somebody who could perform better in bed!" She leaned over to kiss John, "You know I love you, baby," she whispered to him. Then she snickered.

Ellie was used to Margie's frank discussions about sex, but that still didn't prevent her from blushing on the other end of the landline. Margie almost seemed to enjoy embarrassing her younger sister, who was about as sexually *in*hibited as Margie was *un*inhibited. Actually, Margie seemed to enjoy embarrassing *anyone*—close friend or perfect stranger—with her frank conversations about sex.

"If I were you, honey, I would pawn every last bit of shit that prick of a husband owns, before he comes back. After all, it's your stuff, too! You worked your ass off for twenty-five years as a teacher. Where was he? Sitting on *his* ass, leeching off of you all his life! The only thing he ever managed to do is get his ass shot off in the war and impregnate you with Stanley Junior! Why don't you sell his gun collection? Surely someone in the town is interested in buying that crap. Have an auction or something."

Ellie argued with Margie about the feasibility of selling Stanley's things, especially when he left explicit instructions to leave all his possessions alone. Margie knew that Ellie had no intention of selling Stanley's things, even if it meant that she might starve and freeze over the winter.

"I'm telling you—Ellie, honey—listen to me! Sell his shit! Sell the farm! Do what I did, and move out of that God-forsaken hell hole before he gets back. Look, you can't be afraid of that asshole. Just do it! Come live with us. We have an extra room here, and we'll have the new house built soon. Let me know what I can do, honey.....Listen, Ellie....I gotta go. Hell, this must be costing you a fortune. But I'll call you soon, okay?" In a sing-songy voice, she abruptly terminated the conversation. "Okay—love you. Buh bye." Then she hung up the phone.

John sat down next to his wife at the breakfast counter, which was really just a short partition between the kitchen and the tiny trailer's living room. He had heard enough of Margie's end of the conversation to figure out what went on.

"Stanley left Ellie, eh?"

"Yeah, she should have left him twenty-five years ago. It's hard to read Ellie, but she's probably devastated," Margie answered.

"Ah, he was a bonehead, anyway. She is better off," John agreed.

John moved closer to Margie and whispered into her ear. "They never had what we had, right Margie, baby?" He started to breathe heavily and nuzzle his nose against her neck.

Margie smiled. "Except for the night that they made Stanley Junior, I'm not sure they *ever* had that." Then Margie seemed to pick up on her husband's romantic advances. "Why, Mr. Carter, are you trying to tell me something? Ooooh, you naughty man!"

John Carter grabbed his wife's hand, leading her into the back bedroom of their Wauchula trailer house. "Miss Johann Sebastian, I think your organ is now ready for the concert!"

"Am I playing for the funeral? We're going to bury a stiff!" Margie laughed and pushed her husband into the back bedroom. John let out a couple of good whoops and hollers, before they finally shut the bedroom door.

Chapter 4

> "De skin will break when dey're just right. You drain all de water out, and let dem cool. Den, you peel dem. De skin comes off real easy, and you can peel dem pretty fast. Sometimes you can just rip de skin right off wit' yer bare hands." SIGRID SEVERTSEN

Ellen Severtsen-Peters stood at her kitchen sink and peeled a pot of boiled and cooled potatoes. She had just hung up the phone from a conversation with her sister, who lived in Wauchula, Florida. Ellie had hoped that Margie might have some extra cash to share with her, which might help her make it through the winter. As a last resort, she reluctantly called Margie after her husband had left her destitute over two weeks ago.

Unfortunately, Margie was not in a position to help Ellie with her financial woes. All her cash was tied up in an investment annuity that her husband had purchased. This had depleted their life's savings. Ellie worried about her overdue bills which needed to be paid. Her monthly teacher's pension would not arrive until the first of November.

As Ellie stood at the sink, she peeled potatoes with her bare hands. She considered her relationship with Stanley. They had been married almost twenty-seven years, during which time she and their young son had endured so much abuse, it was harrowing for her to even recount.

Stan Junior resembled Stanley in some ways, but never in attitude or demeanor. Both men had piercing blue eyes and a pointed nose with a narrow bridge. Stanley had a son by his previous marriage, named Robert, who had been killed in Vietnam shortly before he and Ellen married. Several months later, Ellen gave birth to her son. Stanley insisted on naming him Stanley Junior, which Ellie reluctantly agreed to. She resolved to avoid confusion by referring to her husband as Stanley or Stan Senior. She always referred to her young son as Stanley Junior or Stan. When she was asked by a stranger how to keep the two names straight, she would offer up her simple mnemonic. Stanley was a big man. He got the longer version of the name. Stan was an abbreviated version of his father, so he was given the abbreviated version of his father's name.

To Ellie, the simple act of naming a son after his father was not so much a sign of respect as it was a recipe for disaster. If Stanley had not been so insistent upon naming his son after him, she would have chosen any other name. It was always a difficult thing to explain who was who, when referring to either her husband or her son. But the greater difficulty of naming a son after his father lay with a son's early perceptions that he should model after his namesake. If his father was a good man—or if the son idolized his father—he may have inadvertently set the bar too high. A son's goals of emulating his father might be virtually unattainable. Conversely, if a boy's namesake had the reputation of Ellen's husband, Stanley, the poor child might be forever cursed. Such was the plight of Stan Junior.

Stanley's abuse of Ellen was mostly psychological, but he did strike Stan Junior often as young boy. Like Ellie, Junior's demeanor and personality was very reserved and quiet, and he generally learned how to avoid standing in Stanley's crosshairs early on. Although Ellen tried to set a good example for her son by not speaking a cross or unkind word against her husband, Junior soon realized how despicable his father actually was.

Ellen recalled several occasions where Stanley Senior raised his cane against Stanley Junior, if he somehow managed to commit some unforgiveable offense to enrage him. Usually the offense was something inconsequential, which shouldn't have provoked a conscientious and loving father to ire. But Stanley needed very little provocation to set him off. When Ellie's husband disciplined her son, he was unmerciful, and he usually used his cane to aid him in these unwarranted beatings. In private, Ellen would often sob to herself, sympathizing for her young son, who was such a sensitive and caring boy. He was nothing like Stanley Senior. He was a very good boy.

One particular day, when Stanley Junior was about sixteen, Ellen's husband became infuriated about some infraction that her son had allegedly committed. She couldn't remember what he actually did—maybe he disturbed one of Stanley's precious tools. Who knows? Ellen recalled standing at the kitchen window, watching this exchange as her son and husband stood out in the front yard.

At sixteen, Stanley Junior had grown two inches taller than his father. By this time, Stanley Senior had become obese and out-of-shape, and Junior had decided that he had finally endured enough abuse. As Stanley Senior—once again—raised his cane against his son, Stanley Junior stopped him, grabbing the cane from his father. Junior then raised the cane to threaten Stanley Senior.

"I am only going to tell you this once. I have had it with this shit! If you ever—I mean ever—raise this cane to anybody, including Mom, I will lay you out and not think twice about it, old man! Don't you ever—*ever*—strike me again!"

From that point on, Stanley Senior never threatened his son again.

Stanley Junior turned eighteen in 1983. The day after he graduated from high school, he moved out. Ellen was inconsolable. Her only son—her life—was walking out on her. In reality, he wasn't walking out on his mother at all. It was his *father* he was leaving. He couldn't bear to witness any more of the repeated abuses his father had piled onto his poor mother during the course of his short life. He had simply had enough.

"What will I do withote you, son?" Ellie sobbed. "I will be all by myself up here."

"Mom, I know you stayed with Dad for my sake. You need to retire from teaching and leave here. Move out. Dad doesn't need you." He held his mother's sobbing face in his hands and gazed into her tear-filled eyes. "When I get settled, I will send for you. You can come live with me."

He moved to Tucson, where he attended vocational school and studied air conditioning and refrigeration, a very marketable trade for someone sweltering in the Arizona heat. After he graduated in 1986 and found his first job, Stanley

Junior had finally extended his invitation for Ellie to come live with him. Each time she declined, believing that Stanley Senior still needed her. Part of her also believed that she was destined to die on the farm. This was where she was born. This was where she had lived her entire life. This was *her* farm. When Stanley Senior married Ellie in 1965, he received it as a dowry from Ellie, who had inherited the farm from Father. This was originally the Severtsen farm. This farm was in her blood.

Also, Ellen felt that, if she did move to Tucson, she would only prove to be a burden to her son. He had endured so much with Stanley Senior during his childhood. He deserved to start a fresh new life for himself. He needed to raise his own family, pursue happiness, and leave his troubled past behind. Having Ellie around would only serve to remind him of his miserable childhood and having to grow up around his cantankerous father.

After extending countless invitations to his mother to move to Tucson, Stanley Junior finally met and married his wife, a Hispanic woman named Rosa Ramirez. Five years earlier when Ellen had retired, she had seriously considered moving there. But she would definitely feel like an intruder, if she tried to live with her son and his new wife. By that time, Junior stopped nagging Ellie to come live with him. But after Rosa came to visit two years ago, she assumed the responsibility of encouraging Ellen to move in with them.

Rosa's inscription on the back of the photograph was meant for her mother-in-law and *not* for Stanley Senior. Ellen knew that Rosa didn't like Stanley Senior at all and would *never* ask him to come live with her. During the short two days that she and Stan Junior spent at the farm two years ago,

Rosa had soon learned to despise the man. It was almost impossible for her and her hot Latin temper to conceal her utter disdain and repulsion for Stanley Senior. But because she was so in love with her husband, she bit her lip and kept these feelings to herself.

Stanley Senior was oblivious to Rosa's contempt for him. He believed she extended the invitation to come live in Arizona to him as well as to Ellen. Even if he suspected that Rosa despised him—which he didn't suspect at all—he really wouldn't have cared. She was merely a woman, and a woman's opinion should never be regarded as *anything* important.

□□□□□□□

Ellen peeled each potato by pulling back the skin and applying pressure with her thumb and index finger. *Peeling potatoes always work well after you boil them*, she thought to herself. *Grandmother Severtsen was right.*

She considered the predicament in which her husband had left her, and she imagined each potato to be a shrunken Stanley head. She envisioned each eye of the potato as Stanley's eyes, puncturing them with her thumbnail and savagely digging them out. She pretended to peel the skin off his face and imagined herself stripping Stanley of his spiteful grin.

When the potatoes were peeled, Ellen washed them in the sink and started to quarter them. She placed each potato on her cutting board and hacked at them with her knife. They were soft, and they really didn't require much pressure in order to cut. But Ellen found this process somewhat therapeutic. She wasn't really cutting *them*. Essentially, she envisioned herself slashing little Stanley heads. She raised her knife above her head in order to gain a more forceful and violent momentum.

As she chopped the potatoes, she repeated the instructions of her current task in her head. *Peel and quarter. Peel and quarter. I'd like to peel the skin off his miserable face. Quarters—he hasn't left me one dime, much less a miserable quarter!*

Ellie dropped her knife as she suddenly remembered the Susan B. Anthony dollars her husband hoarded. They were still hidden somewhere around the house! Where did he hide them? That's right—under the kitchen floorboards!

Over the course of the last thirteen years, Ellie's husband Stanley had accumulated as many Susan B. Anthony dollars as he could lay his hands on. The dollars were minted primarily in 1979, but they were never very popular. A few were minted in 1980-1981 for collectors, but they were disliked as currency by the average shopkeeper, because they were too easily confused with quarters. The dollar itself was eleven-sided, but its size was significantly smaller than the silver dollars minted previously in the U.S.

Stanley's fascination with collecting the dollars was not in the historic significance of Susan B. Anthony. He hated all women, especially the "women's libbers". What he enjoyed about the Susan B. Anthony dollars was that he could torment local shopkeepers by handing them a quarter-sized coin, which they would be forced to accept as dollar currency. Most cash registers didn't have an extra compartment for the coin, which made accepting it especially problematic. Most vending machines would not accept the currency at all.

When the U.S. Mint discontinued the Susan B. Anthony dollar, Stanley decided to start hoarding any that he could find. He was sure that they would become a collector's item, now that they had been discontinued. Therefore, he surmised that it wouldn't be long before they appreciated in value. As a result, he made periodic trips to the State Bank and asked them to sell him any coins they had available. Al-though he hid the coins in places he didn't think Ellie would discover, the situation was much like his Folgers coffee can stash in the barn. Ellie knew exactly where he kept his cash, but she never let on. Stanley, believing himself to be particularly skillful at concealing things from Ellie, had no clue that she knew exactly where he hid almost everything. But Stanley was not particularly intelligent. In fact, his Intelligence Quotient showed that he was mildly retarded and could have been officially classified twenty years back as a moron. But Stanley was so self-centered and sociopathic, he failed to ever notice that almost everyone around him was far more intelligent than he.

When Ellen recalled the Susan B. Anthony dollars and how stupidly paranoid her husband was, she suddenly remembered the episode in the front yard, when Stanley Senior threatened Stanley Junior. Before hiding his coins under the kitchen floorboards, Stanley hid bags of coins under the floorboard of his rusty pickup truck. Stanley Junior had just learned to drive, and he often took the truck out on errands.

Stanley Senior never maintained any of his vehicles. They were often used, rusty, and dilapidated. She recalled one particular time when the passenger's side door latch of his truck was broken. Rather than repair it, he chose to tie the door shut with a bungee cord. Ellen almost fell out of the moving vehicle, when Stanley Senior took a sharp left turn and the cord snapped loose.

Stanley's failure to maintain his vehicle—or the farm, for that matter—stemmed from the fact that he preferred to spend his money buying liquor. On the rare occasions when he was sober, he attended local auctions in order to acquire more things to hoard. He never spent money to maintain his deteriorating vehicles or anything else the family needed. If his vehicles got him from point A to point B, that was all he really cared about. That was the case with his old Chevy pickup truck, which his son used on occasion.

One day, Stanley Senior accused Stanley Junior of stealing the Susan B. Anthony dollars from a stash he had hidden in the floorboard of his old truck. (Ellen suddenly remembered the cause of their last blowout in the front yard.) That was the day that he threatened to strike his son with his cane the very last time. That was the day that his son threatened him in turn, after which Stanley Senior retreated. *It was all because of those gosh darned dollars*, she thought to herself. *How ridiculous!*

As it turned out, the floorboards of Stanley Senior's beat up old pickup had rusted through due to years of neglect and abuse. The result was that his prized stash had slowly fallen through the hole of the rusty floorboard, one by one, until every last coin had dropped onto the street, driveway, or anywhere else Stanley had travelled. When Stanley Senior had discovered what had actually happened—that his coin collection had simply fallen through the rusty floorboards— he never apologized to his son for his wrongful accusations.

But he *did* relocate his stash to the kitchen floorboards to prevent such an incident from ever recurring.

□□□□□□□

Ellen grabbed the Phillips-head screwdriver which her husband had left sitting on the kitchen table. She was going to find those dollars if she had to peel up every floorboard in the kitchen. She retrieved a heavy meat mallet from the kitchen drawer. Then, board by board, she hammered the screwdriver tip into the wooden seams with the meat mallet until she could pry up the floorboard.

Ellen didn't possess a great deal of upper arm strength, but she mustered up almost a superhuman strength, motivated mostly by hunger and cold. She was going to find those coins, if it killed her. She systematically peeled up each board, hoping to find the bag of coins she knew Stanley had hidden. She ripped up each board and peered underneath. But each time she peeled up a board, she found nothing— except for a few cobwebs, bug carcasses, or dust bunnies.

After prying up about twenty boards, Ellie became discouraged. She dropped her meat mallet and screwdriver. She sat on the floor, discouraged and almost in tears.

Exasperated, she gazed to the right of her foot, just under one of the legs of the small kitchen dinette. There she noticed a board, significantly more worn than the other boards of the floor. And it looked to her like this board had been peeled up and sloppily nailed back in place.

She picked up her makeshift hammer and screwdriver and chiseled at the seam of the board. When she could sufficiently reach her screwdriver underneath the board, she tried to bend it back and peer under it. There, in a well-worn burlap bag, lay Stanley's coin collection.

Ellie reached her bony fingers under the board and grasped for the bag. After some finagling and wiggling, she finally retrieved the bag from beneath its subfloor hiding place. Now ecstatic, she poured the bag's contents out on the kitchen floor and counted each coin.

"Fer heaven's sake!" she cried.

There were exactly 73 Susan B. Anthony dollars in the bag. They would be worth 73 dollars *at least*, and that was enough to buy some groceries—flour, coffee, meat, eggs, and more potatoes. That would get her by for a few weeks anyway, carrying her through October until she received her modest pension check at the beginning of next month. *Yes*, Ellie thought to herself. *That might just be enough. Thank you, Stanley. Thanks for being such an obsessive hoarder!*

The Serene Waters RV and Trailer Park in Wauchula, Florida consisted of about 25 single-wide mobile homes crowded onto a five-acre plot of land. At least the park managers *claimed* it was five acres. The way the homes seemed to be piled on top of one another, Margie and John were really not sure. Each home was uncomfortably close to the next, and one's excruciatingly small yard was never really considered private. It was more of a community yard. It was not uncommon for John and Margie to walk out their front door and trip over some neighbor kid's Big Wheel, tricycle, Barbie doll, or action figure. There would often be discarded beer bottles and cans in the yard, left there by residents who found it more convenient to just drop them there than to drop them in an actual garbage can. Sometimes they would trip over live kids, whose mother was cooped up in her trailer, probably watching *Jerry Springer* and completely oblivious to their child's current whereabouts.

Margie and John Carter were now sixty and sixty-two, respectively. They were officially senior citizens. They could have easily found a cozy trailer in a quiet retirement park. But neither Margie nor John considered themselves old. And the idea of being surrounded by LOLs (little old ladies) and crotchety old men, who had nothing better to do than to stick their wrinkled noses into their neighbor's affairs, cramped their free and easy lifestyle. They were technically old, but they felt young. They still liked to go out for nights on the town, late night drinking, and an ever occasional romp in the bedroom. So instead, they chose to live in Serene Waters.

The ironic thing about the name Serene Waters was that Hardee County was located in the dead center of the state of Florida. It was at least an hour's drive to the Gulf Beaches. In fact, there was no body of water located anywhere in or near the park, except for the occasional puddle left behind by the typical summer afternoon deluge.

Neither was the park Serene. It was typically noisy at all hours of the day and night. The younger residents of the park kept their music (usually Country and Western) blaring loudly at all hours. Nagging wives could often be heard ridiculing their poor hen-pecked husbands. Mothers slapped and spanked their children within earshot of their neighbors without fear of being reported to Child Protective Services. And children could constantly be heard yelling and screaming—even at 3 A.M., long after children with good and respectable parents would have sent their little tykes to bed.

This failure on the part of management to enforce any sort of noise ordinance in the park worked to Margie's advantage. This was mainly due to the fact that, on the rare occasion that she and her husband did have a romp in the boudoir, Margie had a tendency to be very vocal. Her groans, grunts, and screams of ecstasy (as well as a few expletives) could easily be heard throughout the trailer park and several blocks beyond that. Simply stated, when Margie had sex, she was extremely loud.

John had been married to Margie for over forty years and was used to the noise. That was one of the qualities that attracted him to her—her lack of sexual inhibition. That was in addition to her beauty and her very sexy and youthful voice. It was true that Margie had gained a few pounds over the years. But her voice was still as sexy as ever, and John found it stimulating to hear her openly discuss sex. It really turned him on to hear her scream in ecstasy during the act of coitus. Sometimes he would simply beg her to "talk dirty" to him for his own personal amusement, no strings attached.

During the time they spent as a young family, Marge's children learned early on to tune out their mother's heated cries of passion, which usually originated from behind the closed bedroom door. They developed a thick skin. Like their mother, they talked about sex and human sexuality openly. When they were young, Margie and John would have intercourse two or three times a day. As John grew older and his sex drive diminished, their encounters became less frequent. Now that he was a senior citizen and his health was failing, Margie was happy to get it once a month.

But what the neighbors at Serene Waters Trailer Park discovered was that, the less frequently Margie Carter got sex, the louder she got when she finally *did* get it. Often, following one of Margie and John's now rare encounters in the bedroom of their cramped trailer house, a few embarrassed parents living in the park would be required to prematurely educate their curious child about the specifics of the "birds and the bees". Needless to say, if Margie's cries of passion were loud enough to embarrass residents of the Serene Waters RV and Trailer Park, she had to be pretty damn loud.

One particular afternoon, John Carter was feeling unusually amorous after his wife had a brief phone conversation with her sister Ellen in North Dakota. They tiptoed to the bedroom hand in hand, shut the door, and stripped down to their naked bodies. As Margie started to warm up, her groans of pleasure could be heard throughout the park.

"Oh, God! John, honey. Oh, yeah, *do* me. Oh, baby. I'm so hot for you right now. Oooh....Yeah, that's it. Do it to me, you bad man! Ummm, ummm, ohhhhhh!"

As Margie and John engaged in intercourse, the headboard of the bed was rhythmically knocked against the paneling of the bedroom wall, causing the entire trailer to shake. As the knocking and shaking of the trailer became more and more frequent, so too did Margie's simultaneously timed "Oooohs" and "Ohhhs". She let out one final and resounding scream, as the noise and the shaking ground to a halt.

Margie's cries of pleasure were followed by a long silence and subsequent cries of terror. Her husband had suffered a heart attack during their episode of heated lovemaking.

In a panic, she called 911. She was scantily clothed when the EMTs finally arrived at her trailer. They pushed their way past concerned neighbors, and she let them in. John lay on the gurney. He was still conscious but sweating profusely and short of breath. He grasped his left arm and chest in excruciating pain. The EMTs strapped oxygen around his face, while he tried to tell Margie he wanted her to put some pants on him before they carted him outside. As the EMTs lifted John's gurney into the back of the ambulance, Margie, dressed only in a sexy silk robe and a black lace teddy, jumped in the back with him. The ambulance driver closed the doors. Terrified, Margie held her husband's hand as she scolded him. "Don't you dare die on me, John Carter! Or I will hunt you down in hell, you son-of-a-bitch!"

Chapter 5

"Back in de day, we didn't have ice boxes. But now, you just quarter dem (the potatoes), cover dem very tight, and stick dem in de ice box for de morning." SIGRID SEVERTSEN

Ellen carefully covered her bowl of quartered potatoes with Saran Wrap, and placed them on the top shelf of her old Frigidaire icebox. As she shut the door, the rotary phone hanging on her kitchen wall rang. She answered it. It was her sister Inga, calling from California.

"Hello? Oh, hello, Inga. Why? What has happened?" Ellen's initial look of concern transitioned to shock, when Inga announced the dreadful news. "Oh dear, how awful. Poor Margie has ta be devastated! How tragic! My dear sister. Oh, I feel so terrible! As a matter of fact, I just spoke ta John a couple of days ago on the phone. Oh, my goodness!"

Inga was Ellen's older and Margie's younger sister. She had moved to California with her third husband five years ago. Neither Ellen nor Margie really liked Inga, because she was always an annoying tattletale when they were growing up. In addition, Inga had always claimed that Grandmother Severtsen loved her more than all the other grandchildren combined. She often bragged about being the most loved, the most beautiful, most intelligent, and the best cook in the family. In reality, none of her brothers and sisters liked her, because she was such a tattletale, a braggart, and a bore. A conversation with Inga always turned into a conversation *about* Inga. And, quite frankly, Inga was just not that interesting.

Inga had two failed marriages before her current marriage. She claimed that she dumped her two former husbands because they were intellectually inferior. The rest of the family suspected that Inga was the one who was dumped because she always failed to acknowledge her own shortcomings. All of her brothers and sisters had secretly confided that it was just a matter of time before her current husband grew tired of her and dumped her just as the first two had done.

Inga's childhood career as the family snitch blossomed into her adult career as the family's "Harbinger of Doom". She perceived it as her job to keep in touch with all her brothers and sisters, who were now geographically scattered. She loved to call each of them periodically. Then she nosed her way into their private affairs and counseled them on the correct and proper way to deal with their current life situations.

Even as a young girl, Margie loathed Inga. And Inga resented Margie. Ellie suspected that Inga was simply jealous of Margie's lack of abandon and her fruitful and happy marriage to John. Inga had recounted the details of John Carter's death, blaming Margie's insatiable sexual appetite for his demise.

Inevitably, Inga hadn't the compassion to leave well enough alone. She always preferred to pour salt in her rivals' wounds. Today was no exception. Often, as she performed her duties as (as Margie called her) "The Angel of Death", she related the news about the recently deceased as a judgment. If somebody died, it wasn't because they lived a long and prosperous life. It wasn't because they were just unlucky and their life was tragically cut short. It was because they smoked too many cigarettes, ate too much pork, were too careless, drank too much—or in John's case—didn't have the wherewithal to deny their spouse's insatiable sexual appetite.

Ellie interrupted Inga's diatribe by attempting to focus on poor Margie's loss. "Well, dear. I probably should give her a call. Land sakes, how tragic. John was a such a good husband ta her. And a wonderful father."

Inga tried to steer the conversation to Ellie's current dilemma. Ellie answered honestly, without elaborating too much.

"Ya, dear. Stanley has left. It's been abote two and a half weeks now, and I haven't heard from him."

Ellie became silent, as Inga began talking. This time, Inga decided that she should start passing judgment on her sister Ellie. Ellie should have done more to prevent Stanley from leaving her. Ellie should have done more to be a better mother. Ellie should have stayed home with Stan Junior and never attended college to pursue a career as a teacher all those years.

Ellen sat on the other end of the phone line, patiently listening to Inga armchair quarterback her entire life. Occasionally, she managed to squeeze a "Ya, hon'." into the phone conversation, which Inga essentially monopolized. And, as Ellie started to mentally tune Inga out, she almost forgot Inga's original reason for calling.

Perhaps fortuitously, as Inga blathered on and Ellen snuggled the receiver under her ear daydreaming, the phone line went dead.

"Hello? Inga? Are ya there?" Ellie inquired. "Inga? Hmm....I guess that we were disconnected." She rattled the receiver switch several times and tried to get a dial tone.

Then it occurred to her. Stanley hadn't paid the phone bill, and now the phone had been shut off.

Ellen Severtsen-Peters stood at the checkout counter of Larson's Grocer and Drug, having walked two miles from her farm to town. Her old friend, Agnes Larson, stood behind the register, waiting to check Ellie out. She transferred several items from her basket onto the conveyor belt of the checkout line. After she had piled the few items she wished to purchase in front of Agnes, she pulled Stanley's burlap bag of coins from her shoulder bag and counted out fifteen shiny Susan B. Anthony dollars.

Agnes Larson was about fifty years old, slightly younger than Ellen. They had both lived in the town all their lives, but Ellen was six years ahead of Agnes in school. Ellen and Agnes often participated in church sponsored bake sales and fund raisers. Agnes's son Andrew was in the same grade as Stanley Junior, so the two women were often involved in school sponsored activities together. Also, Ellie taught two of Agnes's older children, Annie and Bob, when they attended school at Himmel Elementary.

When Agnes grew up and married Bill Larson, she raised a family and helped Bill run the family grocery business. It was a very small store, which carried a small stock of cupboard staples—milk, bread, sugar, potatoes, flour, pop in two liter bottles—and some survival items such as kerosene, Band-Aids, etc. Bill actually had a small pharmacy booth located in the back of the store in order to fill local prescriptions. They only kept the standard and most popular necessities in stock. But the Larsons could always order any nonstandard items special and have it ready for pick-up in a week, at most.

Agnes, like Ellie, was a typical North Dakota wife and mother. She had medium-length chestnut hair, which was now streaked with gray. She usually kept it cut in an outward-flipped, layered bob. She had wispy bangs and usually kept the rest of her hair pushed back with a plastic headband. She also didn't wear makeup, but she had deep brown eyes, full lips, and an almost innocent, girlish face, which was always very animated. One needn't have asked what Agnes was thinking. One could pretty much tell by watching the expression on her face.

Agnes had always been a very amiable woman, who knew all her customers and was always genuinely concerned about their happiness and well-being. She always engaged every customer in some bit of small talk before checking them out and moving onto the next patron.

Sheriff Baker stood behind Ellie in line. He held a cup of coffee and a box of homemade kuchen (a German pie-like pastry) in his hand. As Ellie counted out her coins, Agnes frowned and glanced over at the Sheriff.

"Ya know, Ellie. I hate ta take these from ya. Don't cha think they might be worth somethin' someday?" Agnes inquired.

"I haven't got time fer that, Agnes," Ellie replied. "I need flour now."

Agnes once again looked over at Paul. The entire town was aware that Stanley had left Ellie alone and broke. Then she continued. "I feel bad for ya, Ellie. That rat husband of yours just ran off and left ya. Here ya go, hon'. Don't worry abote it. You keep the coins. Anyways, I still owe ya fer that fabulous wedding quilt ya helped me make fer little Annie. Keep it, hon'."

Agnes pushed over a head of lettuce, gallon of milk, a pound of sugar, and five pounds of potatoes. "If ya want, ya can make some lefse ta sell at the store here. Everybody's just crazy fer yer lefse."

Ellie nodded and smiled, "Okee dokee, hon'. It's a deal. I'll bring some by." She grabbed her sack of groceries and started to leave. Then she stopped and turned around again.

"Oh, gosh! I fergot. I wonder if I can get some change for the phone. I need ta call my sister, and the pay phone won't take these derned coins."

"Sure, hon'," Agnes replied.

Ellie counted out five coins. Agnes opened her register and broke a half a roll of quarters she had in her drawer and handed it to Ellie. She picked up her sack and made her way out to the pay phone, located on the front porch. She set her bag down on the porch, reached into her purse for Margie's phone number, and inserted the proper amount of money in order to place the call.

Sheriff Baker had checked out his items, but he monitored Ellie from inside the store window as she called her sister.

"Hello, Margie? Oh my gosh, hon'. I don't know what ta say. Ya, Inga called me, but they shut off my phone. I'm so sorry, dear. Is there anything I can do fer ya?"

Ellen could barely hear what Margie said on other end of the line. She sobbed so uncontrollably, it was hard for Ellie to make out words in between all the snorting and wailing sounds.

"Are ya gettin' by, hon'? What abote money?"

Margie explained that John had sunk their last $100,000 in savings in a life insurance annuity, which should pay out quickly in the event of his death.

"Well, dear, I'm glad fer that. I wish I could do more. I'm sorry I didn't call ya, but it seems they shut off my phone."

Just then, Ellie could hear the recorded message prompting her to put more quarters in the coin depository.

"Oh, dear. Margie, hon', I've run ote 'o time. I got ta go now. Let me know if I can do anything, okay? I love ya, dear."

She hung up the receiver. Then she pulled out Stanley Junior's phone number. She stood at the phone for a minute, trying to decide if she would make the call. Then she decisively inserted another quarter and dialed the operator. Her hands were now so ice cold, she could barely get her fingers to cooperate. As she spoke to the operator, she could see her breath in front of her.

"Hello, Operator? I would like ta make a collect call ta five-two-oh, five-seven-four, oh-four-six-two. Ellen Peters."

Ellen's daughter-in-law, Rosa, answered the phone. She accepted the charges.

"Hi, hon'. It's Mom. Oh, I got Little Robert's picture. Isn't he just the sweetest thing? Oh, ya. I know ya must be proud. Thanks, hon'. Ya, he's the spittin' image of his poppa. What a sweetheart! Listen, hon'. I hate ta call collect, but I've run ote of coins, and they shut off my phone. Is Stan Junior around?"

Ellen waited patiently as Rosa called Stan Junior to the phone. Her teeth chattered as she stood on the porch in her worn winter coat. Stan Junior answered the phone, and Ellie smiled broadly.

"Hi, sweetie. It's Mom. How are ya, Son?...Oh ya, he did, did he? Oh, my—thirteen pounds, ya say? Oh gosh, he's going ta be a big boy like his daddy! Listen, son, I know this is yer dime, so I'll try ta make it short. I just wanted ta know if Aunt Inga called ya ta tell ya abote poor Uncle John...Oh, she did? I know, isn't it just terrible?...Ya, I just talked ta Aunt Margie...Oh my gosh, she is just beside herself. But, luckily Uncle John left her with a life insurance policy...Oh ya, I wish I could go ta the memorial, but cha know how tight money is."

Ellie patiently listened as her son quizzed her about her health and her financial situation.

"Oh dear, I'm fine. Ya needn't worry abote me." Ellen hesitated. Then she inquired, "Listen, Son. How's yer dad doin'?" She bit her lip.

Slowly, as Stan Junior related the details of past week's events, her look of ambivalence transitioned to concern.

"What d'ya mean, ya don't know where he is?" Ellie raised her brow. "Oh, gosh..."

And while Ellen remained silent, Stanley Junior retold the story of his father's short visit to his son's home.

When Stanley Senior decided to live with his son in Tucson, he announced this decision to everyone—everyone, that is, except Stanley Junior and his family. Senior had packed his small bag of clothes, took his roll of money, and headed off for Tucson two and a half weeks previous. He drove the entire 1,500 mile trip, stopping at rest stops along the highway to sleep. The engine of his battered red Chevy pickup truck sputtered as he wound up the Black Hills, through Wyoming, and south to Denver. His radiator overheated three times. So, what was normally a trip which took 26 hours to drive ended up taking Stanley Senior almost an entire week.

When he arrived at his son's home, he arrived on a Saturday morning. He knocked on the door, and his son answered it.

"Hey there, old man!" Stanley Senior greeted him with a half-man hug and a pat on the back. He smiled sheepishly and teased, "I'll bet you're surprised to see me here!"

Stan Junior was taken completely off-guard. Even more shocked was his wife, Rosa, who had come to despise Stan Senior. But Junior invited Stan Senior in—like the good son Ellie had trained him to be—and permitted his father to stay. He convinced his wife that it would only be temporary, until his father could find a place of his own. Junior also stipulated to his father that he expected him to treat his new wife and son with respect—no cursing, no drinking, and no abusive language. As long as Senior agreed to abide by these rules, he would be allowed to stay.

For the first few days, Stan Senior seemed to be a changed man and a charming guest in the household. But one morning at the breakfast table, Rosa grew short when Stan Senior ordered her to make him a cup of coffee. She had stayed up most of the previous night with Little Robert, and she was exhausted. She also struggled with a severe case of postpartum blues. Needless to say, Stan Senior let some of his old behavior slip out, as he jokingly criticized Stan Junior's failure to "whip his wife into shape". According to Senior, Rosa was too impertinent, and she needed to learn to keep her opinions to herself and do as she was told.

Surprisingly, Rosa didn't lose her cool—at least not in front of Stanley Junior. She left the room and went upstairs to take a long-deserved nap. Stanley Junior instructed his father to tread lightly and departed for work.

Rosa woke from her nap about mid-morning to the sounds of Stanley Senior screaming at the television set. When she went downstairs to see what all the ruckus was about, she discovered a drunken Stanley Senior, reclining in the easy chair in front of the tube. There was an empty fifth of Jack Daniels tipped over on the floor.

This was just too much for Rosa. In addition to the fact that her hormones had been raging, she had tolerated the company of this uninvited guest for her husband's sake. Despite the fact that Stanley Senior had been on his best behavior in recent days, she knew all too well what kind of a man he really was. She had heard her husband retell countless times all the miserable details of his unhappy childhood. She was determined not to let her young family suffer any further abuse from this despicable man. Because he had, once again, made the choice to put liquor to his lips, he had pushed poor Rosa to the brink.

"You're drunk, you slob!" She kicked him in the shin, and he turned to her, surprised.

"Yeah, I've had a little whiskey," he acknowledged.

"A *little*?" She picked up the empty bottle. "This is a *little*?"

Stanley Senior nodded his head, defiantly. "So what, you Mexican cunt! What're *you* gonna do about it?"

With that, an enraged Rosa Ramirez-Peters, picked up Stanley Senior's cane and used the tip to repeatedly poke him in his oversized gut.

"Get up, you fat, lazy drunk! I want you out of this house *now*!" She continued to poke Stanley in the stomach, until he stood up out of the easy chair.

"Watch it, you bitch! You can't kick me out!"

"Like *hell*, I can't. Just watch me! I want you out of here before my husband gets back! I'm tired of your bullshit, you *hijo de tu chingada madre*! Now get out of my house!" Rosa continued to poke Stanley Senior in the rear end, scooting him out the front door while she cursed at him in Spanish. Finally, he opened the front door, and she placed her foot on his bottom to push him out. Then she threw his cane out on the front step.

"And don't ever come back! *Mierda*!" She cried. Then she slammed the door.

The drunken Stanley Senior mumbled obscenities at his disenchanted hostess as he stumbled to his truck. Screeching the tires, he sped off, swerving recklessly along the Arizona city streets, until he was stopped by a police car. He was arrested for drunk driving, drunk and disorderly, and of course—resisting arrest. His truck was impounded, and he spent the night in jail. Stan Junior bailed him out the next day.

When the Arizona Highway Patrol finally released Stanley Senior, his son met him in the front lobby of the jailhouse with his packed suitcase and what remained of his roll of twenty-dollar bills.

"You can't come back, Dad. Rosa doesn't want you around, and neither do I. I don't want you around my son."

Now sober, Stanley Senior feigned a bit of remorse and humility. "But Son, you're not just going to desert me. I have no place to stay and no truck." He looked almost pathetic, as he tried to appeal to his son's sympathies.

"At least you have money. That's more than you left Mom." Stan Junior turned to exit the jailhouse. Then he looked back at his father. "Have a nice life, Dad." Then Stan Junior walked out, leaving his father standing in the jailhouse. With nowhere to go and no means of transportation, Stanley dejectedly stood, holding his wad of rolled-up bills, his antique cane, and his small Samsonite suitcase.

As Stanley Junior related the details of what transpired the previous week, he explained to his mother that he had bailed his father out of jail five days ago. He had no idea where Stanley Senior went, and he hadn't heard from him since. He theorized that his father could possibly have taken a bus back to North Dakota. It wasn't likely that he had bought or rented a car, since his driver's license had been revoked. But driving with a suspended license had never prevented Stanley Senior from driving before. And he had even been known to drive drunk with a suspended license more than once.

Ellie's look of concerned had finally graduated to one of absolute horror, as she listened to the details of Stanley Senior's disastrous attempts to reunite with his son.

But the real truth was not that she was horrified about Stanley Senior's unsuccessful attempts to settle in with his son's family. What terrified Ellen the most was the idea that Stan Senior *might be coming back home.*

Almost paralyzed with fear, Ellen slowly managed to hang up the phone receiver. Sheriff Baker stood several feet behind her on the cold porch, quietly sipping his coffee and snacking on his kuchen. He tried not to eavesdrop on her phone conversation. But as Ellie hung up the phone, Paul couldn't help but hear Stanley Junior's voice on the other end asking, "Mom, are you there? Mom?"

Ellen stood for a moment, in a daze and shivering. Sheriff Baker inadvertently startled her, as he approached her from behind and tapped her on the shoulder.

"Is everything okay, Miss Severtsen?" he asked.

Her heart jumped. "Oh, my gosh, Paul! You startled me! Oh ya, hon' Everything is fine." Still flustered, she bent down to pick up her bag of groceries.

"Aw, Miss Severtsen. Don't tell me yer goin' ta walk those groceries the two miles to yer house, now, are ya?" Paul looked concerned.

"Oh, I'll be fine, hon'."

"Naw, now I insist on giving ya a ride. Why don't cha come with me?" Paul took Ellie's bag of groceries and put his arm out to invite Ellie to take it.

"Land sakes, Paul. You always were a kind boy." Ellen gratefully took the Sheriff's arm as they descended the porch steps to his patrol car.

"Are ya kiddin', Miss Severtsen? Doris would never forgive me, if I let ya freeze ote here in this cold." He smiled.

□□□□□□□

Paul Baker had been the Himmel County Sheriff for the last eight years, having begun his career in law enforcement shortly after he graduated from high school. He joined the Police Academy, subsequently serving as a local law enforcement officer. During his career, he became acquainted with and trusted by everyone in town and practically everyone else in the other neighboring towns of the county. He won the Sheriff's seat in a landslide election in 1986, when he ran for office. His record was spotless, and his character was so squeaky clean, it was almost as if he ran for office completely unopposed.

Paul was always a nice looking young man. He was now thirty-six years old, but he looked much younger. He kept his dark brown hair cut short in a youthful but conservative cut. Perhaps his apparent youthfulness lay in the fact that he smiled most of the time. He had a pleasing face and broad smile and chin, but his green eyes also seemed to smile warmly, curving down at the edges to add a friendlier warmth to his already pleasant demeanor. People always felt at ease with the Sheriff. It was this genuine smile which seemed to allay the doubts and fears of those dwelling in his county. And this smile, when combined with his unimpeachable character and good manners, helped win him votes for office time and again. Almost every woman voter who knew him—married or single—secretly had a crush on him. And every male voter trusted him.

Paul Baker was a couple of years older than his wife, Doris. He had always been sincere and sensitive, and he sympathized with Doris's plight of having to grow up half-Indian in a mostly white school. Paul found Doris intriguing, beautiful, intelligent, and a better conversationalist than some of his other female classmates. He and Doris were inseparable during recess and lunch. They sat together and simply talked about life. When plenty of other girls of more traditional family backgrounds expressed a romantic interest in him,

Paul gently but politely declined their advances. Instead, he chose to pursue a romantic relationship with Doris during the latter part of elementary school and then officially during high school. Doris was Paul's childhood sweetheart and the only love of his life.

Paul and Doris had two boys, who were now a Freshman and a Sophomore in high school. Ellen often asked about the boys. As they rode the two miles in his squad car back to her farm, she asked about them again.

"Oh, Mike and Johnny are doing great. They're on the football team and doing well in school." Paul was obviously proud. He reminded Ellen of his own father, who often beamed when Ellen discussed Paul's stellar performance in her classroom.

"I figure Stanley left ya withote a car? Doris and I have missed ya in church. Our bake sales aren't the same withote ya there." Paul glanced at Ellen with his charming smile. "Just let me know if ya need a ride, Miss Severtsen. Doris and I will pick ya up anytime."

"Ya were always such a good boy, Paul. Thanks, hon'."

Sheriff Baker pulled his patrol car up to the front entrance of Ellen's farmhouse and shut off his car engine. "No, Miss Severtsen. Allow me." He opened his door, wound around the front of the patrol car, and opened the car door for Ellen, grabbing her bag of groceries.

"Oh, thanks Paul, hon'. I'm fine, now. Go on home." Ellen patted his shoulder, taking the bag of groceries back from him.

"I mean it, Miss Severtsen. Just give us a call."

"Okee dokee, Paul hon'. Thanks again."

Chapter 6

Ellen Severtsen-Peters stood at the end of her driveway on November 2nd, waiting for William Knutson to bring the Monday afternoon mail. She was cuddled in her worn winter coat and boots and stood on one-half inch of newly fallen snow.

One could actually set one's watch by how punctually William delivered the mail each day—2:15 P.M., give or take ten minutes. Ellen didn't have to wait long before William drove up in his mail delivery shuttle. Normally, Ellie wouldn't have waited at the mailbox to get her daily mail. But she was anxious to get her teacher's pension check today.

As William pulled up to the mailbox, he noticed Ellen standing next to it, waiting. "Nice ta see ya here, Miss Ellie. Expecting some good news?" he inquired innocently.

Ellen smiled at her old classmate, while he handed her a stack of letters. She shuffled through the stack with her mittens on. After she read the return address on the final letter, her faced dropped. "Oh, dear," she lamented. Then she turned her back as she disappointedly sauntered the quarter mile driveway back to her farmhouse.

Ellen said nothing to William as she turned to leave. He felt pity for Ellie tugging at his bosom. Then he shook his head, as if to clear his mind of this sudden feeling of sadness, and drove on to the next mailbox in his scheduled route.

When Ellen returned to her farmhouse, she stoked the small fire in her potbellied stove, located in the corner of the living room. She removed her coat and mittens and warmed her hands at the stove. She rubbed them together as she stood thinking.

"I could really have used that check taday," she whispered to herself, sadly. She thought about how frustrated she had become, having been left alone. She had been in such a hopeful mood, waiting at the mailbox for her monthly check, only to be let down once more.

Ellen's mind turned to her sister Margie. As the thought of being alone during the coming winter chilled her, she imagined her poor brother-in-law's body, naked and cold in some morgue, awaiting embalming. Her heart went out to her poor sister, Margie. John was her life. During their forty years of marriage, he made her so happy. What would she do without him? How could she survive? Ellen ached for her sister and her enormous loss. *If only I had the money, I would go down to Florida to be with my sister during this terrible time.*

Thinking about Margie, Ellen suddenly felt herself becoming entrenched in her own self-pity. She surveyed the living room as she struggled to control her emotions. She noted the room filled with stacked piles of Stanley's junk. She considered her estranged husband and his inevitable return. What would she say to him? He had robbed her of her youth and happiness, taken her for granted, and left her for dead. She had wasted so much of her life with Stanley. Ellen had never been happy living with him. Unlike her older sister Margie, who actually *grieved* over the loss of *her* spouse, Ellen grieved that *her* spouse might eventually *come back*.

Ellen fought back her growing urge to cry by deciding that she wasn't going to allow herself to become embittered about the lost years of her life. She wasn't going to allow Stanley to get the best of her. And, as she studied the piles of unwanted garbage that had consumed every bit of living space, she resolved to convert her rage and resentment into nervous energy. She would clean.

She walked to the kitchen and retrieved a box of trash bags under the kitchen sink, which she kept next to the old box of rat poison. She filled the bags with every item strewn on the floor. She discarded the pistachio nut shells, knick knacks, pictures, dirty socks, and several pairs of Stanley's shoes—all trash. As she filled each trash bag to capacity, she tied the bag up and carried them out behind the house to toss on the burn pile. Soon the pile grew into a burn *heap*. Then a burn *mountain*.

She dragged all Stanley's other items—like piles of *National Enquirer* magazines, out to the barn. Next went the *TV Guides*—into a trash bag, out to the barn. The old books he never read and their accompanying bookshelves—out to the barn. If the larger items were too large for her to manage, she dragged them inch by inch out to the barn, leaving a snow trail which lead from the front porch steps of the house all the way out to the barn door. When she got out to the barn, she spent ten or twenty minutes making various clanking and banging noises. Then she walked back toward the house to find another of Stanley's large possessions to drag back.

She decided that she would store his duct-taped easy chair out in the barn. She only made it halfway around the house, holding it by the back and dragging its rear feet through the snow, atop the frozen and hardened earth. Exhausted, she gave up and left it in the snow, exposed to the winter elements. The mildew-infested monstrosity still blotted the landscape, but at least it no longer disgraced her living room. As long as she didn't leave the house, she wouldn't have to see it and be reminded of Stanley.

As Ellen relocated each of Stanley's belongings to the trash pile or the barn, a tremendous sense of self-satisfaction filled her. She had quietly reclaimed every inch of the living room of her family farmhouse.

Next, she moved every one of Stanley's possessions out of his first floor bedroom, located off the living room. She opened his closet door. She grabbed every last winter coat, boot, hat, glove, and scarf, and threw everything out into the snow in the front yard. She scattered a pile of Stanley's discarded clothing, which stretched from the front of the porch, past the worn easy chair, and ended just at the open barn doors. Everything that ever belonged to Stanley was disposed of—except for the framed canvas portrait of Stanley's first son, Robert, which sat on the bureau at the foot of his bed.

Ellen picked up the portrait of Robert Peters, which had been carefully hand painted on a small slip of canvas. He was in his Army uniform and had posed for the picture before his service in Vietnam. As she studied Robert's portrait she held it in her hands and reminisced. She collapsed and sat on the edge of Stanley's bed.

□□□□□□

When Ellen graduated from high school in 1955, all her older siblings had moved away. Margie had married John, Morton and Normann had both joined the military, and Inga had married her first husband and moved to Wyoming. Ellen stayed at home with Grandmother Sigrid to care for the twins, Lars and Gunnar, who were now fourteen. In reality, the boys were self-sufficient and didn't require much care. They were almost as tall as Father and were considerably stronger than he was. They spent most of their extra time helping him on the farm, when they weren't in school.

Initially, Ellen wasn't permitted to go to college. Grandmother Sigrid felt it would be better to keep Ellen at home, so that she could perform necessary domestic tasks. Sigrid spent a great deal of time teaching Ellie how to cook, sew, clean, and perform these various household chores. She handed down her recipe for lefse, taught Ellen how to sew quilts, and even showed her how to knit. Many of Grandmother's daily household chores were menial, and she had performed them willingly for many years without assistance. But Ellen was older, and all those tasks seemed to be less of a burden to Sigrid when Ellen was working with her. Ellen was now a young woman. And her grandmother, who never had a daughter of her own, relished Ellie's companionship.

Two years after Ellie graduated from high school, Father hired Robert Peters to work on the farm. He was a young man three years younger than Ellen, who had recently moved to the town with his mother to live with his mother's parents. Robert's parents had lived in Texas and were recently divorced.

Ellen recalled meeting Robert for the first time. Anders had mentioned that he had "hired a man" for the summer—a young boy who had moved to the town of Himmel. Sigrid sent Ellen out to the field to bring her father and the twins some water. Robert stood there with her brothers. The summer heat that day was blisteringly hot, and Robert wore overalls with no shirt underneath. His huge pectoral muscles were clearly visible beneath the straps of his outfit. His broad shoulders gleamed with sweat and were well-tanned from working long days in the North Dakota sun. It was hard to believe that Robert was only fifteen at the time. Ellen was eighteen.

Father was somewhat klutzy in social situations and was often preoccupied with his work in the field. He failed to introduce his youngest daughter to his new employee, so Robert politely introduced himself. Struck by his masculine physique, dark tan, and attractive features, Ellen began shaking. She dipped the drinking ladle into her water-filled stock pot.

She passed the water-filled ladle to Robert and invited him to sip. He acknowledged her gift with a nod. She watched him. As he kept his eyes fixed on her, he drank, and Ellen was hypnotized by his brilliant blue eyes. When Robert had sipped enough water, he gingerly handed the ladle back to Ellen and thanked her. She turned to leave and was suddenly aware that, not only had she had held her breath during their entire meeting, but her heart was pounding forcefully.

Ellen was immediately taken in by Robert's soft spoken nature and good looks. His temperament was much like Father's was. He was a man of few words. Yet in private, he was surprisingly articulate. He and Ellen spent many hours at night on the farm, watching the stars and talking. She talked about life growing up on the farm, about her sisters and brothers who had moved away, about the loss of her mother, and about growing up with Sigrid. Robert confided in her the specifics of his life in Texas, his hateful and abusive father, and his mother's choice to pack everything up and move back to North Dakota to live with her parents.

Robert and Ellen both loved to read books and poetry. At night, they sat on the porch as he read to her. He enjoyed reading aloud. Ellen found something very comforting in the sound of his voice. She watched how animated his face became as he grew increasingly engrossed in the story. His transparent, blue eyes twinkled as he read. His broad jaw, blonde hair, and massive shoulders exuded strength, without him ever feeling the need to prove his masculinity to anyone. He read whatever classic novel he could lay his hands on, stories from the Old Testament, and even excerpts from the *Sears Catalogue*. Ellen didn't much care what he read. She was soothed by the mere sound of his voice.

She cherished the two years that Robert spent working on the farm. So did he, and the two fell madly in love. Father and Grandmother knew the two were fast becoming an item, and both Anders and Sigrid had grown very fond of him. He was honorable and sincere, and he was also a diligent and hard worker. Father had secretly hoped that Robert would eventually marry Ellen and take on the responsibilities of maintaining the farm.

Unfortunately, Anders passed away unexpectedly during the 1957 flu pandemic, leaving ownership of the entire farm to Sigrid and the remaining children. Sigrid was grief-stricken over the loss of her only son, as were Ellie, Lars and Gunnar. Robert had grown close to Ellen's father during the two years he worked on the farm and considered Anders to be a male role model. That was something his own father had never been.

Lars and Gunnar were separate and distinct identical twins, but the family often joked that they were conjoined by an invisible thread. One twin never went anywhere without the other. They always pursued the same interests. They took the same courses in school, and they even fell in love with the same girls. When they finally decided to attend university shortly after Father's death, Ellen and Sigrid were left at home alone. And it was Robert who kept the family farm going.

The following year, Sigrid had decided that Ellen should, in fact, attend college. At first, Ellie was reticent to leave Robert. But Sigrid assured her that Robert would be waiting for her when she returned.

Grandmother's plan for Ellen was that she should study education at nearby Dickinson College in order to become a teacher. That way, Ellen could eventually return to Himmel and help mold the young minds of their close-knit community. Although Sigrid believed that a woman's place was primarily in the home, she felt there were two acceptable professions for women outside the home: nurse and teacher. Sigrid was now sixty-one, but she was determined that her advanced years would not prevent her from living vicariously through her favorite granddaughter.

Robert encouraged Ellen to leave for school. He knew how intelligent she was, and he assured her that he would be waiting for her on the farm when she returned. Ellie reluctantly went off to school, returning to the farm on weekends and vacations to visit her aging grandmother and her strapping young beau. When she had to be away at school, they exchanged letters. Robert sometimes received two or three letters from Ellen in the same day.

Ellen kept every bit of correspondence she received from Robert. She treasured each word, reread each letter, and repeated the contents until each word was imprinted in her memory and heart. She still had every letter Robert had written to her hidden from Stanley in a box beneath her bed.

When Ellie graduated in 1960 with her teaching degree, both Robert and Sigrid stood proudly. They applauded as Ellie marched across the platform to accept her diploma. She had worked very hard in college. During her education at Dickinson College, she earned several scholarships and grants. She ultimately graduated Summa Cum Laude.

That same year, Robert's grandfather passed on, leaving him with enough of an inheritance to attend school himself. He attended North Dakota State University and also graduated with honors in 1964. Also during that time, Robert and Ellen continued to write letters to each other, taking every opportunity to spend vacations and holidays together.

Ellie was now a respected schoolteacher in the town. Robert—always the gentleman—took her on dates during his breaks. Although Ellen had sometimes wished Robert had tried something more, he never acted inappropriately toward her, for fear of muddying her squeaky-clean reputation. Robert was twenty-four and Ellen was twenty-seven. But he stood almost a foot taller than she. At the end of their evenings together, she stood on the porch, one step above him, so that they could kiss face-to-face. There, with Grandmother Sigrid monitoring them through the kitchen window, Robert tenderly kissed her goodbye. He graciously waved goodbye to Sigrid while Ellen went inside. As she waited in the kitchen to turn off the porch light after Robert drove off, her grandmother whispered to her.

"He's such a goot boy. I t'ink he's de one fer you, Ellen. Yer fadder would have wanted you to be togedder."

"Oh, ya. I think so, too." Ellen replied. "I think he's the one."

Robert obtained an educational deferment for the draft during his time at university. When he graduated in May of 1964, he decided to enlist in the Army. During his studies, he kept abreast of current affairs. He grew well aware of the growing protest of the war, but he felt it was his duty to serve his country. Rather than avoid the draft, he enlisted. He felt that, for a North Dakota farm boy, this was the best career opportunity fate had to offer him.

Ellen was devastated. She wanted him to marry her and settle down to have a family. Of course, Robert assured her that, by enlisting so early, he would serve his time and return to her after his tour was over. Later, they would have plenty of time to settle down and start a family.

Robert was sent to Fort Benning, Georgia to serve as infantryman in the 1st battalion, 7th Cavalry. He enlisted immediately after graduation at the beginning of the summer of '64. He and Ellen continued their correspondence during the course of the next year. Despite his rigorous training in the field, he still found time to write Ellie.

Tragically, as U.S. involvement in Vietnam escalated, Robert's unit was one of the first to be sent to there. In mid-August of 1965, his battalion sailed from Charleston, South Carolina to Qui Nhon, Vietnam. He was killed in the infamous battle of Ia Drang on November 14th of that same year.

Ellen recalled the day news broke of Robert's death. The Army had notified his mother and grandmother at their North Dakota farm. Ellen taught school that day, and Sigrid walked to the school to give her the awful news. Although Grandmother was almost as devastated as Ellen was to hear the news, it was Ellen's life that was forever changed by the horrific events in Vietnam. Whatever hopes that Ellen may have coddled for Robert's safe return from the war to her patiently waiting arms—had been mercilessly dashed forever.

Ellie was inconsolable. The best that Sigrid could do during that time was to offer a dry shoulder for Ellie's endless font of tears. Ellen hardly ate, and her grandmother prepared small palatable bites of nourishment to ensure that she didn't starve herself through her period of mourning. She sank into an abysmal depression and eventually missed two weeks of teaching classes at the school.

Robert was dead, and Ellen knew she would most certainly die alone. She had nothing to live for. Her career was meaningless. She was an old maid by North Dakota standards—now twenty-eight years old.

Ellen would have been content to wallow, immersed in her own profound loss, if Grandmother had not reminded her of one very important thing to live for. Yes, she would have to pick up the pieces of her shattered life and move on so that she could preserve Robert's one lasting legacy. This was the only reason she had to be alive.

Chapter 7

"First t'ing in de morning when you get up, you take de cold potatoes out of de ice box. Den, you rice dem. You stick each potato quarter in de ricer, and you squeeze de handle very tight. Dat's why you make sure and cook de potatoes soft, eh? Dat way you don't have to work so hard, squeezing dem. Yer arm will be goot and tired by de time yer done wit' ten pounds. Maybe if yer lucky, you can get one of de boys to help you out. Dey love to smash t'ings." SIGRID SEVERTSEN

Robert Peters' memorial service was held in Himmel, shortly after his remains were brought back home. Robert's mother and grandmother graciously asked Ellen to sit with them during the service. Seated also next to Robert's mother was a very unwelcome Stanley Senior, who made his first appearance in the town. He had nothing to do with Robert from the time he was fifteen, but he not only finagled his way into the memorial service, he claimed direct responsibility for Robert's achievements and sacrifices for his country. He also used the opportunity to brag about his own injuries, which he sustained during World War II. He even had the audacity to sit in the Seat of Honor, accepting his son's folded flag on the family's behalf. The whole thing made Ellen sick to think about it.

"Can ya believe that bastard?" Robert's mother whispered to her.

Ellen shook her head in disbelief, as she sat weeping for her dead lover.

Sitting on the edge of Stanley's bed, holding the portrait of Robert, Ellen thought about her relationship with Stanley's first son and their almost continual exchange of letters from the time she left for Dickinson College in 1958. She had often wondered if he had kept and treasured each of her letters as she did his. Even after he went off to college and enlisted in the Army, she thought of him almost every waking moment and wrote him nearly every day.

She considered her final letter to Robert, which she sent a week before he was killed. She knew that he probably never received it. She wondered, if he had managed to keep of any of those letters during his short time in Vietnam, what might have become of them. Had he even received *any* of them?

Then Ellen suddenly remembered that Stanley had received the entire contents of Robert's footlocker after they sent his body back. And he kept it all hidden in the barn!

Since Stan Senior had claimed ownership of the dilapidated family barn, this space had long been declared off-limits to the rest of the family. Of course, he had hoarded so many tools in there during the course of their marriage, there wasn't really much room for anyone to use the space for anything else—much less as an actual barn. Stanley regarded the building as an oversized warehouse for all his stuff. The barn itself hadn't been painted since Father was alive. The roof now leaked terribly, and the loft sagged. If a large crow were to perch himself there on top of the boxes Stanley had stored there, the entire thing might come crashing down at any minute.

Determined to satisfy her curiosity, Ellen marched back to the decrepit barn, making her way up the rickety wooden ladder to the loft above. As she stood upright on the loft, the creaking beneath her feet made her feel especially uneasy. There were piles of old, musty boxes stacked on top of one another. Some boxes were so worn and deteriorated, they were completely crushed under the weight of the old musty boxes stacked above them.

Ellie started her search at the top of Stanley's stacks of boxes. She grabbed the top box, pulled it down, flipped open the flaps, and examined the contents. The first box was filled with small hand tools. When she had concluded that the box did not contain that which she sought, she cast the box and its contents from the loft onto the floor below and proceeded to search through the next box.

Some of the boxes contained possessions Stanley had acquired long before he married Ellen, which he had carted with him when he moved from Texas. One box contained some World War II memorabilia Stanley had carried with him from his time during the Service. There was a small collection of photographs from his previous marriage to Robert's mother and of Robert when he was small.

Most of the boxes contained items of little value to anyone but Stanley. In truth, most of the items should have been hauled to the trash heap twenty-seven years before. She briefly studied the contents of each box, deciding that she had no interest in it. Then she tossed the box off the loft, onto the floor below. As she tossed the boxes and their contents—some of which were breakable—to the main floor, she felt herself being expunged of all her intense rage. Sometimes, when she heard the sound of breaking glass below, she felt vindicated and let out an almost corrupt and distorted belly laugh.

As Ellen surveyed the remaining three boxes left on the upper loft, she spotted another musty cardboard box with the name "Robert" etched in Stanley's handwriting. She gasped, knelt down in the straw, and gazed into it. There in the crushed and mildewed box were the contents of Robert's footlocker.

Ellie pulled each item out of the box and handled them gingerly, as if they were prized antiques. *These were the items that Robert had kept with him during the war*, she thought to herself. She studied a photo of her as a young girl he had probably kept in his breast pocket. She pulled out his musty Army uniform, his dog tags, even his socks. She smiled, as she caressed each item. And, as she lamented about the life that she and Robert could no longer have together, she wept pitifully to herself.

Finally, at the bottom of the box of Robert's belongings, Ellen discovered—tied together with a small strip of twine—every letter she had ever mailed to him during his time in the Army. She held her breath as she kissed the stack of letters she had penned to her lover. She lovingly rubbed them against her tear-stained cheek and carefully untied the twine knot, freeing the collection from its twenty-seven year bondage.

Robert had kept every letter that Ellen had written to him in his footlocker, and the entire stack had been returned to his father after his death. After Ellie had freed the lost letters, she read each one to herself. Each letter had been carefully opened at the flap by Robert's loving hand, read and reread by him during his rare moments alone. As she read, she imagined him lying on his lonely bunk or in his trenches somewhere, dreaming of Ellen and the life they would share together when he returned.

Each letter had been carefully opened at the flap by Robert and then was restored back into its sacred envelope hiding place. Each letter, that is, except for the *last* letter. *That* letter—Ellen's final letter to Robert—was never opened with his careful and loving hand. In her final letter to Robert, Ellen revealed a tragic secret—a secret which Robert would never survive to learn.

But *someone* had read the letter. It had been barbarically torn at the short end and savagely extracted. And that letter was so clumsily extricated that there was no hope of ever restoring the contents safely to its tidy and carefully sealed envelope. No, Robert never lived long enough to understand the truth about Ellen's dark secret, but Ellen was now sure that *Stanley* had read the letter.

Ellen seethed in anger. She had endured twenty-seven miserable years of continued abuse from her husband. She was constantly ridiculed by him. Stanley watched Ellie slowly die for over the years, riddled by guilt and the belief that she harbored this terrible secret. But now she realized—*Stanley has known my secret all along!*

Fuming, Ellie now channeled her inconceivable rage and resentment toward Stanley into herculean power and might. She threw the remaining boxes of the loft down into the growing heap below, without even taking the time to examine the remainder of the contents therein.

Descending the steps of the loft, she dragged every tool to the center of the barn floor. She started with the larger items—plows, tractors, wheelbarrows, saws, his old worn workbench, and even an old buggy carriage. She piled each tool precariously and dangerously onto the heavier tools below. All these things Stanley had acquired—an old lathe he purchased at an auction—were relocated there, in the center of this huge pile. She carried, lugged, pushed, and dragged every piece of miserable equipment Stanley ever purchased to the center of this growing mound. For years, the presence of Stanley's endless collection of belongings had defiled Father's barn, had wrecked her home, and had ruined her life.

After Ellie had dragged the larger tools and equipment to the center of the barn floor, she relocated all the heavier hand tools on top of the largest items—wheels, scythes, hoes, pitchforks, machetes, rakes, shovels, gears and pulleys. All these lighter, but more dangerous items were stacked onto the growing heap. In fact, this heap was so tall, Ellen now employed the use of a barn ladder to add to it. She ignored the agonizing pain in her back. Her arms throbbed from overexertion. She mourned for her lost love and her wasted youth. *Stanley knew how deeply I loved Robert. Stanley had always known!*

Stanley's mountain of tools now soared beyond reach, almost to the barn ceiling. And Ellen, perched on her tiptoes at the very top step of her ladder, daringly piled the final item at its peak. She deliberately set Stanley's empty Folgers coffee tin on top. And in the tin, Ellen placed the opened stack of letters she had written to Robert so many years ago. *Yes, you want your beloved tools, Stanley? Come get them. They're yours to take!*

After she had placed the pièce de resistance on top of her monument to Stanley's wastefulness and selfishness, she clapped her hands together, admiring her work. It was bitterly cold in the barn, but she was warmed by a sense of self-satisfaction—almost as if she had placed the final star on her annual Christmas tree. She grinned, descended her ladder, took it down, and then hid it out behind the barn. She left the barn doors wide open. She then followed the trail of old clothes she had left strewn in a path all the way back to the front porch of the house.

It was now dusk. She had spent the entire day relocating every bit of Stanley's crap out to the barn or tossing it into the trash heap. She flipped on the kitchen lights in order to see more clearly, as she entered her dilapidated farmhouse.

Click, click, click—nothing happened.

"Oh, my goodness!" Ellen declared. Beat, she flopped herself on her favorite wing chair in the darkness of her living room.

While she had kept herself embroiled in her day of rediscovery and redecorating, the power company had shut off her power.

Later that evening, in her kitchen now illuminated with emergency candles, Ellen Peters moved the groceries from her Frigidaire icebox to the heap of snow outside her front door. She shut the door, stoked a small fire in her potbellied stove, and suspended several of her best knitted blankets and quilts over the old windows of her home, in order to help insulate herself against the invading winter blast.

Exhausted, she sat in front of the potbellied stove and picked up her knitting needles. Her hands were frozen, but she was determined to finish knitting Margie's hot-pink sweater—this time, by firelight.

The next morning, Ellen rose and left the warmth of her stove and ventured out onto the front porch. Her potatoes had cooled in the snow and were wrapped under plastic. The temperature outside was far below freezing, and the potatoes were now partly frozen through. She needed to let them thaw inside a little before she riced them.

She let the cooked potatoes thaw about an hour. Afterward, Ellie assembled her ricing equipment. This was a heavy-duty stainless steel hand ricer, which she operated by inserting the potato quarter into the opening, closing the lid down, and squeezing the spud through a series of holes in a die. When enough pressure had been applied to the soft potato, the squeezed potato emerged as a bunch of soft noodles, which were then incorporated into the flour dough for lefse.

The ricing process required a considerable amount of manual strength, which Ellen did not have. She had spent the previous afternoon toting large pieces of machinery and tools to the center of her huge barn, forming a colossal mountain of Stanley's tools at the center of the main floor. In addition, she had spent the previous morning exhaustively clearing every bit of Stanley's possessions out of her farmhouse. She wasn't really sure what had possessed her to do all those things. She admitted to herself that she found all yesterday's activities somewhat therapeutic. But today, Ellie simply had no energy left.

She tried to muster any bit of arm strength she could manage in order to rice the potatoes. At one point she was so frustrated, she placed an empty bowl down on the floor and tried smashing the ricer handle down with her foot. Exasperated, Ellie tossed her ricer and frozen potatoes on the kitchen floor. She sprawled out on the floor and leaned her head against the kitchen cabinet, whining miserably—like a toddler having a tantrum.

A quarter of a mile down the driveway, a Roadway tractor trailer pulled up to the mailbox. Stan Senior jumped out of the passenger's side of the cab, holding his Samsonite suitcase. When he had slammed the cab door shut, he tapped on it with his cane and saluted the trucker. The trucker nodded and drove off. Then Stan hobbled his way up the cold driveway to his North Dakota farmhouse.

As Stanley Senior neared the farmhouse, he noticed the trail of clothing, which led from the front porch of the farmhouse, winding its way around the back of the house and leading out to the barn.

"What the—" he whispered to himself, puzzled.

His eye followed the tempting trail of "bread crumbs" around the side of the house. He cursed when he discovered his favorite armchair had been mercilessly discarded in the snow, exposed to the harsh North Dakota elements.

"That fuckin' bitch!" he cried.

He continued along the trail of clothing, observing that his other prized possessions had been disposed of in the trash heap and were now scheduled for incineration.

"I'm gonna fuckin' kill her!" he screamed.

Furious, he followed the clothing trail still further, as it stretched directly through the open barn doors. Now he was compelled by both anger and curiosity. And, as he entered the barn, he marveled at the massive mountain of machinery and miscellaneous matter his poor, frail wife had assembled the previous day. Perched atop of this precariously situated colossus was his makeshift safe deposit box—the old Folgers coffee tin.

He could see that there was something in the can. He just couldn't see clearly what it was.

"What the fuck? What the hell did that bitch put up there?"

He dropped his cane to search for a ladder, but there was no ladder to be found. He decided that he could cautiously climb on top of his saw, then step up to the workbench, carefully moving onto the next higher item for support, securing his foothold and eventually making his way up the pile. Then he could examine whatever prize lay in store for him, after he retrieved the coffee tin.

Stanley was both slothful and crippled, but his intense curiosity motivated him to maneuver this pile of crap his wife had brilliantly assembled. As he reached the halfway point of his machinery mountain, he stretched the tips of his fingers toward the coffee can, now just barely out of reach. He leaned over ever so slightly. Unfortunately, he lost his balance and his foothold and fell almost twenty feet before hitting the ground and landing with a loud thud.

After Stanley Peters plummeted to the ground below, the hazardous stockpile of tools and equipment his wife had so deliberately arranged began to shake. Seconds later, the massive pile came crashing down on top of him, tragically crushing his body beneath its tremendous weight.

Chapter 8

> "Den, you wrap everyt'ing up goot and tight and put it back in de ice box until yer ready to make de dough." SIGRID SEVERTSEN

When William Knutson dropped off Ellen Severtsen's mail on Tuesday, November 16th, he noticed that she had not fetched the mail from the previous day. He noted this as something of an anomaly. It wasn't like Ellen to forget about the mail. But he failed to mention this concern, fearing he would be perceived as a busybody. That day, he simply proceeded to the next mailbox on his scheduled route.

But when William Knutson dropped off Ellen's mail on Wednesday, November 17th, not only did he observe that Ellen had not picked up her mail for the previous two days, his level of concern had piqued to the point where he chose to deviate from his scheduled route, drive up to Ellen's house, and check in on her.

He parked his mail truck at the top of the driveway and left his engine running. There didn't seem to be a soul around the farmhouse. *Perhaps Ellen gave up and left town.* He approached the front window, which was obscured from the inside by the numerous blankets Ellen had suspended inside two weeks earlier. He tried to peer in several windows, but he couldn't see inside. He noticed that there was a stock pot filled with frozen and riced potatoes in the yard. A carton of milk also sat in the snow, frozen into one massive block of cold, white ice.

He opened the storm door and knocked on the front door. "Miss Ellie! It's William Knutson! Just checkin' ta see if yer okay!"

There wasn't any answer. Perhaps she did leave for warmer climates and failed to inform anyone in the town. He wouldn't have blamed her.

He knocked again. "Miss Ellie? Are ya there?" Boldly, he tried the latch. The door opened. He hesitated, and then he poked his nose inside the door, now cracked open. "Miss Ellie?"

There was no answer. Why would she leave town and leave the door unlocked? He would have to investigate. He politely kicked the snow off his boots and entered Ellen's kitchen. The kitchen was deserted, and Ellen had suspended a rope in the threshold between the kitchen and living area, using it to hang a bunch of blankets.

William pushed aside the blankets to discover Ellie— nearly frozen and unconscious—sitting in her wing chair and huddled under a multitude of quilts. The fire to her potbellied stove was completely cold, and she seemed to have run out of firewood. The tarnished silver cobra head of Stanley's cane sat on top of the cold stove. It looked as if she had sawed off the wooden stick to fuel her fire.

"Oh, good Lord!" William cried. He patted Ellen's chin lightly to get her to respond. "Oh Jeez, I'm goin' ta have ta get some help here!"

William tried to use Ellen's kitchen phone, only to realize there was no dial tone. Instead, he enlisted the help of Sheriff Baker using his two-way radio. He then tried to revive and warm poor Ellen while he waited for help.

Sheriff Baker arrived a few minutes later in his squad car.

"Miss Severtsen? Say something. Can ya wake up?"

At first, Ellen was unresponsive. Then she opened her eyes and sleepily gazed up at William Knutson.

"Who *are* ya?" she asked.

"I'm William Knutson, Miss Ellie. Sheriff and I are goin' ta get ya ta the hospital now."

The Sheriff and William each wrapped one of Ellen's arms around their necks and lifted her up.

Confused, she smiled at the Sheriff and stated weakly, "Oh, Mister Baker! Yer boy Paul is so sweet. He's really one of my best students. He's just so derned polite."

Ellen's rescuers carried her out to the Sheriff's squad car while she continued to brag about her favorite student, feebly unaware that her star pupil had now grown up to be the town's Sheriff.

William glared at Paul, disgustedly. "Poor thing doesn't even know where she is," he commented. "Stanley just left her here fer dead. Is it any wonder she's lost it now?"

The two men loaded Ellen into the back seat of the squad car, covering her in additional blankets to warm her.

"William, go down ta her mailbox and get all her mail. Then meet me at the hospital," the Sheriff commanded.

"But Sheriff, mail tampering's a federal offense!" William warned.

"I know the law, William. Just do what I ask!" Then, Paul Baker got in his squad car and drove Miss Severtsen to the hospital.

"Miss, Ellie?" Doris Baker stood over Ellen as she lay in her hospital bed.

Ellen drowsily opened her eyes and recognized Doris. Sheriff Paul also stood behind his wife.

"Oh, my goodness! Where am I?" Ellen inquired.

"Ya gave us quite a scare there, now Miss Severtsen."

"You're at the hospital, Miss Ellie," Doris added.

"Hospital?"

"Yes, Miss Ellie. Paul brought you here."

"Well, really it was William Knutson who found ya, Miss Severtsen. He saved yer life. I just brought ya here, don't cha know," Paul said modestly.

"Oh, dear. I'm sorry ta be such a bother."

"Miss Ellie, why didn't you tell us they turned off your power? We would've been glad to help you out," Doris inquired.

"I was fine, dear. You didn't need ta worry abote me."

"Nonsense," Paul scolded. "We'll get yer power turned back on, and yer phone, too. Doc says you'll need to be here a few more days 'til ya get yer strength up. Then ya can go home."

"You just rest, Miss Ellie. Call us if you need anything." Doris gently kissed Ellen on the forehead.

When Margie Carter's husband passed away three weeks earlier, Margie understood that John had sunk their entire savings into a life insurance annuity funded by an offshore investment account in the Turks and Caicos Islands. The agent who sold him the annuity assured John that, because the investment account was offshore, it would accumulate tax-free, thereby maximizing their investment and potential profits.

John was a cute and loveable guy, but he was a horrible businessman, mostly due to the fact that he was so gullible. He had been repeatedly burned during his many failed business endeavors. Unfortunately, he quickly forgot the valuable lessons he should have wisely gleaned from these grave errors of judgment. He was naïvely blinded by the overabundance and charm of these South Florida con men, who were always quick to deceive him out of whatever hard-earned cash he and Margie had managed to save. John Carter always expected the best out of people, even though he usually saw them at their worst.

Three days after John passed away, Margie phoned Dan Sanders, John's life insurance agent, notifying him that her husband had died. Dan expressed his condolences and informed Margie that John's life insurance annuity should pay out quickly, as soon as she brought John's death certificate to his office.

When Margie acquired John's death certificate, she called Dan's office, which was located in a ritzy Sebring hotel. She left a message informing him that she would be by in the morning to show him the death certificate and pick up her check.

The following morning Margie reported to Dan's office with the promised documentation, only to discover that the door to his former office was now locked. Not only was Dan not in the office, he didn't leave a forwarding address or number. When she pounded on his office door and looked inside, she noticed that all his office furniture was gone.

"Holy crap! Where is this guy?" she asked herself. Dumbfounded, she walked down to the lobby, hoping to quiz the hotel concierge.

"Hey," she asked. Can you tell me where Dan Sanders is?"

The concierge hesitated. "Well, ma'am. He's moved out."

"What d'ya mean, he's moved out? I just talked to him on the phone last week."

"I'm pretty sure he's left the country."

"What??? You gotta be friggin' kidding me."

"I believe he's moved to the Turks and Caicos Islands."

Margie was livid at the realization that John had—once again—been swindled. Enraged, she marched behind the concierge counter. She grabbed the desk clerk by the necktie and twisted it violently with her left hand. She pulled his face four inches from her own and lifted her brow in her customary threatening manner. But she spoke with a monotone level of unsettling calm, as she grabbed a pair of scissors off the desk with her right hand.

"You listen here, because I'm only gonna tell you this once. And if you don't tell me what I wanna hear, I'm gonna slice off your testicles with this very sharp pair of scissors. Now—where the hell is Dan Sanders?"

The concierge started to tremble and held up his hands in surrender. "Look, ma'am. I'm sorry. All I know is he left the country. He cleared out his stuff, and he didn't leave a forwarding address. Please don't hurt me, lady! I'm just a desk clerk!"

Shocked, Margie put down the scissors and started to bawl. "Oh my God! I'm so screwed!"

"Sorry, ma'am. I guess he split, when he realized he was going to have to ante up. He was bound to leave the country, if he didn't wind up dead first. He took a lot of rich and powerful people for a ride—even a couple of well-educated doctors who should've known better!"

"We're not rich! That was *everything* we had! My bastard of a dead husband croaked on me and left me with nothing! *This* was all we had—this and a bunch of shredded-up boards which used to be a house in Homestead!" Margie was now blubbering.

"Look, ma'am. I'm really sorry." The concierge tried to console Margie, who sat perched on the reception desk. She grabbed up handfuls of Kleenex as she snorted into them. He tried to reassure her by placing his hand on her shoulder. But he was cautious about getting too close, because he was still a little afraid she might become violent again.

"You just don't know what it's like. This has been a really bad year for me." Margie choked on her words, then pitifully and loudly blew her nose again.

"I know it's not your fault," the concierge added sympathetically. "But—well—honestly ma'am. Didn't it occur to you that the guy might be a little shady, when he was running his office out of a hotel?"

Embarrassed by the fact that her dead husband had been swindled of their life savings, Margie Severtsen-Carter holed herself up in her Wauchula trailer house for an entire week. During that week, she rarely left the trailer, and she refused to talk to anyone. Most of all, she wanted to avoid her jealous sister Inga, who would gladly have poured even more salt into her already painful and gaping wounds of grief. If word got out that Margie and John had been duped by another South Florida con man, Inga would most certainly broadcast her unsolicited "I told you sos" to the rest of the Severtsen family.

She spent most of her time in her trailer, but Margie occasionally stepped out to take short trips to the Circle K and grab some smokes. She never smoked before John died, but she decided that, since she was destined to live the rest of her life alone and in poverty in some God-forsaken trailer park, she was going to do whatever she could to curtail the agony of living. Not only did she suddenly pick up the smoking habit, she started smoking Pall Mall unfiltered cigarettes with the hope that she would develop lung cancer sooner and die as quickly as humanly possible.

Ellie was the one friend and family member that Margie felt she might have been able to confide in. Unfortunately for them both, Ellen's phone had been cut off a few days after John's death. Margie believed that Ellen was actually in worse shape than she was. Not only had her husband left her broke and starving, but Ellen didn't even *like* her husband. At least Margie had *happy* memories of living with John.

Distraught, Margie wrote a long letter to Ellen, confiding in her the fact that, like Ellen, *she* was *also* broke and alone. She missed John, and she missed her sister, too. She wished that she and Ellen could be miserable together and comfort one another. Or at the very least, she wished Ellen could get her phone turned back on so that they could talk about it.

When they were young girls, Marge and Ellie talked together a great deal. Ellen was soft-spoken like Father. Even though she was Grandmother's favorite grandchild, Ellen was not ostentatious like Inga was. Margie never felt as though she was being judged by Ellen—only accepted by her as a beloved friend and sister.

Margie always felt the need to protect Ellen, who was painfully shy and overly sensitive to anyone's plight but her own. As she thought about Ellen's current predicament, Margie wished that she had the fortitude to have done Stanley Senior in years ago, when he first married Ellen. *Ellen would have been so much better off if Robert had lived.*

Margie had just returned from the Circle K with a pack of smokes and some lottery tickets. Lisa and Rachel Myers, who lived two trailers down, were playing Barbies on Margie's doorstep. The girls were four and five respectively. They both had long dark hair, which their mother kept tied into tangled ponytails and seldom brushed. They were slightly plump, but they were also adorable and played on Margie's stoop quite often. They liked Margie, who often invited them in for snacks and probably spent more time with them than their own mother did.

"Where's your mom?" Margie asked the girls.

"She's watching *Oprah*," Rachel answered.

"You guys wanna come in and watch cartoons with me?" Margie inquired.

The sisters jumped up excitedly. "Sure!"

Margie's trailer park did have cable TV access. Like most little kids, Lisa and Rachel often enjoyed watching Nickelodeon cartoons. Margie didn't seem to mind frying up an occasional hot dog meal for the girls and letting them hang at her place once in a while. She often wished that her grandchildren lived closer to her, so that she could spend more grandma time with them. But her two little neighbors were charming substitutes. Right now she just needed their company. They seemed oblivious to grown-up problems and issues, and Margie craved a temporary respite from her own adult misery.

"Girls, come here." Margie took Rachel and Lisa into her bedroom and opened her closet door. "You guys wanna play dress up?"

The girls were ecstatic. Margie salvaged several hats, dresses, and several pairs of high heels after the hurricane, but not much else of real value. Most of her wild stuff was pink, which Lisa and Rachel also loved. She grabbed a bright pink, feather boa and wrapped it around Lisa's neck.

"Well, there. Aren't you pretty?" she complimented.

Lisa stood, modeling her gorgeous boa in the floor mirror, as the kitchen wall phone rang.

"I'll get it!" Rachel volunteered.

"If it's a telemarketer, tell 'em I'm poor!" Margie joked.

Rachel answered the phone, while Margie grabbed a large, oversized straw hat off her closet shelf and placed it on little Lisa's head. "There," she said. "You look just like Princess Diana. Well, with that straw hat, maybe her overpriced gardener."

Rachel held the phone out at arm's distance, as she called to Margie from the kitchen. "It's for you, Mrs. Carter!"

"Who is it?" Margie yelled back.

"Some Sheriff guy," she answered. "—from Na'kota."

Chapter 9

Two hours after she received a call from Sheriff Paul Baker, Margie Carter had squeezed all of her remaining possessions into the trunk and back seat of her baby blue Lincoln Towncar. She weeded out most of the outfits in her closet and donated them to her dress-up playmates, after deciding that they wouldn't fit in her trunk. These donated items included: several pairs of peep-toed heels and sandals, her bright pink feather boa, three sets of hats, and various sequined purses, skirts, and dresses—all of which Lisa and Rachel wore in multiple layers, while they stood to bid Margie a bon voyage.

"Where are you going, Miss Margie?" Lisa asked.

Margie knelt down and took hold of Lisa's small hand. "Well," she explained, "you know when your Mommy doesn't want to do something for you, and she says she'll do it when hell freezes over?"

Lisa nodded.

"Well, that's where I'm headed."

Margie kissed Lisa on the cheek and gently tapped her nose. "I'm gonna go take care of *my* little sister."

Rachel handed Marge a worn and dirty Pound Puppy. An ear had been torn off, and his stuffing had been shoved back in. A rusty safety pin secured the seam in place.

"Here, Mrs. Carter. Rover can take care of you."

"Ohhhh..." Touched, Margie choked back her tears and hugged little Rachel. "I'm gonna miss you girls."

She stood to bid the girls a final farewell. "Once you girls grow into those shoes, you are so gonna knock some little boys' socks off!" She then turned and marched to her Towncar. She opened the driver's side door and yelled, "Turn left at Champaign!" She positioned Rover face-forward in the passenger's seat, started the engine, and spun her tires out in the red Florida clay.

While she drove off, Rachel and Lisa waved goodbye and clumsily shuffled home in their oversized shoes. Rachel held a newly acquired gold sequined purse, and Lisa now sported a hot pink feather boa.

Sheriff Baker stuck his head into Ellen Severtsen's hospital room and knocked lightly on the door jamb. Ellie sat upright in her hospital bed watching television. Her arm was still hooked to an IV, but she was obviously feeling better and seemed to be in good spirits. She was now well enough to be discharged.

The fragrant smell of flowers permeated the room. She was surrounded by at least a dozen get well bouquets sent from former students, various Himmel neighbors, and fellow church members at Himmel Lutheran. At the center of Ellen's nightstand stood a gorgeous bouquet of two dozen yellow roses. Attached to the arrangement was a simple handwritten card—"Get well soon, Miss Ellie. Love, William Knutson."

"Miss Severtsen? Yer awake?" Paul asked.

Ellen grinned, "Oh my! Hello, Paul dear."

Paul stepped into the doorway. "Yer looking very well these days, Miss Severtsen. It looks like ya got yer color back."

"Why, thanks, hon'. Ya know, I'm so grateful ta you and William both."

"Miss Severtsen, I brought ya a surprise. Somebody's here ta visit." He coached Margie into the room.

Surprised, Ellen bounced up and down in her hospital bed. She immediately recognized her sister. "Oh, my goodness!" she cried ecstatically. "Aren't ya just a sight fer sore eyes!" Ellen and Margie talked on the phone regularly, but Ellen hadn't seen her older sister in person in over ten years.

Margie stepped over to Ellie's bed. She grabbed her hands, leaned over, and puckered her lips. "How are ya, lass?" she inquired. And with the customary greeting she reserved only for her little sister and her two daughters, she pressed her cheek to either side of Ellen's face, loudly smacking her lips in the air.

"Land sakes! I'm just beside myself!" Ellie exclaimed. "What brings ya here, Marge?"

"Well, apparently someone has been reading your mail," Margie answered. She mischievously winked at Paul. "Sheriff Baker called me in Florida and asked if I would come look after you."

Ellen commented worriedly. "Oh, dear. I didn't mean ta be a bother."

"Don't be silly, Ellie dear. There's a lot more to the story. We'll talk later."

Sensing that he might now be intruding on the sisters' reunion, Paul Baker excused himself. "Ladies, I will let ya catch up. I have ta get back ta work now. Nice ta finally meet ya, Marge."

Margie sat down at the edge of Ellen's bed and shook her sister's hands excitedly. She bit her lip as Paul exited the room. Her gaze was fixed on the lawman's rear end, as he vanished down the hallway.

"Ellie, honey. He's dreamy. Is he married?" Marge was, of course, referring to the Sheriff.

"Oh gosh, yes. He's married ta Doris. They were both once my students. Plus—well, isn't he just a little young fer ya, Marge?"

"I'm gonna let you in a secret, little sister. I've been super horny since—well, since I don't know when! I'm about ready to whore myself out for free, just to get myself laid!"

"Land sakes! John's not even cold, dear. Don't ya need some time ta grieve?"

Margie laughed loudly. "Hell, no! I need a penis! I need me some action!"

She stood and quickly changed the topic. "I hear you're gonna bust out of this joint today. Let's get all these posies together and load them into the Towncar." She leaned down to sniff the yellow roses William Knutson had sent. "Hmmm...who are these from?" she inquired. She pulled out the attached card.

"Oh, heavens, Margie!" Ellie reached for the card in her sister's hand, trying unsuccessfully to snatch it away from her.

Margie glanced down to read the card. "Oooooh...It says '*Love*, William Knutson.'" She grinned devilishly, and in a sing-songy voice began teasing Ellie. "Ellie and William up in a tree....K-I-S-S-I-N-G!"

Embarrassed, Ellie gasped shyly. "Oh, my gosh..."

When Ellen's admitting physician informed her that she might be ready to go home in a few days, she was filled with a sense of dread. She didn't entertain the idea of returning home to her farmhouse alone. Even after Paul Baker had the phone and power turned back on, she hated the idea of being there—all winter, all by herself.

But Paul had the good sense to appeal to Margie and ask her come to North Dakota to live with her sister. True, he had opened Marge's letter to Ellen and read her mail, but Ellen didn't mind in the least that her privacy had been violated. Thanks to Paul Baker's intrusions, she was not going to freeze, starve, *or* spend the winter alone. She now had her big sister with her to keep her company.

The Severtsen sisters returned to Ellie's farmhouse, after she had been released from the hospital. It was hard to believe that Ellen had been admitted just a week earlier, both malnourished and hypothermic. She was now home—reenergized and comforted in the knowledge that her favorite sister would be staying there with her. The dilapidated farmhouse was now illuminated with electricity and heated by the warmth of the electric furnace. Ellen had made up Stanley's bed for Margie to use. She lovingly provided several layers of her handmade quilts in order to keep her sister warm in her new bed.

Margie had no bedroom attire to speak of. She historically slept in the nude, because she didn't like the restrictiveness of clothing keeping her awake at night. Of course, that worked fine for Margie when she lived in South Florida, but that wouldn't work for her in North Dakota. And, despite the fact that Paul Baker had turned the power back on, it was still quite chilly in the bedroom. Margie donned a pair of sweat pants and t-shirt she had packed in her suitcase. These were the warmest items of clothing she owned. She needed to invest in some warmer winter garments.

Margie readied herself for bed, but her teeth began chattering. "My feet are friggin' freezing! Can I borrow a pair of socks?"

Ellen loaned her a thick pair of socks to keep her feet warm.

Margie put them on, all the while still shivering. "Tell me why I came up to this frozen tundra again?" She crawled under the covers. "Vvvvvvv!"

Ellie turned to ascend the stairs to her own bedroom.

Margie cried out to her, "No! Wait, Ellie! I'm too cold! Come keep me warm!"

"What? C'mon, Marge!" Ellie stated in disbelief.

"Seriously, Ellie—I'm not kidding. I need your body heat."

Ellen climbed under the quilts of Stanley's queen-sized bed and snuggled up to her sister, who still shivered.

"Land sakes, Margie! Ya think ya hadn't ever lived in the cold, the way ya carry on!"

Margie laughed. After about a minute, she warmed up, and her teeth stopped chattering.

Exhausted, Ellen drifted off to sleep.

"Ellie?" Margie whispered in the silence of the dark room.

"Hmm?" Ellie answered sleepily.

"You wanna spoon?" Margie chuckled.

Ellen chuckled, too. "Oh my goodness, Margie. Go ta sleep!"

Chapter 10

> "Dis is de part where you got to prepare yer work surface. I just use dis here rag over and over again. I wash it, and den I iron it out real goot fer de next time I need it. I weigh it down on de ends and flour it up real nice so I can roll out my lefse. You need to use unbleached white flour. And I have dis special sifter, where you turn de crank and de flour comes out fine. De finer de better. You don't want any lumps in yer flour." SIGRID SEVERTSEN

As Ellen Severtsen stood at her kitchen sink, she gazed out the window. For the first time in a long time, she now had a partner in the lefse-making process. She had performed this task alone for years. But today, her big sister Margie was reluctantly helping her.

She poured some unbleached white flour into her special hand sifter as she noted the snowfall outside. Because the temperature was so far below freezing, the flakes fell to the earth outside in a very fine powder. She tipped the flour sifter upside-down in the sink, while she tested it. Finely sifted flour rained down into the sink, coating the bottom of the basin with fine, white powder.

"It is almost as if God has his own special flour sifter, sifting snow on this fine day, eh?" Ellen contemplated.

"Give me a friggin' break, Ellie!" Margie snapped, as she grabbed the flour sifter from her. She shook the sifter above the rolling board, which was covered with a pastry cloth.

"Let's just get this whole thing over with," she angrily commented.

Ellen frowned. Her sister was clearly an unwilling participant in the preservation of the Severtsen family tradition, but she tried to remain optimistic. *Perhaps the joy of preparing lefse will rub off on Margie, after she's been baking a while.*

Ellen tried to coach Marge. "Ya've got ta weigh down the edges or tape them down, if ya want to roll the lefse ote right."

"Yes, sir!" Margie sarcastically saluted her sister with a floured hand.

"Well, there's no need to be snippy, hon'. I'm just tryin' ta help here." Ellen stated defensively.

"Where's the friggin' tape? Hand it over!" Margie barked.

Ellie handed her the tape.

As she defiantly taped the pastry cloth down to the wooden table, she mimicked her little sister's commands behind her back. "Do you think you're the only one who knows how to make lefse?" Margie inquired indignantly.

"Well, I have made it a lot more than you have, hon'."

Margie mixed some flour into the bowl of measured and riced potatoes. "Hand me the cream mixture," she commanded.

"Oh no, Margie hon'. Yah've got ta wait five minutes first ta let the potatoes warm," Ellen instructed. She turned her back to her sister to place the cast iron griddles on the stove top.

"Aw, who cares! It's all gonna get hot on the griddle anyway."

"Oh no, Margie hon'. This is Grandmother's recipe," Ellen assured.

"Hey, *I'm* the older sister. *I'm* supposed to be the boss here."

"Well, Margie hon'. It's clear ya don't know what yer doin'."

"Did you talk to your students this way? You know, like they were super retarded?" Margie snapped.

"Now, yer just bein' difficult!" Ellen shook her head as she set the heating dials on the stove.

Childishly, Margie picked up her wooden spoon and scooped up a lump of the potato mixture. Using the spoon, she catapulted the mixture across the room, striking her unsuspecting younger sister on the back of the head. The potato wad splatted on the floor behind her in a sticky, gooey glob.

Ellen turned around, reaching around her head to feel the stickiness which remained in her hair. "Oh my goodness, Margie!" she cried, insulted.

"Is that the best you can do, Ellie? I mean, don't you *ever* curse? C'mon, let me have it!" Margie teased.

Ellen remained silent. She simply walked over to the bag of flour next to Margie on the old wooden table. She lifted up the bag and turned it upside-down, pouring the entire contents onto Margie's head.

Margie stood as Ellen slowly and deliberately poured out her wrath and the entire bag of flour onto her big sister's head. Margie laughed—almost demonically—as she scooped out eye holes to see through the floury mask. She peered out from beneath her white eyelashes, now drenched in doughy tears of laughter. Ellen carefully set the empty bag of flour back down on the table and clapped off the excess flour from her hands.

"I think we need another bag, eh? This one's empty." Ellen looked at Marge, covered in flour. She also started to chuckle.

That morning, as the Severtsen sisters mixed, rolled, and grilled, they reminisced about their childhood together. They laughed about growing up poor, about the countless antics which prompted Father to discipline them, and the countless other antics which they managed to commit while miraculously skirting justice. And as they walked themselves through the lefse-making process which had been handed down from their grandmother, they reminisced about Sigrid.

"Ya know," Ellen recalled, "I think the last time I ever made lefse with anybody was with Grandmother, before she died. Stanley never did like lefse, so I didn't make so much after that."

"Did Stanley ever like *anything*?" Margie asked rhetorically.

"Well he did seem ta love Grandmother. He was always very nice ta her. Even though *she* didn't like *him*. After Stan Junior was born, she tried ta convince me ta divorce Stanley. She said she could take care of the baby, while I went back ta work."

"It was real hard when we first got married." Ellen chuckled as she continued her story. "After we built the inside bathroom…Well, ya know how Father built the crack ta the door so high? Stanley would go in there after supper and stink the whole bathroom up, and the smell would come creeping out from under the door. One day, Grandmother grabbed a can of Lysol and started spraying it under the door, while Stanley sat on the can.

"And ya know Grandmother starts yellin' at Stan with her Norwegian accent abote the stink. 'Yer stinkin, up de whole house!' she'd say ta him. Oh, my goodness! It was so derned funny!"

Margie laughed boisterously as her sister recounted the story. "So *then* what happened?"

"So, Stan comes ote, bucklin' his pants, and he turned three shades of bright red. And he says, 'It can't be any worse than that fish stuff ya eat!'"

"Lutefisk!" Margie cried. "I hated that crap!"

"Well ya, hon'. Everyone did. But Grandmother loved it. She ate it 'til she died. After that, Stan threw ote all the pots and pans she used ta make it and forbade me from bringing it inta the house. He says, 'That stuff is poison. It'll kill ya.'"

Ellen paused thoughtfully. "But he never did say anything cross ta Grandmother. Ya know, Margie—Stan was cross ta plenty of people, but he never spoke an unkind word ta her. And I'm pretty sure he knew she didn't like him. Go figure."

"Hey!" Margie blurted, still laughing from the retelling of the previous anecdote. "Do you remember those worm pictures we made?"

"Oh, gosh yes!" Ellen answered. She smiled as the sisters recounted the infamous worm picture they had made fifty years before.

Ellie, who was six years old, stood on a stool next to Sigrid at the kitchen sink and rinsed dishes. Margie—then twelve—had just finished painting the barn with her father and brothers. Her tomboy overalls and shoes were covered with splotches of red barn paint.

Margie poked her head in the kitchen door. "Psst!" she cried to her sister, trying to raise her attention.

Sigrid warned her oldest granddaughter not to track paint onto the kitchen floor.

"Ellie, come out here. I've got a surprise fer ya!" Margie commanded.

Ellen looked at her grandmother with a pleading face, and Sigrid granted her permission to play outside with her older sister.

"Don't get yer nice new dress dirty, Ellie!" her grandmother scolded.

"I won't!" Ellen promised, as the two girls scooted out to the stump behind the barn.

"Look what I got!" Margie held up a can of red barn paint, which had been leftover from her chores. She also held up an old can of whitewash she had found inside the barn. She had salvaged an old pine board, partially rotted on the edges.

"Look—white and red make..."

"Pink!" Ellen screamed ecstatically. "What are ya goin' ta do, Margie?"

Margie stuck her hand into a rusted and empty can of beans she found to retrieve the contents. She pulled out a dirty handful of fat Canadian night crawlers. "I found worms!"

"Eww!" cried Ellen, thoroughly repulsed.

"We're goin' ta make worm pictures!" Margie announced enthusiastically.

"What's that?" Ellen inquired.

"That's when ya dip the worms in the paint, and then ya let 'em squirm around on the board. Then they paint pictures," she answered.

Margie mixed the whitewash and red barn paint into varying shades of hot and pastel pink. Then she dipped selected worms into each color, while Ellen directed her. She placed each struggling, paint-encased worm down on the board to wriggle out a pattern. The two sisters watched their painting come to life.

"Now you try," Margie coached.

"Oooooh. No, Margie. I can't. Grandmother Sigrid said not to get dirty."

"Oh, yer such a scaredy cat!" Margie teased. Then she dipped another worm in the whitewash and dropped it on the board. "Oh, that's a good one!" she exclaimed, while the squirming worm desperately wretched out his pattern of color.

"Margie?" Ellie asked.

"Huh?"

"What happens ta the worms?"

"Oh, they die."

"Ohhh..." Ellen started to cry.

"They're just stupid worms," Margie stated indifferently.

Ellie sobbed even more sympathetically. "Poor worms."

"What? They die when ya use 'em fer bait! We're just makin' pretty pictures!" Margie exclaimed.

The two Severtsen sisters studied the Pollack-esque work in progress. Ellen, who was still somewhat disgusted by the whole process, pointed to certain likeable features in the developing masterpiece. Of course, Ellie only pointed. She couldn't muster up the courage to actually *handle* the worms or stain her fingers with the paint.

"I like the pink better. He moves around pretty good." Ellen sniffled again, rubbing her wet nose. "Poor worms…"

Soon, the previous blankness of their pine canvas was obscured by splotches of pink, red, and white paint, small clumps of dirt, and several doomed and slowly moving carcasses of the soon-to-be-dead earthworms.

"Okay, I think we're done." Margie pulled each worm, barely clinging to life, off the rotted pine board canvas and displayed the newly-finished masterpiece to her little sister.

"See? Isn't it beautiful?"

Ellen, still a little shaken about having brutally sacrificed half a dozen innocent worms in the name of modern art, admired Margie's creation.

Margie handed the painting to her little sister. "Keep it, Ellie. I want ya ta have it. Ya just got ta let it dry before ya touch it."

Ellen grabbed the painting with one hand, while she half-hugged her big sister. "Thanks, Margie. It *is* beautiful! I'm goin' ta keep it forever!" Ellie glanced down at the discarded and colored globs of worm carcasses, laying beside the old tree stump. "Poor worms…"

"Ya, poor stupid worms…" Margie commented apathetically. As she escorted her baby sister back to the farmhouse, she impishly suggested, "Now let's go show Inga. I'll bet she's goin' ta be so jealous!"

Ellen and Margie sat in the sparsely decorated living room of their farmhouse on Christmas Eve, watching a rerun of *It's a Wonderful Life*. Ellen reclined in her favorite wing chair, and Margie sprawled out in a warm nightgown on a musty but sturdy used couch they had recently acquired at the local thrift shop. She snuggled herself under one of Ellen's homemade quilts and ate a bowl of popcorn.

As Jimmy Stewart raced through the snowy streets of Bedford to be blissfully reunited with his wife and children, Margie's eyes welled up with tears.

She immediately rose to her feet. "Oh no! None of that sappy sentiment is gonna get me down tonight!" She cast off her blanket and turned the movie off. "I've got an idea. Let's exchange presents. I've got something special for you, Ellie."

Ellie was thrilled. It was Christmas Eve, but she had not really received a Christmas gift since before her son left for Tucson. "Oh, gosh!" she surprisedly exclaimed.

Margie retrieved an envelope upon which she had handwritten Ellen's name. "Open it!" she coached.

Ellie enthusiastically opened the letter. Inside was a card, which she read aloud:

"To My Dear Little Sister Ellie,

This is my Christmas gift to you. This is our opportunity to be successful female entrepreneurs. We have to muster our wits about us and use our brains to take care of ourselves. We're all we have left.

Love, Your Big Sister, Margie"

"What is it?" Ellen inquired, as she curiously pulled out the enclosed letter.

"They're the 900 numbers John and I bought," her sister replied.

Ellen looked puzzled.

"Don't you get it, Ellie? We're gonna start our own 900 number sex chat lines!" Margie tried to channel her excitement into her perplexed sister while explaining further. "You and me. You know—We answer the phone and talk about sex, and guys pay us."

Ellen shook her head. "I can't do that, Margie. I wouldn't know what ta do."

"Don't be silly, dahlink. I'll teach you everything you need to know."

Ellen hesitated.

"Really, Ellie. There are plenty of women who make decent money doing this." Margie assured.

Ellen smiled, but then looked suddenly concerned. "What abote our neighbors in Himmel and at church?"

"They don't need to know a thing. We can just tell them we're sharing lefse recipes or some dumb junk like that. We don't have to tell a soul. We'll just put ads in skin rags in big cities in other states, and the people here won't have a clue!"

"I don't know, Margie. Isn't that kind of dangerous, hon'? Ya know, there are a lot of weirdoes ote there nowadays."

"Naw. We just pretend we're living someplace else. We use assumed names. We make up crap, and we don't give out any personal information."

Ellen hesitated as Margie continued. "For Chrissakes! We're out in the middle of friggin' nowhere, Ellie! Whose gonna come all the way out here?"

Ellen thought for a moment then decisively consented, shrugging her shoulders. "Okee dokee. What have we got to lose? If it makes ya happy, I'm willing ta try anything."

"Now I've got somethin' fer you, Margie." Ellen ran upstairs to her bedroom, and brought down two wrapped gifts for her sister. "Here. Open this one first." She handed Margie a meticulously wrapped gift box. Marge held it to her ear to as she shook it up and down. It obviously contained clothing, but she smiled and asked, "A priceless Ming vase? Gold bars?"

"I wish!" Ellen stated, giddily unable to contain her joy. "Open it!"

Margie unwrapped the gift and opened the box. She gasped as she pulled back the tissue paper to reveal the hot-pink sweater that Ellen had labored over for the past few months. It was fashioned of a very loud pink yarn, but the knitted eyelets and scalloping appeared almost as delicate as finely woven lace.

Margie stood, as she donned and modeled her skillfully crafted sweater. "It's absolutely gorgeous!" She examined the stitching closely then sighed heavily. "Thank you, Ellie dear. This is beautiful."

"I was workin' on this when Stanley left. But when ya came ta stay, I tried ta sneak-knit under the blankets in my bed—so ya wouldn't see. I finally finished it last night."

Touched, Margie twirled around again, proudly modeling the sweater.

Ellen handed her the second gift. "Ohh, I know yer goin' ta like this one."

Margie impatiently tore at the shiny red and green Christmas wrap to discover an aged and rotted board, coated with smears of white, red, and various shades of pink paint.

"It's the worm picture!" Ellen exclaimed happily.

"Oh my God…" Margie cried in amazement. "You kept this all these years?"

"Of course, hon'." Ellen grinned proudly, hugging her sister.

Marge stared down at the childhood Van Gogh, bearing the faded impasto of various shades of pink paint. She lovingly laid her hands on the textured surface and suddenly burst into uncontrolled sobbing.

"Oh, goodness," Ellie stated remorsefully. "I didn't mean ta upset ya, Margie dear!"

Marge wailed, "Oh no, Ellie, honey. It's just—I'm so lonely!"

"Oh, I know, hon.' But ya do have me, dear."

"It's not the same. I miss John! I guess I've been trying to kid myself, pretending I was okay and that I didn't need him. But I just feel so empty and dead and depressed inside. I'm so *sorry*."

Ellen was perplexed. "*Sorry*, hon'? What have ya got ta be *sorry* for?"

"Well, when John and I were having sex for the last time—you know—just before he died? Just before that I said that I was going to bury a stiff." Margie wailed even more pathetically now. "—But I meant his *penis*! I didn't mean *him*!"

Ellen sat on the old sofa next to her distraught sister, who sadly dropped the worm picture to the floor. Marge hid her face in her sister's shoulder. Ellen reached around her to assuredly pat her sister on the back.

"There now, hon'. I know it's hard ta lose somebody ya love. Especially somebody who loved ya as much as John did."

Margie looked up at Ellen, her face now wet with tears and her nose now bright red from sniffling and wiping it repeatedly on the sleeve of her new pink sweater. "Ellie?"

"Ya, hon'."

"Did you ache this bad when Robert died?"

"Oh ya, hon.' I cried fer years and years after Robert died."

"How'd you get over it?" Margie asked.

"Oh, well. I'm not sure I *ever* got over Robert. He was special. But after he died, I met Stanley. And then Stan Junior was born soon after that." Ellen wiped a tear from her sister's cheek as she looked into her tortured eyes. "It'll get better, I promise ya, hon'. With time, it'll get better."

Margie stretched out on the worn out sofa and placed her head on her sister's lap. As midnight passed and Christmas morn crept quietly in, Margie mourned herself to sleep. Ellen stroked her weeping sister's hair and empathetically grieved for her own lost love, who passed away over twenty-seven years before.

Chapter 11

Alan Dickinson sat alone at his computer desk in the ad layout division of the *Himmel Chronicle*. In reality, the ad layout division was a tiny 5' x 9' cubicle in the already small office for the weekly town newspaper. The paper itself was only a two to four page weekly foldout. Most of the time there wasn't a great deal for Alan to do. Today, like most other days, he reclined in his comfortable desk chair and propped his feet up on the edge of his desk. He draped his keyboard in his lap and played a game of *Legend of Kyrandia*.

Alan was a very tall, overweight young man of sixteen. Like his father, Erik, Alan had curly red hair and blue eyes, which were framed by long eyelashes so white, they almost seemed like silk webs. He was now a young man, but he looked like a child in a grown man's body. This was due to the fact that his entire body was still dotted with a million freckles. His already out-of-shape physique indicated that he had always been the artsy, computer-geek type. Like his father before him, he was an ex-student of Ellen's, who studied under her tutelage from the first through the sixth grade, until just before she retired. He was not Ellen's favorite student, but she did acknowledge that Alan was a bright boy, even though he was somewhat of a troublemaker.

The *Chronicle's* art department did not drum up a sufficient amount of business to justify the salary of one full-time ad artist. As a result, Alan was known to do freelance layouts and photography for individuals placing ads in other newspapers. When he wasn't involved in doing layouts for the paper or drumming up freelance work, he whiled away the hours playing PC games on his DOS computer.

He sat alone, playing with and cursing at his game. His former teacher and her older sister entered through the *Chronicle's* front door. Since he was the only person in the office, he put down his keyboard and stood to greet them.

"Well, hello ladies," he greeted suavely. "What can I do for you?"

Margie was intensely preoccupied with the business at hand. "Ellie tells me you do freelance work. Is that true?"

"That depends on what you need," Alan answered.

She handed him an old boudoir picture she had given to John in 1958. She had the photograph taken privately by a discrete Florida photographer after giving birth to her fourth child. She had formerly presented the photograph to her late husband on their seventh anniversary. Even after four children, Margie still had a knockout figure. In the picture, she was tastefully and sexily posed on a romantic antique day bed. The photograph was fairly well-preserved, despite the fact that the outer edges were worn. It also contained a few spots of moisture from being stored for over thirty years in the Florida humidity.

Alan examined the photo, and his eyes widened. "This is you?"

"Yes. Tell me. What can you do with this?" Margie inquired.

"When was this taken?"

"Shut-up! Just tell me what you can do with this."

"Well, I'm not sure what you need, ma'am."

"First, you've got to promise me that you won't tell a soul about this," Margie demanded.

"Sure, if the price is right, I can keep a secret," Alan promised. "What are you gonna do?"

"We're going to place ads in a couple of skin rags for two 900 numbers we own. I need you to touch this up. Can you fix the photo and update my gown?"

"You mean, make it look less fifties-ish?"

"Yeah, update it and fix the worn spots."

"Sure, no problem," Alan assured.

"Then, I need you to add some text," Margie added.

"Like what?"

"1-900-HOT-MAMA. Just ask for Gabrielle. Let's talk about your wildest fantasies." Marge's puckered her lips sexily, as she dictated the copy for the ad.

"Whoa," Alan moaned. "You're sure you want to do this? How do you know I can keep this a secret?"

"Maybe this'll help." Marge snapped her fingers, and Ellen revealed a rolled up wad of twenty dollar bills, tied together with a rubber band. Ellie handed it to her sister.

Marge whipped out several large bills and handed them to Erik. "Will that keep your trap shut?"

"Sure, ma'am." Alan smiled, crumbling the stash of cash in his jeans pocket.

"That's not all," Margie commanded. "I need you to do an ad for Ellie."

Alan looked surprised. "What? For Miss Ellie?"

"Yes," Margie answered. "I need you to take a sexy school teacher photo of Ellie."

"Aw, shucks. I can't do that. She's my teacher."

"No, she's your *ex-teacher*. Get over it and grow up! I need you to take some hot photos of Ellie looking like a sexy, strict school marm."

Ellen stood, frozen with embarrassment. Her sister continued to bark out orders for Alan.

"You mean she needs an ad, too?" he asked nervously.

"Yes. That one will say '1-900-OLD-LADYs. Nasty school marm ready and waiting to punish naughty school boys. Ask for Miss Elsa Dietrich.'"

Alan glanced over at Ellen in disbelief. "Miss Ellie?"

"Yes, Alan dear," Ellie answered. "Desperate times call fer desperate measures. Ya will keep this quiet, won't ya?"

"Well, that depends." Alan held out his naked palm.

Margie rolled her eyes and pulled out a few more bills, slapping them in his hand. "You little shit! Now let's get moving."

"Right this way, ladies...Miss Ellie..." And with that, Alan Dickinson directed Ellen and Margie to his studio to produce one of the all-time best quarter-page ad layouts of his meager graphic design career. This was an ad he could *never* show anyone in the town of Himmel—*ever*.

Alan Dickinson finished the ad proofs for Margie and Ellen within three days. Of course, he didn't really have anything else to devote his time to. The two sisters marched their addressed ad proofs to the post office to mail to a select few entertainment publications in the country. All of these newsletters catered to the younger crowd and specifically featured 900 ads for sex chat lines in the back. In addition, Margie had selectively chosen a variety of magazines in larger and distant cities, where she knew no one would possibly recognize her or her sister's image. Hopefully, if Alan could keep a secret, no one inside the state of North Dakota would ever know about their new business venture. They could reside as two respectable old ladies in the tiny town of Himmel, while they conducted their sleazy 900 chat lines in the privacy of their own home.

The publications Margie selected to advertise in included: *Creative Loafing* in Charlotte, North Carolina and Tampa, Florida; *Riverfront Times* in Saint Louis, Missouri; and various cheap ad campaigns along the Las Vegas strip. Those ad campaigns usually involved non-English speaking vendors who simply handed out business cards and flyers to passers-by and encouraged them to dial the sisters' 900 number. These cards were often discarded just a few feet away on the edge of the sidewalk. But occasionally an interested recipient would stuff the advertisement in his pocket.

This was all the initial advertisement the sisters could afford. Of all their ad campaigns, the Las Vegas campaign was the riskiest and most expensive. Despite the questionable nature of their advertisements, the other aforementioned publications were quite reputable. Margie's plan was to place two 1/4 page ads side by side with 1-900-HOT-MAMA and

1-900-OLD-LADYs. Margie would answer the HOT-MAMA line as a young seductress named Gabrielle. Ellen would answer the OLD-LADYs line as repressed old school teacher, Elsa Dietrich, who threatened to punish naughty, masochistic bad boys by slapping a ruler to their naked bottoms.

The sisters stood in front of William Knutson at the postal window. Margie had lined up her pre-addressed envelopes, which contained the advertisement proofs that Alan had expensively but confidentially prepared. Of course, William had no idea what the envelopes contained. As Margie read off the names on the unsealed envelopes, Ellen read off the amount due to each magazine. William issued money orders payable to each vendor. Ellen then retrieved her roll of bills. William totaled the cash due, and Ellen paid him, along with a small money order issuance fee.

William said nothing, but Ellen could sense by the way his eyes darted across the envelopes that he was curious.

"We're starting some 900 numbers," she volunteered, trying to assuage his curiosity. Margie glared at her, wary that her sister might give away too much information.

"Yes, uh—we're puttin' my recipe for lefse ote. Ya know, so people call in ta get some cooking tips." Ellen seemed to be flirting with William, who warmly smiled back at her.

"Oh, ya. I see. I'm sure that plenty o' people 'round here would like ta call in."

"Oh no, hon'. My recipe's free ta anyone in Himmel. They just need ta ask."

After William issued the final money order and Margie sealed it into its respective envelope, William bid the sisters goodbye. "Good luck, there with yer new business, Miss Ellie!"

"Yep," Margie answered sarcastically. "We'll need plenty of that there luck, don't cha know. Thanks, William."

"Yer welcome, ladies! Have a great day!" William saluted his love interest and her sister as they headed out the front door.

Margie and Ellen left the post office. Margie quietly nudged her little sister to tease her about William. "Ellie and William up in a tree..."

"Goodness, Marge. Why d'ya have ta be that way? He's just an old friend."

"Maybe you should tell *William* to call in. I'm sure he'd *love* to talk to *you*!" Margie joked.

"Marge!" Ellie snapped. "Can't ya stop yer teasing fer once?"

"Hell, no! If Stanley ever comes back, you need to dump his sorry old ass and trade him in for William Knutson. You know he's sweet on you."

Ellen grew impatient, as she boarded the passenger's seat of Margie's baby blue Lincoln Towncar. "Margie, hon'. Give it a rest! Last thing I need is another man right now. We've got work ta do!"

It was the first week of March, and Ellen Severtsen once again trekked the quarter mile hike to check her afternoon mail. This month had been filled with record warm temperatures for North Dakota. In fact, Ellen now required only her favorite pink sweater to warm her.

Margie stood in the kitchen, while she made lefse and answered the phone. The 900 line she had advertised had already generated a few regular callers. They all wanted to speak to Margie. And Ellen had to admit, her sister was very good at sounding sexy. Some of her callers might have even been considered somewhat obsessive about the attention she was doting on them. Of course, it was all for money.

Ellen opened the mailbox. She discovered Marge's very first revenue check, since they had established their 900 number and put ads in a few select entertainment publications. She opened the envelope and reviewed the check. It was not a sizeable sum, but it was certainly nothing to scoff at. As Marge's number grew in popularity, Ellen was sure that the size of the checks would also grow exponentially.

She trotted back to the farmhouse, kicked off the dirt from her shoes, and removed her sweater. It was no longer wintry outside. In the past month, average temperatures had finally climbed well above freezing. It was indeed an early spring in the town of Himmel.

Marge heated up a butter and cream mixture to be used for making lefse. She nuzzled the cordless phone on her right shoulder, while she simultaneously carried on a phone conversation with a 900 caller.

Ellen quietly showed her the sum contained on their latest check. Marge nodded and smiled.

"Oh yeah. Ummm, that's so good, Jack. Mmmm—that just turns me on." She commented to her caller, while quietly acknowledging her sister's good news.

She warmed the butter lightly on the stove to soften it. "Yeah, you're just trying to butter me up, aren't you?" She added the cream mixture to the warmed butter. "Yeah, Jack. You make me want to cream in my jeans! What? Oh no, I'm not wearing jeans! I'm not wearing anything. My pussy is ready and waiting for your big, massive dick."

Ellen shook her head. She wasn't quite sure she would ever get the hang of this. She hadn't answered a call yet. And she didn't know what to do, if somebody *did* call. But Margie seemed comfortable with it, and her success with 1-900-HOT-MAMA was making money.

"Ooooh, yeah. That's right. Give it to me, Jack!" Margie added the salt to the butter cream mixture. "Oh yeah, honey. Talk dirty to me like a salty sailor!" Margie held up the phone, so that Ellen could hear the grunts and groans from her caller on the other end. Ellen snickered quietly in her palms as she listened.

"Oh yeah, Jack baby. That was good for me. Huh? Oh yeah, I'm just going to shower and lay out nude at the pool for awhile. You just think about me. And I promise the next time I touch myself I'll be thinking of you. Mwahhh. Buh bye..."

Marge hung up the phone. She set down the butter and cream mixture, grabbing their first check from her sister. Elated, she danced around in circles.

"Hell yeah! We're going to be rich! Oh my God, Ellie! We're going to be friggin' rich!" She grabbed Ellen's hands and joyously spun her around.

Just then, the phone rang. But it wasn't Margie's line, it was *Ellen's* line. Ellen stood looking like a deer in the headlights. She panicked and stuttered. "M...Margie, I ca..can't..."

"Nonsense," Marge commented. She answered the ringing line. "1-900-OLD-LADYs....Yes—just a minute."

She handed the phone to Ellen, still frozen in terror. "It's for you, Miss Dietrich!"

Ellie rolled her eyes and took a deep breath. She hesitantly took the phone from her sister. Margie grinned impishly.

"H..Hello? Y...Yes, this is Miss Elsa Dietrich. What is yer name, ya naughty boy?" She took in another great sigh, as the caller answered her question. "Oh. Dan, eh? Well, Mister Dan, what have ya done ta be such a naughty school boy?"

Ellen was clearly uncomfortable, as her caller related the pornographic error of his ways. Her eyes widened as she shook. Marge watched, amused by the exchange.

She picked up a lefse stick in her hand. This was a long wooden stick with a handle, which was used to flip the delicate flatbread on the griddle. The edges of the stick were smoothed so as not to tear the rolled bread. Ellie snapped it hard against the kitchen table.

"You hear that? That is my ruler, eh? I want ya ta pull down yer pants and bend over fer me. I'm goin' ta spank yer bare bottom. That'll teach ya a thing or two abote ever doing *that* again, don't cha know!" She snapped the wooden stick repeatedly against the hard surface of the kitchen table as she yelled into the phone. "Don't ya ever—*ever* do that again. Ya hear? Yer a very, very naughty boy!"

This time, Ellen held the receiver out as she continued to yell and smack the lefse stick down on the table, making a loud "thwapping" noise, which the caller could clearly hear. In turn, Margie put her ear to the phone, as she quietly chuckled to the noises of heavy breathing on the caller's end of the line.

Marge nodded to her sister, acknowledging that the caller's breath sounds had subsided. Ellen held the phone back up to her ear. "Now, don't call here again until ya think abote what you've done, eh?" She hung up the phone.

After Ellen restored the cordless phone back into its cradle, Margie laughed hysterically. "Oh my God! That is so funny! Ellie, dahlink. You were great!"

"Well, maybe I need a little work, eh?"

"Did it make you think about teaching school again, dear?"

"Goodness no, Margie! I never treated my students like that."

"No, you're a natural, Ellie. I didn't know you had it in you. I can only recommend one thing, dear."

"What's that, hon'?"

"You've gotta drag it out for at least five minutes. Give 'em their money's worth!"

The sisters joyously clapped each other's hands above their heads.

"Sister, we are gonna be so friggin' rich!" Margie cried ecstatically.

Chapter 12

> "Pull yer potatoes out of de fridge two cups at a time. Mix two tablespoons of unbleached flour in wit' de potatoes and let dem sit out for at least five minutes to warm. It's got to get warmed and comfortable introduced to de flour before you add more." SIGRID SEVERTSEN

Revenues from the April 900 number check were so much higher than the March check that Margie and Ellen decided to expand their advertising budget. In addition to the previously mentioned ads, they added two more entertainment publications in the New York City and Los Angeles areas.

To celebrate their growing success, Marge took Ellen out on a shopping spree, 66 miles east of Himmel to Bismarck. She also talked her sister into a coiffure and manicure at a prestigious Bismarck salon. Slowly, Ellie had transformed herself from the haggard old school marm she played on the 900 line (and in life) to a lovely and sexy new single woman. She now wore her naturally wavy blonde hair about her shoulders. She updated her attire, began to wear makeup regularly, and even bought a few significant and expensive items of jewelry. In the past, these luxuries were unheard of.

But Margie's constant coaching convinced Ellen that she now deserved to treat herself to some of the finer things in life.

Even though the sisters were becoming successful, Margie had some growing concerns about Ellie. For one, there was really no telling whether or how soon Ellen's estranged husband, Stanley, might return. No one had heard from him since he left Tucson in late October. He had repeatedly warned Ellie to steer clear of his belongings, which Ellen had stashed in the barn. The few times Margie suggested venturing out to the barn for something needed, Ellen stubbornly refused to cooperate. "Stanley left explicit instructions not ta mess with his things, dear," she warned her sister. "He will be furious if anything is ote of place."

But Marge was even more concerned that the almost twenty-seven years of abuse that her younger sister had endured with Stanley had taken its toll on her sister's sanity. At times, Ellen seemed distracted and even irrational. Marge had also noticed that Ellen struggled with apparent lapses of memory. She forgot the obvious—like the names of people she had known all her life. She misplaced things often. She noted on two occasions that Ellie had completely forgotten the lefse-making process—something Grandmother Sigrid had ingrained into her psyche from childhood. Ultimately, Ellen seemed to be someone very different from the young, innocent girl of thirteen that Margie had deserted, when she left the farm to make a life for herself in Rapid City.

But Ellen was now the only thing constant in Marge's life. True, Margie was lonely, and she missed *male* companionship. But her sister seemed to fill that void in her life—at least temporarily—preventing Margie from experiencing an otherwise unbearable loneliness. At the very least, Ellen needed Margie, and Margie needed to be needed. So for now, Marge had resolved that—whatever the cost, whatever the risks—she would be there to support her little sister. She would protect little Ellen from harm, from her mean husband Stanley, and from poverty and destitution. And if that meant that Marge would eventually have to finish Stanley off—if he ever did decide to return—then so be it.

Margie sleepily checked her watch. It was 6 A.M. when the 900 line rang. She angrily answered the phone.

"What??? What? I told you I'm not a morning person, Jack! Why do you have to call this early? Seven? Oh yeah, it *is* seven. But it's still too goddam early."

Ellen was already awake making breakfast.

"I know, but I already told you I'm not a morning person. You know I'm up all night partying in South Beach…"

Margie had her callers convinced that she still lived in South Florida. Most of the time, she had them envisioning her lying naked or in a scant bikini beneath a palm tree on the beach. Because she had a youthful voice, they believed she was as young and sexy as her ad picture. They weren't aware that her featured picture was taken over 34 years ago.

Margie wasn't even sure that Jack was the caller's real name. But the man who claimed his name was Jack called from Pineville, North Carolina, a town just south of Charlotte. He soon became an obsessive caller, sometimes calling her two or three times per day.

Ellen was deeply concerned by the tone of Margie's voice. Something in her conversation told Ellie that Margie's caller was not interested in the usual sex chat they had so often engaged in. He was concerned about his phone bill.

"What d'you mean your mother is pissed? You live with your mother? How old are you?.....Thirty-five and you're still living with your mother?.....Three thousand dollars?....Oh, my God! Are you nuts?"

Ellen could hear Jack on the other end of the phone, loudly cursing at Margie. Marge was, in turn, becoming furious.

"Fuck you, you impotent asshole! You can't threaten me! Come get me, you son of a bitch! I dare you! They can shut her fucking phone off for all I care. At least then you won't wake me up at a six 'o clock in the fucking morning with your Ted Bundy phone calls, you sick son of a bitch!"

Margie slammed down the cordless into its cradle. "Shit!"

She glared at Ellen. "His phone bill was three thousand dollars last month. He still lives with his fucking mother, for Chrissakes! –And he's thirty-five! What a loser!" Margie let out one long, exasperated heave of disgust. "Oh, Ellie. I'm so glad these assholes don't know where I live. They haven't a clue."

"Well, look on the bright side, Margie, hon'. His phone'll be shut off soon, and he won't bother ya anymore, eh?"

Ellen handed her sister a breakfast plate and smiled. "Have some eggs, hon'?"

Stanley Peters, Junior was a bit hungover. He drove eight hours the previous day with three buddies from work in his Dodge Caravan to Las Vegas. They hosted a bachelor party for his work buddy, Steve, at the Tropicana Hotel. The chosen hotel was clearly outdated, but it wasn't quite a rat hole and was still within everyone's modest entertainment budget. Steve and Mona were to be married the following evening in the Las Vegas Drive-Thru Wedding Chapel, after which they planned a three day honeymoon in Vegas. Immediately after the ceremony was over, Stan Junior had to return to Tucson and report to work on Monday.

It was 3 A.M. on Saturday morning, and Stan Junior attempted to work off his inebriation. He ventured out for fresh air with another buddy and walked up the Strip.

Las Vegas was a town that truly never slept. Neon signs blinked constantly—even at 3 A.M. The Strip was still packed with bodies. The traffic was congested. Ambulance sirens were perpetually ignored. And rows of Hispanic men and women still lined the street sides to torment passers-by with their endless supply of advertisements—strip clubs, escort services, in-room massages, and 900 numbers.

As Stan Junior's buddy passed a vendor, a short Mexican man in a polo shirt stopped him. "Hey," he invited, "Look."

Stan's buddy took the flyer from the man, as the two men walked on.

"Damn," Stan commented. "I can't believe Rosa let me come to this. I've forgotten how bad it is to be hungover."

Stan's single buddy stuck in a little jab. "At least *I* can do something while I'm here." He pointed to the piles of discarded cards for strippers and prostitutes littering the streets. "I just hire one of *these* girls. All *you* can do is get drunk, call up Rosa, or call up one of *these* ladies." He pointed to the two pictures side by side on the bright yellow flyer, which was handed to him moments earlier.

"I suppose, if you called up one of *these* ladies on the phone and spanked your monkey, it wouldn't be like you were *cheating* on Rosa." He looked at Marge's picture in the ad. "Of course, I could spank my monkey to *this*." Then he pointed to Ellen's picture on the right. "But you would have to be some sick, perverted school boy to want *this*. Huh?"

He briefly showed the flyer to Stan Junior, who ignored it. He was still reeling from his hangover. "Oh man," he moaned, "I think I'm gonna be sick..." Stan leaned behind a trash can to vomit. He coughed up a few chunks of all-you-can-eat shrimp and what remained in his stomach of the six shots of tequila he had downed at the bachelor party.

"Sorry, man. Whew! Never again. I don't know how my dad's been doing this crap for all these years," Stan Junior commented.

His buddy chuckled at him and shook his head. "You just don't have this in you, do you Stan? You can't cheat on Rosa, and you can't handle your booze, either. He pointed the flyer at Stan's chest, in an accusatory manner—as if fidelity and sobriety were both things to be ashamed of.

Stan snatched the flyer from his friend. "Give me that! I'm just saying. You might as well dip the pen in the inkwell, if you're gonna call these broads up. I mean, look at them!"

Stan Junior glanced at the picture of Margie on his flyer, pointing. "I mean, sure she's hot, but—"

Then, he did a double-take. As he recognized the portrait on the advertisement, he commented, "What the—Aunt Margie??"

Then Stan Junior glanced over to the picture on the right side of the yellow flyer. Immediately, he recognized the picture of Ellen. "—Mom???"

Margie Carter sat at the kitchen table, with her foot propped up on the chair. She filed her toenails as the cordless phone rang.

Ellen sat opposite her, thinking to herself as she knitted a small cap for her young grandson. *He's eight months now. His head circumference will be larger, but I'm not sure he'll ever need a winter cap.* She nodded to herself. *Well, maybe if he comes to visit.*

Margie answered the phone, almost apathetically. "Yeah, 1-900-HOT-MAMA...Uh huh. Oh yeah, do it to me. Oh God, yeah." She sounded bored and detached from the conversation.

Ellen was immersed in her knitting, paying little attention to Margie's call. These days, she was almost as apathetic as Margie, but not quite. Ellen didn't field nearly as many calls as Margie did. Perhaps if she did, she would be pitifully bored, too.

Margie hung up the phone, more focused on polishing her toenails. "Oh, Ellie. I didn't think I'd ever say this, but I am so bored talking about sex."

Ellen looked up, shocked. "Well, that doesn't seem like ya at all, dear."

Margie answered, "It's one thing to sit and talk about it all the time. It's quite another thing to actually *do* it. I miss *doing* it. Don't you ever miss doing it, Ellie?"

Ellie shrugged.

"Yeah, I didn't guess so. I don't think I'd ever miss doing it with Stanley, either." She laughed to herself.

"Maybe ya should take a small vacation, Margie hon'. Ya know, get away fer a bit. They've opened that big mall in Minnesota. Wouldn't ya like ta take a trip?"

"Right. Who's gonna answer this line? It ain't gonna answer itself! You can go, Ellie. This phone is like a big old anchor for me." She picked up the handset. "It would be one thing if it vibrated like a dildo. Then it would be useful. But it doesn't even do that!"

"Cheer up, hon'. We should get another check soon. Maybe it'll be even bigger than the last."

"It's gonna have to be like a bajillion dollars to cheer *me* up." Margie joked.

Just then, the phone rang again.

"Aw hell," Margie cried. She picked it up. "1-900-HOT-MAMA. This Gabrielle. Tell me your most intimate sexual fantasies."

Margie's face grew pale, as she recognized the voice of the caller on the other end. "Stan?" Panicked, she immediately hung up the phone.

After a few seconds, Margie's phone rang again. But this time, she didn't answer it. It rang fifteen or sixteen times before the ringing finally ceased. All the while, Margie bit her lip.

Then Ellen's phone rang.

"Don't get it!" Margie snapped.

"Dear, I have ta get it. What if it's a caller?" She cautiously picked up the phone.

"Hello? Oh ya, hi Stan, hon.' What? 900 number? Now, Son! What kind o' nonsense is that, eh? No, I don't know what yer talking abote, dear. Say, how's that grandson of mine?"

Ellen looked a little nervous. "Heck no. Why, I've never heard of such a silly thing. Oh, yer father? No, I haven't seen Stanley since he left last October."

Marge anxiously listened as her younger sister waded through a river of bullshit. "Oh, no dear. Don't get me wrong. I'd love ta see ya. But Aunt Margie and I are just fine. Ya. No, ya don't need to check up on us. We're doin' A-okay."

Then Ellen started to panic. "Listen, Son. I already told ya. There's no need ta come up here, now. Don't ya worry yer little head abote me. Ya just need ta worry abote that little boy 'o yers, now. Hear?"

Ellen was suddenly quiet, and then she carefully hung up the phone.

"What did he say?" Marge inquired.

"Oh, dear. I'm afraid he's comin' up ta visit."

"Holy crap!" Margie cried.

Ellen sat down, beat. "Holy somethin'—that's fer sure!"

Chapter 13

> "In de meantime, you can heat up yer griddles and get dem to a steady, medium hot temperature. Dis is important, now. Are you listening, Ellie? Get it hot, but steady hot. Odderwise, yer bread will burn or be too soft on de inside."
> SIGRID SEVERTSEN

The North Dakota climate had heated up comfortably the first week of May. In fact, it could have been considered pleasantly, toasty warm. Summer had set in, and Marge and Ellen once again received an even bigger 900 revenue check than they had for the month of April.

But Ellen knew it was only a matter of days before her son appeared on her doorstep. He had inadvertently discovered the truth about her and her sister's 900 sex chat line. Ellen had always tried to set a good moral example for her son. How was she going to explain this?

Stan Junior had packed up Rosa, Little Robert, and two week's worth of clothing and supplies. He took a leave of absence from his A/C installation job, claiming that he "had a family crisis to attend to." He then drove his family in their Dodge minivan from Tucson to Himmel in three days.

Ellen anticipated that she would reluctantly have to let Stan Junior in. She didn't anticipate that he would also bring

Rosa and Little Robert with him. When he showed up on her doorstep with Rosa and Little Robert in tow, she happily let him in. She greeted them all ecstatically with hugs and a big grandma kiss.

"Oh my gosh! Isn't he just a sight fer sore eyes? Oh, Marge, look at this little guy."

Margie cooed at the little eight-month-old infant, as Ellie took him from his mother.

"I can't tell ya how good it is ta see ya!" Ellen cried joyously.

At first, Stan Junior looked amazed when his mother greeted him at the front door. "You look different, Mom. You look—younger."

Rosa added, "You look great, Mom. Very sexy."

"Ya think so?" Ellie responded, blushing. "Ya, somethin' different."

Of course, this blissful reunion brought almost everyone joy—except for Stan Junior. He somehow had assumed the role of disciplinarian, and he couldn't fathom the idea that his mother had been reduced to engaging in such a deviant line of work as conducting a sex chat line in order to pay the bills. He also seemed a little shaken by the idea that she had discarded her North Dakota schoolteacher appearance for a more updated and youthful image. This was not how he remembered his mother.

Ellen invited her son and his family in, as they gathered at the kitchen table. "Are ya hungry? Ya must be starved and exhausted." She shook her head again, as she handed Little Robert to Marge. "I'll make ya somethin' ta eat real quick."

Stan Junior chimed in. "No, Mom. We need to talk." He pulled out the yellow flyer he had procured in Las Vegas. "Explain this," he demanded.

Ellen's face fell. Resigned, she sat down. "Well, dear. Aunt Margie and I—well, we needed ta make money. My pension was far too small fer the both of us ta manage, and yer dad left me with almost nothin'. As it turns ote, Uncle John was also swindled by some insurance guy before he died."

Stan Junior appeared clearly disillusioned by his mother's confession. "Mom. You mean, men actually call you? —*You?*"

"Why, Son? Is that so hard ta believe?" She paused before continuing her explanation. "Look, hon'. I know ya think I'm an old lady. And probably I am. But everybody—young people, old people—we all need ta feel special. We all need ta feel loved. Honestly, Robert. Stanley leaving was probably the best thing that could've happened ta me."

There was an uncomfortable pause in the conversation, as Stan Junior assumed a look of utter indignation. "Mom—I'm *Stan Junior.*"

"Huh?" Ellen look puzzled, while Margie seemed suddenly concerned.

"Mom! You called me *Robert!* My name is Stan!"

"Oh, fer heaven's sake, Son. Don't ya think a mother knows her own child?" Blowing him off, Ellen rose from the table. "Well, if yer not goin' ta eat, I'll just show Rosa and Little Robert yer room." She retrieved her grandson from Margie's cooing arms and retreated up the stairs to the guest bedroom. Rosa followed behind.

Ellen, Rosa, and Little Robert departed, while Stan Junior and Margie remained at the table to continue their conversation. Now they both were clearly concerned. And Stanley was ready to lay a large portion of the blame on his wayward Aunt.

"Aunt Margie. How could you let this happen? This isn't Mom. Why didn't you guys ask us for money? We would have sent you something."

"You know it's not like your mother to ask for anything. That's not what we Severtsens do. Hell, Grandma Sigrid died of God-knows-what in her bed for months and refused to see a doctor. We've always done things on our own, and we've never expected anything from anybody.

"You know your father left your mother for dead. Christ, Stan—she almost died of hypothermia! I'm only grateful that I had these two 900 numbers to use. That was the one thing John had left me after over forty years of marriage.

"If you ask me, *you* should be ashamed of *yourself.* You don't need to make your mother feel guilty for this. She always did what was best for you. She stayed with that old codger all those years for *your* sake! Now you've got to do what's best for her and let her live her life."

Stan Junior gazed down shamefully at the flyer, which he still held in his hands.

Marge continued her speech. "Look, Stan. What I'm really concerned about now is that..." She bent down to whisper to her nephew, afraid that her sister might eavesdrop. "Between you and me, I think Ellie is losing it."

"What d'you mean?" Stan asked.

"I mean, she's not playing with a full deck. You know, the wheel is turning, but the hamster is dead? Seriously. She's so friggin' scatterbrained, I'm gonna have to start writing Sven and *Ellie* jokes up here. I think she might have Alzheimer's."

"What makes you say that?"

"You just heard it, Stan. She called you *Robert*. You know—Robert, her old boyfriend from thirty years back and your half-brother? She does that all the time. She forgets things—like how to make lefse. She has never forgotten how to make lefse! Sometimes she gets up in the morning, like she's getting ready to teach school. Hell—she's been retired for over eight years!"

"You really think she's senile?" Stan inquired.

"Think? I know. Look, Stan. She's endured so much crap from your father, it's not even funny. You know. You grew up here. Is it any wonder she's lost it? *You* would've lost it if you stayed!"

"What do we do, Aunt Marge?" Stan Junior was obviously overwhelmed.

"I don't want to put her in a home. I can't *afford* to put her in a home, if I wanted to. Your father left her with nothing. I don't know, Stan. But if I can help it, that won't happen. Ellie is the only thing I've got now, and I'm not about to lose her."

Stan suddenly looked bright-eyed, as a tremendous idea crossed his mind. "What if we have an auction? Sell all Dad's junk out in the barn?"

"Hell, no!" Margie replied. "Your mother would never go for that. The few times I mentioned going out to the barn, she went crazy. She said that Stanley would be pissed when he came back, if people were messing with his shit. See, Stan? This is what I'm saying. *Your mother is not your mother.* She's someone else. And I think it's because she's loony. Lord only knows how long she's been like this."

"What if she doesn't know, Aunt Margie?"

"What d'ya mean?"

"Here's my idea. Let's send her to town tomorrow with Rosa. You and I can break into the barn and see what's in there. If we decide there's enough there to auction, we'll send her on a trip somewhere, sell all Dad's stuff, and give her the money to support herself. Then she won't have to do all this 900 nonsense." Stan related his well thought out plan as if he had spent every moment during his journey to Himmel devising it.

"How much do you think all that crap is worth?"

"From what I remember—with the antique guns and machinery and equipment—I'd say we might raise forty or fifty thousand dollars."

"Holy crap! That much for all Stanley's junk? You sure?" Marge asked.

"I'm positive. Maybe even more than that. We need to find it all, sort it all, and sell it all."

Early the next day, Rosa Peters was instructed to create an all-day diversion for her mother-in-law, using her young son as bait. She drove Ellen to Bismarck for a day of shopping.

Immediately after the trio departed, Marge and Stan Junior made their way to the dilapidated barn. The doors were closed and padlocked shut. This wasn't the old combination padlock that Stan Junior remembered. This was a new padlock, which required a key.

He managed to borrow a pair of bolt cutters at the local machine shop in town. He cut the lock. The great doors to the old barn swung wide, as they creaked. And as they opened, a horrendous stench of decay wafted out from inside the barn. Overcome by the odor, Margie gasped. Stan Junior shielded his face under the neckline of his t-shirt.

They each stepped five feet inside, still overcome by the tremendously overpowering odor.

"Christ, something died in here!" Margie cried.

Stan Junior stood aghast, as he surveyed the mountainous assembly of tools and machinery before him. "What the hell?" He questioned, obviously perplexed.

"How did all this crap get like this?" Margie asked.

"Heck if I know. Haven't you come in here at all?"

"Hell, no. Your mother would freak if she knew we were here now! It looks like a huge pile of dog shit. Look! There are even flies circling overhead." Margie started to pull at some smaller tools to loosen them from the enormous heap.

Stan Junior followed the swarm of flies overhead toward the rear of the humongous pile of tools. Horrified, his face immediately lost all its color. He stepped back and leaned against a beam. He struggled not to faint.

Margie glanced up from the heap at her nephew. "What is it?" she asked.

Stan only grunted as he pointed to something buried at the bottom of the heap. He was obviously sickened by this discovery, which lay entrapped beneath the twisted mire of rusted tools and machinery.

There, under the huge heap of metal, lay the rotting corpse of his dead father. Stanley Senior had died there in the barn just as he had lived—buried beneath a monstrous pile of crap which he had possessively regarded as his entire life's work.

A half hour after their traumatic discovery, Stanley Junior and his Aunt Marge showed up at the Himmel County jailhouse. He was still white as a sheet, and she was almost hysterical.

"We need to speak to Sheriff Baker!" Margie demanded.

The desk clerk went to the back office to fetch the Sheriff, who came out moments later.

"Sheriff, I don't know how to tell you this, but we found Stanley Peters dead in Ellie's barn," Margie blurted.

"Is that so?" Paul Baker asked. He didn't seem surprised.

"Yes, Sheriff. And it looks like he's been dead for some time."

"How'd he die? Can you tell?"

"Looks like he was buried alive under all his tools." Marge volunteered. "He must've been there all winter long. I don't think that Ellen even knew he was out there."

The Sheriff grabbed the keys to his squad car. "Well, let's go take a look."

They returned to the barn. The Sheriff surveyed the damage inflicted by the heavy pile of tools onto the rotting corpse which was once Stanley Senior's body.

"Yep. Looks like he was buried alive." The Sheriff commented, studying the pile of metal and the decaying flesh and bones beneath. "Lord knows how long he was out here before he died. Could've been minutes. Could've been days. Hard ta tell at this point. I imagine he was partly frozen during the winter, and he probably started ta thaw a couple of months ago, when it started ta warm up 'round here." He stated his theory very matter-of-factly, as though he was emotionally desensitized to the horrific scene.

Stan Junior remained silent, still in shock and almost on the verge of tears.

"We're goin' ta have send him off ta Bismarck for an autopsy." Paul Baker commented.

"Bismarck?" Margie asked. "Can't we just bury him?"

"Not likely. What if there was foul play? Ya know, it's hard to tell with this much decomposition what actually happened. Better ta send him off ta the Medical Examiner."

Margie, at first almost pervertedly amused by the idea that Stanley had finally gotten his comeuppance, now became seriously concerned for her sister's welfare.

"What? You think Ellie…" She entreated Paul Baker for an explanation.

"I'm not sure." Paul glanced back at Stan Junior, who was still in a state of shock. "Are ya goin' ta be okay, Son?"

Stan nodded.

Marge interrupted the Sheriff. "Wait, Sheriff. Can you— Well, do you think we can just dig him out quickly and cart him away before Ellie gets home?"

"Dig him ote?" The Sheriff quizzed.

"Yeah." Margie began her feeble explanation. "Honestly, Sheriff. I'm not sure Ellie is in her right mind. Stan will corroborate. Won't you, Stan?"

Still speechless, Stan nodded in agreement.

"I think she's lost it. I really don't think she knows Stanley died in here, and I can't begin to believe that she had anything to do with it. You know Ellie, Sheriff. You were the one who called me up here. This is not her doing. She wouldn't hurt a fly."

Margie continued. "Can't we just ship him off to the Coroner without her knowing about it? That way, we can find out what actually killed Stanley first. Once Ellie is cleared of any wrongdoing, we can break it to her gently. I really don't know—in her present state of mind—if knowing Stanley is dead wouldn't just send her off the deep end for good."

The Sheriff considered Margie's request. He pensively walked around the heaped pile of twisted tools and metal and shook his head. "I just don't understand how this happened."

Then he decisively looked up. "I tell you what. I'll bring my officers ote here, and we'll take some crime scene photos. Survey the contents of the barn—if that's even possible. How long will Miss Severtsen be gone?"

"She's in Bismarck. She'll be gone all day." Marge answered.

As he turned to leave, the Sheriff shook his head one last time. "Tsk, tsk." He patted Stan Junior reassuringly on the arm. "Sorry again, Stan. Must be terrible ta see yer dad this way. Let me know if there's anything I can do."

The Sheriff left, and Margie breathed a sigh of relief as she spoke to her nephew. "You see what I mean? This is just gonna kill your mother!"

Stan finally managed to muster up the courage to speak. "D'you think Mom had something to do with this, Aunt Margie?"

"I really don't know. If she did, you know Stanley drove her to it. Chances are, if she *did* kill him, she might not even remember doing it. I saw this happen to guys in Korea. Shell shock." She paused for a moment. "Shit! I should've known, when she pulled out that roll of twenty dollar bills!"

"Roll of bills? Dad had a roll of bills with him when he came to Tucson. I gave it back to him when I bailed him out of jail. He usually kept it in that empty Folgers coffee can, over there on the ground."

"Holy crap!" Marge cried, exasperated. Then she closed her eyes, as she fought back her overwhelming tears of frustration. "Oh, Ellie dear, how am I gonna get you out of *this* long, hard, dirty, dildo of a pickle?"

Chapter 14

"When yer potato and flour mixture has set for five minutes, you mix t'ree tablespoons of de cream and butter mixture. But you have to watch and adapt. If it's winter or de potatoes are dry, you may have to use more. If it's a year where de dairy cows' milk has been t'in and de milk is not as creamy, you may have to use less. You'll have to figure out what works for you, when you get used to doing it enough times. Mix two more cups of flour. Did I tell you to use unbleached flour? Make sure it's unbleached. Mix well, and knead it fifteen times on yer floured rag. You don't want it sticky, but it's got to be wet enough to hold togedder."

SIGRID SEVERTSEN

When Ellen and Rosa returned late in the evening after a long day of shopping in Bismarck, Marge was exhausted. Both she and Stan Junior had broken into the barn, discovered Stanley's rotted corpse, reported it to the Sheriff, gave him access to perform an abbreviated crime scene investigation, and helped him ship the body off to the Bismarck Coroner's office. They did all this without Ellen ever suspecting a thing.

As in childhood, Marge was seldom squeamish about anything. She resolved to play it cool. It didn't bother her at all to find Stanley's body in the old barn. On the other hand, after discovering his father's lifeless and rotted corpse, Stan Junior found playing it cool a very difficult thing indeed. At this point, he wasn't sure his mother wasn't at least clued into the details of his father's untimely demise.

Marge and her young nephew had devised a plan for a more lengthy diversion to get Ellen out of town for two weeks. During that time, she and Stan Junior could clear out the barn, survey its contents, and hold an auction of all Stanley's belongings.

For many North Dakota farmers, auctions were a lucrative, all-day affair. They took a great deal of planning and work on the part of the sellers, usually required the enlistment of an auctioneer, and ultimately offered spectators a huge opportunity for socialization and entertainment. An auction in North Dakota was regarded more like an "estate carnival"—a once in a lifetime opportunity to gather and bicker over the spoils and fruits of the seller's lifetime of labor.

Rosa agreed that Ellen should take Little Robert on the trip with her, while she stayed behind to answer Marge's 900 line. Of course, Stan Junior reluctantly consented to this arrangement after his wife stubbornly insisted on doing so. Rosa argued that their plan for auction would be best served if she answered the line for Marge, thereby freeing Marge to help Stan prepare for the sale. And if Ellen took Little Robert with her, Rosa might get a long-deserved break from the tedium of motherhood.

Marge dialed the phone to call her son Joseph in Minneapolis. He worked as a site foreman for her twin brothers, Lars and Gunnar, in their very successful and profitable construction business.

"Hi, baby. It's Ma. Listen. I need you to do something very important for me….Well, I need you to take your Aunt Ellie off my hands for two weeks and get her out of this state. You need to come pick her up and take her to the Mall of America…No, I need you NOW! I need her out of my hair today. I've got some stuff I need to take care of here with your cousin Stan, and I need her gone."

Joseph was obviously reticent to drop his work obligations in order to create a diversion for his Aunt Ellie. Clearly, this task just wasn't as important to Joseph as it was to his mother.

"What d'ya mean Uncle Lars won't let you go? Listen to me. Get my little prick of a brother on the phone now!" She commanded.

Lars reluctantly answered the call from his big sister. Even after fifty years, he was still a little terrified of his older sister's wrath. "Hello, Lars? What's this I hear about you not letting Joseph get off work?"

She listened impatiently as Lars feebly tried to explain his apparent unwillingness to cooperate with Marge's plan. Finally, she interrupted him rudely. "Listen, you little imp! I need you to give my son time off to drive his little fanny over here and pick up *your* sister to take her to the Mall of America! You hear me???"

Marge angrily slammed down the cordless phone and yelled, "Christ! I should've dunked that little weasel in the latrine when I had the chance!"

Marge informed Ellen of her pending plans for a brief vacation out of state. She also informed her sister that she was expected to care for her grandchild and cart him around with her on her trip.

At first, Ellie argued against leaving Stan Junior behind. He explained that he needed to stay behind and "fix things up" on the farm. He especially needed to fix the storm door for starters. In fact, he stated that there were so many items which had been neglected and needed his attention, he wasn't even sure two weeks would be enough time to accomplish everything he needed to do. He would simply have to prioritize and get through as much work as he could.

After a good bit of persuasion, Ellie acquiesced. Marge had convinced her that she truly deserved a vacation and that everyone left behind would be just fine without her. She informed Ellie that she could stay with Margie's eldest son in Minneapolis. Soon, Ellen's initial concern transitioned to elation, when she realized that she would be going to Minneapolis to visit the brand new mall. And she was even more excited to be spending quality time with her new grandson.

"Gosh, I hear ya can spend days in that place," Ellen confided. "Goodness, I'm so excited." She made happy faces at Little Robert in his high chair. "Grandma and Robert are goin' ta have so much fun…" She winked at the infant, and he smiled back.

When Marge's son Joseph arrived at the farmhouse the next day, Marge greeted him at the door. Ellen had excitedly packed her belongings for the trip the night before.

"I'm so excited, John dear. This is goin' ta be the best trip ever!"

"The name's *Joseph*, dahlink. And yes—it's going to be the *best* trip, because it's the *only* trip you've ever had." Marge kissed her sister goodbye by pressing her face against either side of Ellen's cheek. "Keep an eye on your Aunt Ellie, dear." Then she whispered quietly to her son. "Make sure she doesn't accidentally burn the house down or forget Little Robert at the Mall."

"Yes, Ma," Joseph obediently replied.

"You're a good boy. Now—Go! Get lost!" his mother commanded.

At Marge's bidding, Joseph, Ellen, and Little Robert left the State of North Dakota on the trip of a lifetime—a quest to the Mall of America in Minneapolis.

At first, Marge was worried that Rosa Peters would not do well at answering her 900 line. But after listening to her field a few calls, Marge's fears were soon assuaged. As a matter of fact, Rosa was almost more talented at answering Marge's line than Marge had been lately. Rosa addressed the task with a renewed enthusiasm. For her, it was a refreshing respite from the boredom of housewifery and motherhood.

Stan Junior, of course, could not bring himself to listen in on his wife's explicit phone conversations. He knew that Rosa was far from being a saint. But Stan unrealistically put his wife on a pedestal—much like he did with his mother. He still couldn't fathom the idea that *any* woman might stoop to having to sell sex chats to horny men, when they knew full well that they were probably masturbating on the other end of the phone line. He tried to convince himself that, if his efforts to raise cash from the sale of his father's estate were successful, it would have all been worth it. This entire plan for the 900 numbers would be stifled, when he presented his mother with enough cash monies upon which she could comfortably retire.

Once Margie was assured that she could hand the reins of her burgeoning business over to Rosa's capable hands, she paid a concerned visit to the Sheriff. She knew that Paul Baker and his wife Doris had always been fond of Ellen. After all, it was Paul who contacted Marge to convince to her move clear across the country to take care of her sister.

Marge also understood that Paul might be able to offer her some insight into the details of Stanley's demise. Her plan was to coax Paul out of a little additional information in order to hurry the case along. Perhaps if Margie intervened, a just and speedy outcome might be arrived at for all affected parties.

She sat at Paul Baker's desk, but she tried not flirt overtly with the attractive, yet highly esteemed Sheriff.

"What brings ya here, Mrs. Carter?"

"Well, Paul—I'm just a little concerned for my sister. I don't know what I would do without her."

"I see. Do ya think that Miss Severtsen might have murdered her husband?"

"Honestly, Sheriff. I just don't know. Now that I think about it, it's possible. If she did, you know—everybody in this town knows—she was probably driven to it. I'm not sure, if she *did* do it, she would even remember it at all. She's definitely losing her mind. I mean, just today, she greeted my oldest son, Joseph, by calling him by the name of my dead husband, John.

"I tell you, honestly, Sheriff. I don't know what to do. If I could just get some idea of what actually happened—how Stanley might have died—I might be able to answer some questions. I mean, I'd hate to see that you went through all the trouble of getting me up here to take care of my sister, only to see her get carted off to some state loony bin for the criminally insane. Ellen's much too fragile for that kind of place. That wouldn't do anybody any good. Would it?"

"Nope. Yer right, Mrs. Carter. I'd hate ta see that happen ta Miss Severtsen. We all love her dearly. Unfortunately, the case is now in the hands of the Bismarck Coroner. We'll have ta see what he decides."

"What *he* decides?"

"Ya." Paul scratched his chin for a moment. He opened a manila file folder and read his report. "It looks like Jim McDaniel has been assigned the autopsy at the Bismarck Medical Examiner's office."

Margie seemed interested. "Really? Maybe you could tell me a little about this guy."

"Well, he's a pretty nice guy. Not originally from here, of course. Only been here fer abote ten years. I think he came from Atlanta. He's mid-fifties, single. I understand he has a penchant fer loose women and a really good cigar."

Marge started to lick her lips. "Really? And he's good looking?"

"Well, now, Mrs. Carter. I couldn't tell ya one way or the other abote that. But the ladies sure seem ta like him." Paul grinned nervously.

"Okay then. One more thing. Where does he like to hang out?" Marge inquired.

"I've heard he frequents Peacock Alley on Main Avenue. Their steak sandwich is pretty good."

"Hmm. I'll have to give it a try. Thanks for the info, Sheriff."

Ellen Severtsen rested her elbow on the passenger's side door of her nephew Joseph's car. As they raced eastward on Highway 94 in his metallic blue Ford Taurus, she opened the window all the way down and stuck her hand out. The warm summer wind brushed against her palm and blew through her hair.

She, her nephew Joseph, and her infant grandson were on their way out of the state, on an eight-hour journey to Minneapolis. She sat quietly enjoying the scenery. A few times they passed sunflower farms. The fields were freshly plowed, and no plants were yet apparent. They had not reached their full growing potential, since the harvest season was still five months away. Soon the green flowers would emerge from their gestating pods. Their infantile stalks would grow strong and thick, and the mature flowers would climb to heights taller than a fully grown man.

As Ellen felt the heat of the summer sun beating down on her face through the dirty car windshield, she closed her eyes. *I'm a lot like a sunflower,* she thought to herself. *I'm waiting to emerge and show my true character, in all my beauty and ravishing glory. I am pointing my face toward the sun.*

Then she smiled at her nephew and looked behind her to address her grandson. Little Robert was strapped obediently in his infant car seat. He looked up at Ellie and smiled. "Oooh, Little Robert. We are going ta have such fun! I haven't travelled this way in a very long time."

Soon the car of weary travelers passed a great sign on the highway. Ellen pointed to show her little grandson. "Look, hon'. It says, 'Welcome ta Minnesota!' Oooh, how exciting. Clap yer hands. Can ya clap?"

She unfastened her seat belt and reached back to hold her grandson's pudgy hands. She clapped them together. "Good boy!" She turned back around in the passenger's seat and refastened her seatbelt. She smiled at Joseph. "He's a good boy—just like his poppa. –And his grandpoppa."

After another hour of driving, Ellen and Little Robert fell fast asleep, while Joseph drove the last leg of their journey to Minneapolis.

Joseph had delivered his Aunt and her grandson safely to his home. He called Marge to let her know he had arrived in one piece. His wife, Melinda, had graciously situated Ellen in the guest bedroom.

"Look, Ma. I think Aunt Ellen is going senile. Didn't you say she'd never left the State of North Dakota?"

"Never. She's never been out anywhere. Why do you ask?" Margie inquired.

"Because she acts like she's been out here before. She talks about some old places and stuff like she might have been over here eons ago." Joseph stated to his mother.

"See? That's what I'm talking about. I'm telling you she's never been out of the state. The only long trip she ever went on was when she went to college in Dickinson."

"Not only that, Ma. She talks to Little Robert about his 'grandpoppa'—Uncle Stanley—like he was some kind of great man, instead of the low life that he was," Joseph added.

Margie shook her head in disgust, as she held the phone to her ear. "There wasn't anything great about Stanley, except his size."

"So, what do you want me to do, Ma?"

"I don't know, Joseph. Your Auntie is friggin' losing her mind. Just keep an eye on her. Don't let her stray too far or leave the oven on. And make sure she puts her pants on before you go out. Other than that, I'll keep you posted on things here. Love you, Son. Mwahh. Buh bye."

"Okay, Ma. Call me."

Chapter 15

Marge Carter stood before the small mirror above the sink in the bathroom of the old Severtsen family farmhouse. She wore her best dress—a slimming little tea-length black number with a plunging neckline and ¾ length sleeves. She fluffed out her shoulder pads and pushed up at her bosom to enhance the boosting effect of her new Wonderbra. She admired her "udders", which was her North Dakota farm girl pet name for her boobs. After breastfeeding four children, she had to admit—they still looked pretty amazing.

For a woman of advanced years, Margie Carter was hardly a wrinkled hag. True, the last few months of misery brought with it a few added frown lines, but she was still a handsome woman. She looked far more youthful than all of her peers— even some celebrities, whose youthfulness was often the result of some deliberate surgical intervention.

Marge was all-woman and an all-natural woman at that. She exuded sex appeal, and she knew it. She convinced herself that her youthful appearance had more to do with her youthful mindset. She truly felt that her active libido and sex life had a rejuvenating effect on her mood and appearance.

She stepped into a shiny pair of silver heels and picked up her black silk clutch purse. She had spent the entire grueling day helping Stan Junior weed through his father's belongings. And just an hour ago she had a very emotionally draining conversation with her son Joseph, who was babysitting her loony sister in Minneapolis. Rosa was answering the 900 line, which enabled Margie the chance to sneak away at last. It was only 7:30 P.M., and it was still light outside. She planned to drive the Towncar 66 miles east to Bismarck and order herself a steak sandwich at Peacock Alley American Grill and Bar. If she got herself laid in the process—well, *that* would be an added bonus.

She was on a mission. She drove the hour long journey in her Lincoln and rolled down her car windows. *I'll fix my hair when I get there*, she said to herself. She cranked up the car radio full blast and boldly sang along with the music as she sped down the highway.

Her destination—Peacock Alley—had a rich history in the city of Bismarck. It wasn't exactly a five star restaurant (nothing in Bismarck was five star), but it certainly wasn't a dive by any stretch of the imagination. Originally established after prohibition in 1933, it reportedly served alcohol and hosted gambling secretively during that miserable period of American history. It was located in the historic Patterson building in Downtown Bismarck. The food was top-notch, and many menu items had received rave reviews.

Marge finally arrived at her intended destination. She rolled up the car windows and turned off the ignition. She glanced into the rear view, tousled her hair, and applied one final coat of pink lipstick. Of course, pink was always her favorite color, but Marge also remembered reading in a fashion column that pink lipstick made older women appear younger. Red—old. Pink—*young*.

This color suited her fine. *Yes, I look super-hot*, she thought to herself. She smacked her lips, checked her eye shadow, stuffed her lipstick in her clutch purse, and headed through the front entrance to the Peacock.

The restaurant was divided into two sections. One side consisted of a dining room with booth-style restaurant seating and tables. This was the more elegant side of the restaurant. Seating in this section required reservations.

The other section of the bar and grill had more of a pub-like atmosphere. It was a little bit more homey, and a single woman could safely hang out at the bar all night, without a reservation and without fear of possibly being groped. But Marge had been sexually frustrated by her recent, involuntary life of celibacy. Being groped by a stranger might actually do her some good.

She marched past the hostess and made her way to the bar. She shuffled her bottom onto a stool, next to a somewhat scruffy-looking man in his mid-fifties. His hair was a dirty blonde—a little longish, perhaps. But Marge could read from his manner of dress that he seemed more of a casual professional. He wore Docker khakis, penny loafers, and a brown tweed sports coat with leather patches on the elbows. He had an unruly beard and sad, brown eyes. She decided that, underneath all the excess facial hair, he was not at all bad looking.

He sat, pensively glaring across the bar, holding an unlit cigar in his right hand. He briefly glanced at her out of the corner of his eye, as Marge scooted onto the stool to his left. She nodded, but she didn't say hello.

The bartender handed the man a glass of single malt scotch. "Here you go, Doc."

"Thanks, Glen." He lifted his glass, taking a swig.

Glen raised his brow slightly, acknowledging Marge's presence.

"I'll take a bourbon," she said. "Make it a double. Jim Beam, please."

The bartender nodded and turned his back to prepare her drink. He poured a glass and handed it to her.

"Can you run me a tab, please?" She took a hard swig of the bourbon.

The man next to Marge cleared his throat, as he spoke to the bartender. "Hmm. The woman can handle her liquor."

Glen smiled and nodded.

"What?" Margie looked up but seemed disinterested.

"Usually single ladies sit here and end up ordering something fruity."

"Yeah, right. I've got enough fruity in my life right now." Margie opened her clutch purse and retrieved her pack of Pall Malls and a Bic lighter. She tapped the box on the counter and pulled out a cigarette with her lips. She lit the cigarette and inhaled one long drag. She then stuffed the remaining pack and the lighter back into her clutch purse. She blew out a long puff of smoke.

"That stuff'll kill you, you know," the man next to her informed her.

"That's kinda the point—isn't it?" Marge still seemed a little put off by the man. She took another drag of her cigarette with her right hand, then downed another swig of bourbon with her left "Anyway, what would you know about it?" she inquired.

"I guess you could say it's my business," he answered.

Marge moaned, still only half-interested.

The man continued his feeble attempt at making conversation. "I suppose I'm not one to talk. I have my own vices."

"Like sucking on an unlit cigar?" she sarcastically quipped.

The man chuckled. "I can see you're amused. But there's really an art to savoring a great imported cigar."

"Really? What kind of secret is that?" And then she added, again sarcastically, "Wait—will you have to kill me after you tell me?"

He ignored her snide comment and began his monologue. "Well, you almost have to spend time sampling the flavor before you light it. You sniff the aroma. You imagine what it will be like, when you *do* smoke it. You take it on your lips. You lick the tip. You bite it, and you savor it."

Marge felt herself becoming aroused, listening to the man just talk about cigars. She was now clearly engaged in the conversation, as he continued his description.

"Finally, you light it. You're into the 'down-and-dirty' of the moment—the intense heat of the flame and the stench of the smoke filling your lungs and the surrounding air."

"And then?"

"And then….it's all over. You're left holding your smelly butt in your hand and a brief but lasting memory of what once was. It's like a really great one-night stand—perfection."

Marge chuckled at his wit. "How charming!"

The man smiled, as he extended his right hand to shake his neighbor's hand. "Doctor James Lee McDaniel the Third, MD/PhD, at your service madam."

"Margot Carter the First, B.I.T.C.H. But I'm no madam, sir—I can assure you."

The man looked apologetic. "I'm sorry. I suppose that was a little pretentious of me, wasn't it?"

"Slightly."

"Okay. Let's start again." He extended his hand once more. "I'm Jim."

She took his hand and smiled. "Margie."

"Nice to meet you, Margie." He glanced down at her empty glass and pointed to it. "May I?"

"I was trying to figure out what the hell you were waiting for."

He motioned for Mike to bring a second drink. "You can really put that stuff away, can't you?" he asked.

"Honestly? I'm not usually this thirsty. I haven't had a drink in over six months. I've got two weeks to make up for that."

"How so?"

"Well, I'm living with my sweet sister, Miss Goody Two-Shoes, and she doesn't permit drinking or smoking in the house. Her late husband was a drunk."

"I see. He died of cirrhosis?"

"I'm not sure *what* he died of. Anyway, she's in Minnesota for two weeks, so I need to get my fill of all my vices before she gets back."

There was a slight lull in the conversation, as the waiter brought Margie's new glass of whiskey.

"So what exactly are you a doctor of, James Lee McDaniel, MD/PhD?"

"I'm a pathologist for the Bismarck Coroner."

"You play with stiffs all day?"

"Oh yeah," Jim commented cynically, lifting his glass. "All day, everyday."

"Me too. You single?"

"Divorced."

"You're obviously not from around here," Margie commented.

"No, I divorced my gold-digging bitch of a wife and left her in Atlanta ten years ago," Jim answered. Then he shook his head. "Sorry. I'm still a little bitter. And you—single or divorced?"

"Neither. Widowed."

"Oh, sorry." Jim paused, a bit uncomfortable. "How long ago?"

"Six months ago. I *killed* him," Margie boldly declared.

"What d'you mean, you *killed* him?"

"I had sex with him. He had a heart attack and died."

"Oooh. Rough." Jim took another swig of his scotch and stared straight ahead. "Wow. Then—you must be pretty good."

Margie chuckled. "Damn right, I'm good. I'm a little out of practice, but I'm still pretty darned good."

"So, you said you're into stiffs? What exactly do *you* do for a living, Margie Carter?"

"I own a 900 sex chat line," she informed him, proudly.

"Really? Here in North Dakota?"

"Uh huh. 1-900-HOT-MAMA. I'm Gabrielle."

"I see." Jim thought for a moment, then he nodded. "Yeah, I could definitely see you doing that. You have a very sexy voice," he complimented.

"I have a successful ad in some skin rags across the country. I put in a picture of me taken thirty-four years ago. But the caller doesn't know that. I've certainly aged a bit since then and put on a few extra pounds."

Jim leaned back to get a good, long look at Margie's derrière. "Naw. I think you're shaped just right. I kind of prefer that Rubensian look. It's supple and soft. It suits you."

Marge paused again, looking suddenly serious. "Say, how's your heart?"

Later that evening, a very drunk Doctor James Lee McDaniel and his also drunk companion, Marge Carter, stumbled down the hallway to their room in the Radisson Hotel Bismarck. Jim backed Marge against the door and kissed her deeply on the lips. As he fumbled for his room key, she laughed out loud at his clumsiness.

"Ha! Maybe you're too drunk for me to take advantage of!"

He finally pulled the key out of his pocket. She tried guiding the key into the keyhole to help him. They both laughed. "Well, if you can't get your key into this hole, how're you gonna get *that* key into *this* hole?" She pointed to his fly first, and then to her crotch.

He bobbled his head and pointed to himself. "You would be amazed at what I—a trained physician—can do!" he joked.

"Stop!" Marge slapped his arm. She was laughing so hard, she was gasping for breath. She held her ribs in side-splitting agony.

He opened the door. They embraced and clumsily backed up to the bed, falling backward.

Marge stopped laughing and suddenly turned serious again. "Hey, wait!"

Concerned, Jim stopped. "What? What's wrong?"

"What if I get—pregnant???" She again broke out into delirious laughter.

Jim snickered as he reached for his wallet. He ineptly retrieved a condom. "It's ribbed for her pleasure."

"Now that's what I'm talking about!" She chortled, while simultaneously unfastening his pants. Jim lay helplessly reclined on the bed, resigned to letting her have her way with him. All the while, the two were in passionate hysterics, crudely removing items of clothing with little-to-no finesse.

She kissed him again, as she straddled him on the bed. He had been holding the condom in his right hand, while she dominated him. She reached down to feel his erect penis. "Umm, I like that." She grabbed the condom. "Let me see that thing." She violently tore at its wrapper.

Jim lifted up his head, still pathetically intoxicated and helpless. "You need assistance with that thing, madam?"

"Shut up! I already told you I'm no madam," she scolded. Then she laughed again as she successfully retrieved the rubber from its packaging. "No—I can do this!" she assured herself. "I just need to—" .

As she fumbled with the prophylactic, it made a hard snapping sound.

"Oh, shit!"

A few seconds of dark silence ensued.

"Broke?"

Marge stuck her finger through the newly torn hole in the condom. "Uh, got any more?"

"Sorry. That was my spare."

"Oh, hell!" she cried, beat.

Then, she thought for a moment. "Okay, okay. I got an idea," she slurred.

"What?"

"Okay. I gotta ask you something—you know, as a trained physician."

"What?"

"If you give me the clap, can you prescribe me some penicillin?"

And after several minutes of additional boisterous laughter, Marge and Jim continued with their lovemaking session—the first of many to occur that very evening.

Early the next morning, Margie lay naked in the king-sized bed at the Radisson. Yawning, she smelled her breath. "Oooh—Bad cottonmouth," see whispered to herself, sleepily. She stretched, as she opened her eyes. She felt the pillow next to hers. Jim was not there. He sat, fully clothed at the edge of the bed.

Noticing that she was awake, he turned to her, as he slipped his foot into his left argyle sock. "Hey, sleepyhead," he greeted.

"Yeah, I'm not an early riser. I got pretty toasted last night, and I'm hungover." She held her forehead and stuck out her tongue.

Jim leaned over to kiss her on the cheek. "Thanks for the evening. Gotta go."

"Where?"

"I do have a job, Margie. Gotta go to work." He checked his watch, as he slipped it on. "I'm already late."

Reaching into his back pocket, he pulled out his billfold. He pulled out two crisp $100 bills. He quietly opened Margie's clutch purse on the nightstand and gingerly placed them inside.

Marge was clearly pissed. "What the hell is that for?"

"I just thought…I don't know. I thought—"

"You thought what, you bastard? That I was a goddam whore???" Furious, Marge jumped out from under the sheets, snatching up the bills he had so delicately placed in her purse.

He held up his hands to shield himself from Margie's obvious wrath. "Well, Marge. You *did* tell me that you had a sex chat line. I kinda figured you were a working girl." Jim entreated Marge sheepishly, "I'm sorry. I guess I shouldn't have assumed…"

She examined the bills in her hand. "What am I worth?" Enraged, she glared up at him. "I'm a two-hundred dollar hooker?" She fumed as she spoke. "Look, asshole. If you don't want to see me again, that's fine. Just leave. But don't insult me by giving me this shit!" She threw the bills in his face. "Just friggin' leave!"

"Marge—" He tried to explain.

"Get out, asshole!"

Jim hurriedly headed for the front door, leaving his room key. "Can you check out?" he asked.

"Get out!" She stood there naked, with her hands on her hips. Then she screamed as she madly stomped her foot. "Aaaaargh!"

Chapter 16

It was 11 A.M. at the Severtsen farm. Rosa was in the farmhouse kitchen, answering the 900 line for Marge. Her engorged breasts were painfully swollen and about ready to pop with milk. She rested two one-gallon freezer bags full of ice on each boob, as she answered the line. She sat at the kitchen table, drinking a cup of black coffee while she spoke.

"Yeah, this is Gabrielle…What do you mean I'm not Gabrielle? Sure I am."

The caller on the other end did not seem convinced that Rosa was who she said she was. "Who are you? Jack? Tell me about your intimate fantasies, Jack."

Rosa had immigrated to Arizona from Mexico with her mother, father, and younger brother when she was nine. She spoke perfect American English, but she had a very subtle Spanish accent. Even the most guttural English words rolled sexily off the tip of her Latin tongue.

She was a very attractive young woman, a few years younger than Stan. She had very distinct curves and long and straight, dark ash brown hair. Her eyes were a deep brown, and her eyelashes were so thick, long, and curly that they almost looked false. It was not hard to understand how Stan would have been so helplessly captivated by Rosa's luscious and sensuous lips or her golden brown complexion.

"—The other Gabrielle? Oh no, she's not here."

The caller was becoming irate, but Rosa was not going to take any abuse from him. "Look. She's not here. Anyway, don' you wanna discuss your fantasies with me? I'm a lot younger and prettier than the other Gabrielle."

"Well yeah, sure she's the girl in the ad. But that picture was taken a long time ago."

Jack asked her how long it had been since Marge's picture was taken.

She answered, "Over thirty years." She tried, once again, to encourage him to chat with her. "Talk to me, baby. Tell me what's on your mind."

Jack cursed angrily on the other end. Rosa held the receiver away from her ear. "Look, jerk! That's none of your business. I'm not gonna tell you her real name, and I'm not gonna tell you where we are. You don' wanna talk to me, then I don' wanna talk to you." Angry, she hung up the phone.

Just as Rosa finished her heated exchange with Jack, Margie sauntered into the kitchen. She was still fuming from her encounter with Jim McDaniel. She still wore the dress from her date the night before. She wore a pair of sunglasses and moved very slowly. Her complexion took on almost a greenish hue, as she struggled to recover from the previous night's bout of drinking.

"Who was that?" Marge asked Rosa.

"Some guy named Jack. He wanted to talk to you. He tried to get me to tell him your real name."

"I thought they shut that guy's phone off. He kept saying his mother was going to kick him out." Margie stated, disgusted.

"Ah, he's not a problem," Rosa assured. "I can handle it."

Marge nodded at Rosa's makeshift cold packs, still propped atop her chest. "Sore boobs?"

"Yeah. They feel like two big boulders. Very hard and painful. I hap' to sleep on my back. Hurts too much. It's like they're on fire." Rosa pouted, extending her bottom lip. Then, she looked up at Marge. "You're kinda late. Stan wanted you out at the barn."

"Yeah, I know," Margie responded. "Let me get a cup of coffee and put my jeans on. I'll be out there in a second."

Half an hour later, Margie ventured out to the barn where Stan had been working. There were two long flatbed trailers parked in front of the open doors. The auctioneer had backed the trailers up to the barn and instructed Stan to start loading some of the smaller equipment and tools into boxes. Then he was instructed to set the boxes onto the back of the trailer. As the auction opened, buyers would be invited to inspect the goods before they decided on a bid. The auctioneer would hold up the box when the bidding started. The larger tools and equipment could just be laid out strategically along the perimeter of the barn.

Stan Junior stood on the back of the long flatbed trailer, shuffling over a box of half-filled cans of spray paint with his foot. He glared over at his aunt. He was obviously miffed.

"Glad you could find time to join me," he commented sarcastically. He jumped off the trailer.

"Sorry, Stan. Auntie's got a bit of a headache right now." She still wore her sunglasses to shield her sensitive eyes from the glare of the summer sun.

"Out all night, sleazing around?" Stan inquired accusatorily.

"Hey," his aunt cried defensively. "Don't you dare judge me, you little snot-nosed brat! I should take you over my knee."

Stan sat down on an inverted 5-gallon paint can, dejected. "I'm sorry, Aunt Marge. I guess I'm a little overwhelmed right now. I mean, I just found my poor dad's body rotting under a bunch of his crap in this barn. My own mother, who should probably be in some mental hospital by now, is probably the one who killed him. And my wife is answering a slutty sex chat line in the kitchen. And just between you and me, Aunt Marge—I'm not so sure she's not actually enjoying it!" Frustrated, he hid his face in his hands.

Margie patted her nephew on the back. "It's okay, Stan baby. Auntie's working on a plan to get us out of this mess." She looked around at the separated heaps of tools and equipment. She walked over to the trailer and peered into the box of spray paint cans. "Seriously. Who's gonna buy this shit?"

Discouraged, Stan Junior stared down at the ground beneath his feet.

Marge pulled up an old wooden crate and sat down next to her nephew. She wrapped her arm around his back.

"Cheer up, baby. Auntie will make it better. I promise." She spoke in a childish voice, while she pinched his cheek and mussed up his hair playfully. "Now there's a good boy…"

Annoyed, Stan pushed Margie's hand away. "Knock it off, Aunt Marge."

Marge forcefully pulled her nephew's head to her bosom, and clumsily stroked his head. "Wassa matter, widdow Stan? You too big for Auntie to wuv on you? Give Auntie a big kiss," she teased. She puckered her lips and smacked them, sloppy and wet against his cheek.

Later that afternoon, Stan and Marge had almost completely loaded both flatbed auction trailers full of boxes. Stan was a fit young man of twenty-seven. He was used to hard labor. But Marge had been a housewife and mother for the last thirty years. She hadn't worked so hard since she left the family farm at nineteen. Her back was aching. They were both covered from head-to-toe with grime from pilfering through Stanley's filthy possessions.

As she piled each hoarded item of Stanley's onto the trailer, she stopped to examine it and estimate its worth. She convinced herself that the majority of items had no value. All the stuff was just crap, and if she wasn't interested in Stanley's junk, how could anybody else be?

But Stan Junior knew that if his father thought the items were important enough to purchase and collect, surely someone else would take a shine to them. "It doesn't matter, Aunt Marge. Throw it on the trailer!" he directed.

He pointed to a few select items to illustrate his point that Stanley's collection may, indeed, have some monetary value. "See these here?" He displayed his father's antique gun collection, comprised of several pistols (one a revolutionary war set of duel pistols), four hunting rifles, a crossbow, and a few novelty pistols. "Dad bragged about these guns all the time. There are a few guys in Himmel—Paul Baker included—who would love to get their grubby paws on these puppies." He surveyed the contents of the gun collection, then stopped suddenly. He looked puzzled. "Hmmm..." he murmured.

"What?"

"Well, most of his guns are here, but his World War Two Army rifle is missing."

"No kidding. Maybe he sold it," Margie suggested.

"No way. He might've sold one of the other guns, but he definitely wouldn't have sold that. He loved to hold it while he polished it and told me and Mom his war stories over and over again."

"Well, maybe your mom kept it as a memento," Margie commented.

"Mom? What would Mom do with a gun?" he asked in disbelief.

"I guess you're right. Ellie can't even kill a worm," she joked.

"If that's true, Aunt Marge—what makes you so sure that Mom offed Dad?" Stan Junior asked.

"Relax, Stan baby. We don't know if she did."

Stan glanced around the barn. "Maybe it'll turn up," he said, once again distracted by the thought of the missing rifle.

Moments later, Rosa walked out to the barn. "Marge, there's someone on the 900 line asking for you."

"It's not Jack again, is it? I was hoping they'd have shut off his phone by now," Marge complained.

"No, this guy asked for Marge Carter. He says his name is Jim McDaniel from Bismarck."

Margie grinned. "Sorry Stan, baby. I gotta take this." She excitedly skipped up the dirt trail to the dilapidated farmhouse. She rushed into the kitchen and nervously grabbed the cordless phone. At first, her expression was a happy one. Then her face transitioned into an angry scowl. She almost forgot how badly Jim had pissed her off.

"What do *you* want?" she demanded. Her tone was harsh. "Why shouldn't I hang up on you? Listen, I don't mind being a one-night stand, but I'm certainly not a prostitute."

Marge listened silently as Jim McDaniel tried to eloquently apologize for his grave faux pas, committed earlier that morning. He knew Marge was mad at him. He just needed to keep her on the phone long enough to explain.

"Why did you call the 900 number?" she asked.

Jim explained that her 900 number was the only number she had given him. She didn't even tell him what town she lived in. In fact, he knew very little at all about her. He asked Marge how much it was costing him to talk to her.

"It's $5.99 for the first five minutes, and 99 cents for each minute after that," she informed him. "How long have you been holding?"

He told her that Rosa had kept him on hold for twenty minutes.

"Ha! I might get that two-hundred dollars from you after all!"

After her laughter subsided, he tried to very humbly invite her out on a dinner date.

"Tonight? Well, let me check my calendar." She glanced at the 1993 wall calendar, which was tacked to the wall above the kitchen table. There wasn't a mark anywhere on it. Actually, she had no scheduled engagements for the entire year.

"Yeah, I'll pencil you in. What time and where?"

He asked her if she liked barbecue spare ribs.

"Honey, I lived in the South for almost forty years. Now, how can you live in the South and *not* like ribs?"

Chapter 17

There was really no question in the mind of any Bismarckian that BuBBa Q's was the best rib joint in town. Actually, BuBBa Q's might have arguably been considered one of the best barbecue joints in North Dakota. True, the absolute best barbecue had to be Southern, Texas, Kansas City, and then Chicago-style—in that order. But if one craved barbecue and one lived smack-dab in the middle of prairie country, BuBBa Q's was the place to be.

Jim greeted Marge in the restaurant parking lot, as she parked her Lincoln. He opened the door, trying to be gentlemanly, but still looking apologetic. He cowered a little and bit his lip, as he extended a hand to help her out of the car.

"You look lovely. Hard to believe you were up last night drinking—and other things. No bags under the eyes."

"Cover girl concealing stick." She accepted his hand and stepped out of the driver's seat. She dressed a bit more casually today and wore a knee-length skirt and tunic.

"Hey," she said slyly, "Didn't you wear that outfit yesterday?"

Jim looked down at his jacket, a little defensive. "Well, yeah—this is the same coat, but the *pants* are different." He politely took her hand and escorted her into the restaurant. "You see, Marge, the secret is that I never date the same woman twice. That way, she never notices that I don't change my jacket."

Marge voraciously gnawed at the last sauce-drenched spare rib until all that remained was a sinewy bone. She set it down on her plate of bare bones and smacked her lips. She sucked each finger clean by inserting each one up to the second knuckle in her open mouth. Then she wiped her hands on the napkin stuffed into the neckline of her tunic, lifted the napkin to her lips, wiped her mouth clean, and smiled again. Satisfied, she leaned back and sighed.

Jim didn't order ribs. He sat across the booth from Marge, toying at a beef brisket with his fork. The beef brisket was actually better than the ribs at BuBBa's. Very tender and moist. He said little as she ate, but he studied her intently.

"You really don't try to put on airs, do you?" he joked.

"Life's too short, without me having to complicate it with a lot of extra bullshit," she stated emphatically.

"I like that philosophy, Marge. And I like you. You're a genuine human being."

She made a stupid face. "—As opposed to a fake one?"

Jim chuckled. "No, I mean you're fresh. Really, I've never met anybody like you. Where are you from?"

"Here. Where the hell else would I be from?" she snapped. "I mean, who comes here, if they weren't already stuck here in the first place?"

"No, I mean, you *act* different, but you *look* different. Everybody here is either pasty white or Indian. You're neither," Jim remarked.

"Believe me. Some of my younger brothers and sisters are almost albinos," she joked. Then she smiled. "I do know what you mean. My mother was French-Canadian and Mandan Indian. My Norwegian Grandmother always told me I looked more like Mother."

"Your mom still around?"

"No. She died when I was ten. She was very hard-headed and free-spirited."

"You must've inherited those qualities from her. But I mean that in a good way. I like that about you, Marge. But you don't talk like you're from here. You don't have that North Dakota accent."

"I lived in Florida for so many years, I kinda lost it. My younger sister has it bad, though. She never left the state. Been here all her life. She does that 'ya, hon', 'okee dokee', 'eh?', and 'don cha know' stuff all the time.' Pretty amusing. It's hard not to laugh."

"Yeah?"

"Her husband left her not long ago. After John died six months ago, I decided to move up here to take care of her. She's always been supersensitive. Very fragile. Totally not like me."

"I'm convinced that there's nobody like you, Marge." Jim looked deeply into her eyes and smiled.

Marge felt her heart begin to pound forcefully. "Say, Jim. Are you feeling like another roll in the hay?"

"My apartment's just down the road," he answered.

"Well, what the hell're we waiting for?"

Jim McDaniel had rented the same apartment since he moved to North Dakota ten years ago. His apartment was one of many apartments in his large complex. Each apartment looked just like the next—with minor variations. Each building in the complex looked just like all the other buildings in the complex. It was conveniently close to his work, but it was admittedly small. It was a two bedroom, but he mainly used the second bedroom for storage. Jim chose to spend most of his extra cash enjoying the finer, consumable things in life. Things like a fine imported cigar.

Due to his sizeable monthly alimony checks to his ex-wife, he hadn't invested a great deal in furniture or aesthetics for his apartment. Neither of his two grown sons had any interest in visiting him in North Dakota, and he rarely invited friends or coworkers over. And he had never invited a woman over, until now. So, even after ten years, his flat still looked like a bachelor pad. It was clean but very Spartan in appearance.

They had just completed another marathon round of lovemaking. Marge and Jim lay naked, nestled under the sheets. She rested her head in the crook of his arm while they talked.

"That was nice," Jim remarked.

"Just nice?" Margie asked.

"Okay, great." He whispered to her. "But you are pretty loud."

Marge laughed.

He added, "I thought Mrs. Stevens was gonna call the cops. Then, at one point, I heard a dog or a wolf or something howling. Maybe he thought you were in pain."

Marge laughed again. Then she paused for a moment, before changing the subject. "We talked about me earlier. What about you?"

"What do you mean, 'what about me?'" he asked.

"How did you get here?"

"By car."

"No, smart-ass. What made you decide to move to friggin' North Dakota, of all places?"

"Well, it's a long story." He seemed reluctant to talk about it.

"I've got all night."

"It's just that—it's not very interesting," Jim stated.

"I'm easily amused. Try me."

"Well," he started, "I was born and raised in Atlanta—"

"—the son of a poor black family?" she facetiously interrupted. She snickered. "Sorry. I couldn't resist."

"I descended from a long line of Southern gentlemen, who descended from Confederate soldiers. When I say 'Southern', I'm talking about *die-hard* Southern men. You know—they'd go to the Civil War reenactments and proudly wear the Confederate Gray. My granddaddy and his father were clansmen. My parents lived in one of those beautiful antebellum-style houses…"

"Like Tara?"

"Yeah, with the great columns and such. Well, when I graduated from high school, I went to college. I met my fiancée, Lila. She was very Southern belle. You know, did the debutante thing and the finishing school garbage."

"Big hooped skirts with bustles?"

He chuckled and then continued. "Anyway, you get the picture. So, she pushed me to go to Emory University Medical School, which—I wanted to do, don't get me wrong. But she wanted very badly—"

"—to be married to a doctor?"

"Uh huh. So, when I graduated and did my residency, I got a job with the Atlanta Coroner's office. I worked my ass off for sixteen years. I hardly saw my two boys at all.

"Then you had a mid-life crisis?"

"Kind of. Sort of. Between '79 and about '81, I started having to do all these autopsies for the Atlanta child murder cases. You heard about them, right?"

"You mean when all those black kids who were getting killed by that serial killer guy?"

"Yeah. The guy's name was Wayne Williams. Well, I think maybe I had been a bit desensitized by all the violence before. I mean, there was a lot of shit that happened during my college years and early in my career with the Civil Rights Movement. But—having to see these seven, ten, twelve, fourteen-year-old kids, knowing there was some crazy murderer out there just strangling the life out of them—for no good reason? Well, it was just too overwhelming.

"Everyone in Atlanta was going nuts. They wanted to know who to blame. They wanted answers. I was just doing my job." He shrugged his shoulders and continued. "So, I came home one night—late again. And I told Lila that I just couldn't take it anymore. It was just too much."

"And what did she say, when you told her that?" Margie asked.

"She said that if I didn't want to be a doctor anymore, she didn't want to be married to me. And she said that I should be grateful that 'at least those children weren't white. *That* would be bad.' Can you believe that woman? What a heartless bitch!"

"That was why you left her?" Marge asked.

"That and the fact that she was screwing around behind my back."

Marge laughed. "But why here?"

"She told me that she was going to take me for *everything* I had. And she did—she got custody of the boys, she got the house, she got the best divorce lawyer money could buy. She had her nails so deep into my balls, I wasn't ever gonna be free of that bitch.

"I needed to move. I needed to get out of Atlanta and away from that hillbilly mentality. Anyway, I had several job offers at other coroners' offices. I picked the one that was as far away as possible, which paid as little as possible. I wanted to get away from her gold-digging claws, and I wanted to pay her as little alimony as possible to finance her harlot lifestyle.

"I moved up here in '82, and I've been here ever since. To be honest, when I first moved here, I was quite sure I'd made a mistake."

"But your wagon wheel broke, so you stayed?" Margie chuckled each time she rudely interrupted Jim's story.

He was also slightly amused by her wit. But he continued his story.

"I remember driving to Bismarck. I had taken everything I managed to get out of the divorce, and I packed it into my Volvo. It was night, and it was summer. I remember driving down the road and thinking—everything is just so *flat*. I mean—really flat. So, I saw this flashing red light in the distance. I kept driving toward it. 'I just need to get to that red light,' I kept telling myself. I knew I would eventually get there. Wouldn't you know, it seemed like two hours before I finally stopped at that light? I thought to myself, Oh my God! This is hell! Hell is North Dakota!

"So, anyway—Then November came. I had this little dinky apartment, and I would go outside to smoke my cigar sometimes. I go outside—And I have this nice, new winter coat, mind you—and it's freezing and windy outside. I think it was probably thirty below with the wind chill. I tell you. I thought my thin, Southern boy blood was going to have to give up and run back to my frigid ex-wife with my tail between my legs. At least *she* would be warmer than North Dakota."

"What changed your mind? Don't tell me—another woman?"

He laughed. "Don't interrupt. I'm trying to tell you this story. So—I'm standing outside, maybe it's only twenty below. I'm trying to light my cigar, and I look up in the sky, and there are these bright bursts of blue light. It was just amazing. It was like God was speaking to me or something—you know, through the Aurora Borealis. It was like I never noticed them before." Jim's face had grown increasingly animated as he recounted his discovery of the Northern lights. "I guess that's when I decided that I would stay."

"You never found a serious girlfriend since your divorce?"

"Honestly, Marge. I don't think I ever wanted one. I think I have just tried very hard to steer clear of the flame. Probably, I just look for one-night stands so I can remain detached. You know—no commitment, no heartbreak. What about you, Margie?"

"What *about* me?" she asked, warily.

"What're *you* looking for in a relationship?" Jim inquired. He clasped her hand in his, romantically weaving his fingers through hers.

This conversation had gotten a little too serious for Marge. She found herself feeling a bit uncomfortable, so she decided to lighten the mood. "Well, I don't mean to sound trite, Jim. But I was just looking for somebody to push the cobwebs out from between my legs."

Chapter 18

"Now, you take yer log of dough, and you slice it into coins, yah? Six usually do de trick. Dat way, yer lefse is not too big and not too t'in. Den, you place one dish on yer floured board, sprinkle wit' flour, and start to roll. Remember, you got to have yer special lefse rolling pin wit' de grooves. Roll carefully from de center, out to de edges, but don't press too hard, when you get to de edges. Yer bread needs to be round in shape, and de same t'ickness all de way 'round, see? If it's too t'in on de edges, yer edges will get crispy and crack. Same t'ickness all de way 'round. Ya, goot. Just like dat. Well, maybe dat's not perfectly round, but dat's a goot start, eh?"
SIGRID SEVERTSEN

Marge Carter stood at the kitchen sink. She stared out the window, thoughtfully engrossed in the details of her own dilemma, as she dried the small rack of newly rinsed dishes. She held up Ellie's lefse pin. This was a special rolling pin, which her sister used for rolling out the potato flatbread.

Lefse rolling pins differed from conventional rolling pins in that they had to be purchased at a special supplier of Norwegian cookery. Like a regular rolling pin, a standard lefse pin was made of hardwood (usually Maple), but it also had a series of grooves etched into the surface. This enabled one to roll the soft potato dough down to a consistently thin thickness. A skilled maker of lefse knew that perfectly made flatbread was extremely thin—not nearly a thick as a tortilla or pita wrap. If the lefse was not rolled out thinly enough, it came out like shoe leather. This special rolling pin enabled the sprinkled flour to reach deep inside the grooves of the pin to keep the dough from sticking as one rolled it out. As a result, it created fine ridges in the bread.

She retrieved a mesh sleeve from the kitchen drawer. *I guess, since Ellie isn't here, we won't be needing this anytime soon. I'd better put it away.* She examined the pin one last time, before inserting it into its protective cotton glove. She noted its particularly worn appearance. *This sucker looks like it's been beat to hell,* she thought. *Maybe I'll buy Ellie a new one. Yeah. Definitely. If I get us out of this mess, I will **definitely** buy my sister a new lefse pin. As a matter of fact, if I get us out of this mess, we can make lefse **every day.***

She leaned over the sink in despair, as she recited a short prayer in her head. Marge was not a religious woman. She hadn't set foot in a church for over twenty years. But her younger sister was a faithful parishioner of Himmel Lutheran and had attended Sunday services all her life. Marge wanted to entreat God for help, but not for her own sake—for the sake of her sister.

God, I know you're up there. If you hear me, help me save my little sister, Ellen. She has been so good all her life. She's all I have, and I can't lose her. Give me the strength I need to help her out of this disastrous chain of events. Don't do this for me, Lord. Do it for my little sister.

Oh, and by the way, God—I'm still pissed at you for taking John away from me. But we can talk about that later. Amen.

Marge ended her prayer and turned, leaning her backside against the sink. She wiped a tear from her eye, grateful that no one was present to witness her moment of weakness. Then she decisively shook off her blues, determined to set out for the day's chores. She had to drive to town today. She needed to hang flyers for the auction to be held in two days. She and Stan had prepared a list of all Stanley's items to be auctioned off, which included the time the auction was to begin.

She grabbed up her hammer, nails, jar of thumbtacks, and stack of flyers and headed out the front door.

Ellie picked up the phone receiver to her nephew's kitchen wall phone and placed a call to her farmhouse in North Dakota. As she punched out the eleven digit number on the touchtone phone, she thought to herself. *Isn't it delightful? Everybody in the world has their own unique touchtone jingle.* This newfangled technology was nothing like her rotary wall phone—or even the cordless sets that Margie had purchased for the 900 numbers.

She sat patiently as the house phone rang. Rosa answered.

"Hi Rosa, dear. It's Mom. How are things going up there?" Ellen asked.

Rosa was glad to hear from Ellen. It had been almost a week since she left with Little Robert. Her daughter-in-law informed her that she didn't really have time to talk, because the 900 line was ringing. She briefly asked Ellie how Little Robert was doing.

"Oh, hon'. He's such a joy. He's a very good boy. He and Grandma are getting along just fine!"

The young Mrs. Peters was relieved to hear that her son was doing well.

"Listen, hon', I know yer other line is ringing. Is Margie there?"

Rosa called Marge to the line. Ellie grinned broadly.

"Hi Marge. Goodness, it's good ta hear yer voice. Ya, hon'. I'm havin' a marvelous time ote here. It's so different from how I remember."

Marge asked her sister about her tour of the newly opened Mall of America.

"Oh ya. It's huge—big as can be. Almost too big. O' course, they've got lots of frufy stores, but they've got an amusement park and picture shows—all right there in the mall. There must be four or five stories of wall-ta-wall stores! I've never seen anythin' like it. Oh, and Marge, hon'. Ya'd never believe this. They've got one store with just refrigerator magnets! That's it. All they carry in the entire store is magnets fer the ice box. My goodness, it's just the most fascinatin' thing I've ever seen!"

"Oh ya, Little Robert is just a joy. Now, Margie, I don't mean ta brag, but he really is the most precious thing alive. He's even startin' ta talk. I think I can get him ta say "grandma" before long. Oh, and he's so derned bright. Just like his poppa."

"Ya, we went to the Como Park Zoo with Joseph's girls. Oh, Marge, they're just so darling. We saw the tigers and zebras. I think Robert enjoyed the sea lions best. Melinda and I and the kids just had a ball. It was nice going ta the park—ya know—with little ones this time."

"Say, hon'. How's it goin' over there? Are ya lonely?" Ellie inquired of her sister.

Marge answered evasively that she had been dating someone since Ellie left for Minnesota.

Ellen giggled. "Ya don't say! Well, tell me. Who is he? Where did ya meet him?"

Margie explained that she met some guy in Bismarck, and he had been calling the 900 line.

"Well, are ya serious abote him?" Ellie asked, a little cautious.

Margie replied that she didn't really know how she felt about him, but that he was a nice looking doctor. She hadn't decided whether it was serious enough to give him her address and phone number. For now, he would be calling her on the 900 line.

"Oh, I know dear. Ya just can't be too careful anymore," Ellie agreed.

"Say, Margie. How are Stan and Rosa doin'?"

Marge stated that Rosa was answering the 900 line for her, so that she didn't have to be anchored to the phone so much. She was doing very well. At first, Stan Junior didn't like the idea. But Marge noticed that, because Rosa had to talk about sex all day and she didn't have to stay up with the baby all night, Stan might be getting a little more action in the boudoir as of late.

Ellie seemed a bit embarrassed. "My gosh, did ya *ask* him abote that?"

Margie informed her sister that she did. She had no problem asking her nephew about the specifics of his sex life with Rosa. Stan told Marge that, even though he was initially against Rosa answering the 900 line, he resolved that he could "take the crumbs any day."

Ellie giggled again. "Well, dear. I don't want ta bore ya with this stuff. Joseph bought me one of these disposable cameras, so I'll have plenty 'o pictures ta bring back. See ya in a few days, hon.'"

Marge stood in the farmhouse kitchen, after hanging up the kitchen wall phone. She groaned as she hung the receiver in its cradle. Then she rolled her eyes, leaned up against the door jamb, and banged her forehead on the wall.

"What's the matter, Marge?" Rosa asked.

"I just got done talking for twenty minutes with my sister about refrigerator magnets!" she exclaimed, frustrated. "And to top that off, she really is convinced she's been to Minnesota before."

"You didn't remind her that she's never been *anywhere*?" Rosa inquired.

"No. I don't even bother correcting her anymore. She lives in her own little world. There's no point." Marge answered. She threw her head back and whined, "Oh my God, Rosa. What the hell am I gonna do about her?"

Once again, Jim McDaniel called the 900 number to set up a date with Margie. He wanted to see her tomorrow, because he would have to work late tonight on several cases he had backlogged. Margie had informed him that time wouldn't work for her, because they had an auction scheduled for the following day.

Ultimately, they agreed to meet late that evening, about 10 P.M. Jim thought that he might be able to finish up his pending workload by 9:00. After that, he could rush home quickly and shower. Marge could meet him at the apartment then.

Marge agreed to meet him at his apartment that evening. But in reality, she had a much more devious plan in store. She was running out of time, and she needed to dig for information from Jim about Stanley's death.

She thought about the various sex spy stories she had heard of in the news during the Cold War. She found the idea intriguing. Had she not been happily married to John all those years, perhaps she might have been a successful sex spy. She remained faithful to John during their entire forty year marriage. But she also knew that she could be a lioness in the bedroom. She relished the idea of circling her prey thoughtfully, then viciously going in for the kill. The idea of using her feminine wiles to fight for a cause greater than herself intrigued her.

But the truth was that, although Marge liked to tell herself and others that she was a heartless vixen, she had a very soft interior. She allowed only rare individuals the opportunity to catch a glimpse of who she really was, on even rarer occasions. Her late husband and her four children knew that she wasn't a vicious lioness. They knew she was a domesticated pussycat. Her sister Ellen knew that as well. But no one else really understood Marge's vulnerable side. She was much too guarded to show any outward signs of weakness. If she became overwhelmed or frustrated about things, she simply masked her feelings behind a veil of anger or violence.

Marge had resolved to meet Jim. But she wasn't going to meet him on *his* terms at his apartment, as they agreed. She wanted to show up at his work, two hours early. Perhaps she could get some information about Stanley. Maybe she might find out if Stanley was murdered and—if he was—*how* he was murdered. If Ellen did kill Stanley, maybe Marge could sufficiently charm Jim into falsifying the report to save her sister. Ellen was all Marge had now. She wasn't about to give her sister up to the authorities for what, admittedly, should have been done to Stanley Peters twenty-seven years ago.

Chapter 19

Dr. Jim McDaniel stood over the naked corpse of a twenty-four year old male, who was partially draped in blue paper. He also dressed in scrubs and a disposable blue surgical gown. He wore a white plastic apron and a pair of safety goggles to shield himself from blood splatters. A paper mask obscured his lower face, and his hands were covered with partially bloodied latex gloves. He held a scalpel in his right hand and a pair of hemostats in his left.

There was a small microphone suspended above the autopsy table. As he performed the autopsy, he verbally walked himself through the examination, dictating the patient history. For his external examination, he noted details regarding any visual observations, palpations, lacerations, bruises, or scarring of the corpse.

Then he proceeded with the internal examination of the deceased. He made a large, Y-shaped incision which extended from the shoulder blades of the body. His strategic cuts met at the bottom of the young man's breastbone.

He exposed the chest cavity. His Anatomical Pathology Technologist, Kim Jeffreys, stood nearby and handed him a saw. She donned similar attire, wearing a disposable gown, gloves, apron, and mask. Once Dr. McDaniel had freed the ribs and sternum of the young man's body with the saw, Kim assisted him with lifting up the chest plate. That enabled Dr.

McDaniel to visualize all the thoracic organs inside the young man's chest.

Dr. McDaniel was a skilled pathologist, having practiced medicine for almost thirty years. His assistant, Kim, was a young woman in her early thirties. She had been working with him for the last eight years. She was a slender woman of medium height. Her light blonde hair was curly but short. Although she wore round John Lennon spectacles and little makeup, she was quite naturally attractive.

As he meticulously cut, exposed, studied, and weighed the deceased (and various parts of the deceased), the examination room phone rang. He whispered a small curse under his breath, annoyed to be interrupted in the middle of his work.

"Answer it. Would you, Kim?"

"Sure." She set her tools on the nearby metal cart and removed her gloves. She pulled her face mask below her chin to answer the phone. It was the security guard at the front desk, who had recently started his shift for the evening.

"Jim, there's someone out at the front desk waiting to see you," his assistant informed him.

"I don't want to see anyone right now. Tell them I'm in the middle of something."

Kim relayed his message to the Security guard. She looked bewildered and held up the phone. "Ed says the visitor's name is Marge Carter?"

Disgusted, Jim shook his head. He angrily snapped off his gloves into the biohazard trash bin and removed his mask. "Give me the phone," he ordered.

"Put her on the line," he instructed Ed on the other end.

Marge took the phone.

"Marge, I'm in the middle of something. Why couldn't you wait to meet me later? *I told you* I have to work late."

At first, Jim seemed annoyed to discover that Marge had stopped by his work unannounced. Soon, however, his face softened as she spoke to him. "I see. You thought I could give you a tour, huh?" He seemed amused that Marge had such an interest in his work. But then again, Marge was one of the few women he had ever dated who wasn't grossed out by things like dead or dismembered bodies. She seemed to actually enjoy it in a disturbingly amusing sort of way.

For Jim, that was a refreshing change from his ex-wife, Lila. She *never* took an interest in his work. She was repulsed by the mere thought of it. She often proudly told strangers that her husband was a doctor. But when they quizzed Lila for specifics about Jim's specialty, she shamefully admitted, "He's a horizontal doctor."

Jim now smiled. "Okay. You gotta give me thirty minutes, so I can get this guy's chest put back together. Wait out there, and I'll come get you." He hung up the phone.

"New girlfriend?" Kim inquired.

"Something like that," Jim answered.

"That's totally not like *you*, Jim. You sure you know what you're doing?"

"Not at all." he stated. "I don't know *what* the hell I'm doing."

After Dr. McDaniel had weighed and reassembled the organs back into the body of his latest autopsy, he discarded his surgical gown and personal protective equipment. He dismissed his assistant for the evening and met Marge at the Security desk out front.

He nodded to the security guard on duty. "Thanks, Ed."

"Really, Marge. Why did you decide to come here?" he asked.

"You'd been talking about your job, and I thought it might be fun to get a tour. You know, maybe get to know your patients," she joked. She shrugged her shoulders.

He led Marge through the security access doors to his exam room. The acrid scent of formalin, death, and disinfectant filled the room. Marge held her nose. "Ew! It friggin' stinks in here, Jim!"

"You kind of get used to it after thirty years," he stated.

"Phew! No, I don't think I could *ever* get used to that smell. I wouldn't mind the blood and guts and dead people nearly as much as I would that chemical smell. Ugh!" Margie gagged.

The autopsy room had only two bodies lying out on dissection tables. These were long, stainless steel tables which had a reservoir for excess blood to drain, when the bodies were cut open. Of course, dead bodies had no circulating blood, but the removal of vital organs for weighing and tissue sampling could still be quite messy, depending on the manner of death and the corpse's stage of decomposition.

The two bodies were strategically draped in sheets. Marge studied the silhouettes of the bodies in Jim's current caseload. One looked to be rather slender in build. The other was substantially larger. His blackened hand poked out from under the sheet. It was clear *that* body had been decomposing for quite some time.

She walked over to the thin body. "Is this the guy you're working on?" she asked. "Can I see?"

"Well, really, I'm not supposed to—"

Before Jim could finish his sentence, Marge flipped the sheet down to expose the young man's face. "He's kinda young. Too bad. What a waste. Nice looking, too. What'd he die of?"

"Drug overdose, most likely. They found him dead in his apartment a week ago. Really, Marge. I'm not supposed to tell you about this stuff. It's confidential."

"Don't worry. I don't know who this guy is. He could be anybody, for that matter. Tsk, tsk, tsk. It is a shame. I'm surprised. He must not've had a girlfriend, huh?"

"Maybe he did, and that's why he killed himself," Jim smartly remarked.

"Funny." She lifted the sheet up further, to peek underneath. "Oooh, looks like you've been hacking him up quite a bit, eh?"

"I had to weigh his heart and lungs. That's what that scale is all about." He pointed to a large spring-loaded scale, which was suspended from a heavy-duty metal stand.

She lifted the sheet up even further to obviously catch a glimpse of his genitals.

"Marge!" Jim scolded.

She peered out devilishly behind the sheet and grinned. "Just checking things out," she teased.

Marge flipped the sheet back over the young man's face. She looked over at the second draped body. "Who's *this* guy?" She skipped over to the next body, examining the decomposed hand, poking out from beneath the sheet.

"Kinda looks like maybe he's been sitting around awhile. Can I see?"

"Sure. I should warn you, Marge. It's pretty gruesome."

She pulled the sheet halfway down to reveal the decomposed head and torso of her ex-brother-in-law. "Ooooh, he was a fatty! What did *this* guy die of?"

Marge almost seemed as though she was having fun—a little too much fun, in fact. But Jim perceived her level of engagement in his work as somewhat of an ego boost. He concluded that there was really no harm in discussing the case.

"Well, he was fat, but he hasn't quite gotten past the bloating stage of decomposition. The Himmel County Sheriff's office sent this guy to me, because they found this guy's body dead in his barn."

"Yeah? What happened to him?" Margie asked, listening intently.

"He was buried under a mountain of heavy metal tools. Apparently, he hoarded tools and machinery in his barn. It was piled almost to the ceiling," Jim stated.

"So all his tools fell on him and killed him?" Marge inquired.

"Well yes, they fell on him. But the Sheriff was puzzled at how this whole mountain of tools even came to be in the first place. You know—did the guy pile all this stuff up there, or what? I'm not sure they will ever figure that out—how the tools got all piled up on top of each other in the first place. Or even how he ended up buried under the heap. This guy walked with a cane. He was shot up during the war. And you can see that he was pretty obese, so I don't think he was physically capable of moving all that stuff by himself."

"I'm sure he didn't get to be that size, unless he had been sitting on his ass his whole life," Margie commented under her breath.

"What?" Jim asked.

"Nothing. Go on."

"But that's not what killed the guy," Jim added. "Well, I mean this guy was seventy-five years old. He was going to die soon."

"Of old age?" Margie asked. "I should live to be so old."

"No, of cirrhosis. This guy must've been an alcoholic all his life. His liver was pickled. I don't think he would've had much longer, if someone hadn't killed him first," he commented.

Upon hearing this latest comment, Marge's heart stopped. But she resolved to play it cool. Jim wasn't even aware that she knew Stanley. "What makes you think somebody killed him?" she asked intently, trying not to seem suspicious.

Jim stepped closer to the body, as he pointed to it. "You can clearly see that his body had decomposed."

"Yeah. How long do you think he had been dead?" She asked. She felt herself starting to tremble, but she tried to remain calm.

"It's hard to say. I'm guessing that this guy was killed late fall—maybe seven months ago. But it's hard to say. With him being out in the barn, it could've been as late as late winter—as little as two months ago. Basically, somebody killed him, and then his body froze there. When it started to warm up about March, he started thawing again and decomposing. That's why there's really no way to tell exactly when he died."

"Yes, but how do you know somebody killed him?" Margie asked again.

"Well, two things. What killed him was that he was stabbed in the chest. Right through the heart. One blow." Jim acted all this out for dramatic effect. "A very powerful, forceful blow, probably while he was lying there unconscious. He was lying down, but it still must've been somebody with tremendous strength."

"He wasn't impaled by one of his tools that fell on top of him?" Marge inquired.

"No. From photographs that the Sheriff took of the crime scene, there wasn't really anything there in his barn that could've been used as a murder weapon. Must've been something like a screwdriver—probably something with a twelve-inch shaft. There were other screwdrivers in the barn, but they were all considerably larger. Definitely not the murder weapon." Jim explained.

"So you're saying, whoever killed him took the murder weapon with them?" Marge asked.

"Yes," Jim stated. "You're awfully interested in this case."

"Oh, well.." Margie still tried to play it cool. "You know, it's not the typical open-and-shut case, right?" She suddenly turned serious again, still trying to conceal her growing nervousness. "But you said there were *two* odd things. What's the other thing?"

"Well," Jim pointed again. "You see these bruises on his skull?"

"Yes," Marge replied.

"His entire head is black-and-blue. Well, I know he's been sitting around, and dead bodies get blacker as time goes on. But his skull was clearly cracked in several places. Of course, it seems like his body is pretty decomposed. But really, it's actually pretty well-preserved. With the cold winter and it being closed up in that barn, the flies in North Dakota wouldn't have set up maggot larvae until it got sufficiently warm."

"So, what does that mean?" she asked.

"It looks like somebody really whacked the guy on the head—over and over."

"With what?"

"I don't quite know. I would have said with a big, round piece of wood—like a baseball bat or a rolling pin or a chair leg, maybe. Something blunt. The curious thing about that is that whatever the murderer used to whack this guy's head? It wasn't completely smooth, like a bat or a rolling pin. It almost looks like it was something—ribbed."

Marge was visibly trembling now. "What do you mean, ribbed?"

"Let's see if you can see. Yeah—here, on the guy's left temple. I know he's pretty bloated and black, but you can pick out a small area in the skin, where it's broken, and the maggots set in. Several uniform lacerations, spaced maybe 1/4 inch apart."

Immediately, Margie started panicking, as she thought of her sister. *Oh my God, Ellie's lefse pin!*

Jim proceeded to summarize his theory on Stanley's death. "Somehow this guy's crap fell down on top of him and trapped him underneath. But he wasn't dead, just trapped under his own tools. Then someone came along, whacked him on the head with something—something blunt but grooved, fracturing his skull, and eventually knocking him unconscious. They took a screwdriver and—with one heavy thrust—drove it deep into his chest. He was dead in seconds."

As Jim played out the entire, violent scenario of Stanley's death, it dawned on Margie that Ellie must have been his killer. Marge had no clue of how her frail sister might have mustered the energy to not only haul Stanley's tools to the center of the barn, but to whack him repeatedly over the head with her lefse pin, eventually cracking his skull and knocking him out. How could little Ellie have forcefully and unmercifully pierced his heart as she dealt her husband's final death blow?

There was no question that Stanley had it coming to him. If Ellen had selected a different weapon with which to assault Stanley—like a hoe or a shovel—Marge might not have figured that Ellen was Stanley's murderer. Ellen was petite and fragile. She didn't possess the stamina to move all that equipment by herself. But by striking Stanley over and over again with the lefse pin, it was almost as if Ellen had left her calling card at the murder scene. This was her "Columbian necktie." It was simply a matter of time before Ellen was found out.

Jim McDaniel was not a native North Dakotan, and he was unfamiliar with the process of making lefse. He had probably never seen a lefse pin. *I should have known, when I put Ellie's pin away yesterday, that it didn't get that way from rolling potato dough. She had used it to smash in Stanley's skull!*

Marge started to swoon and her hands began to shake. "Holy crap!" she cried.

Jim grew suddenly worried. "Hey," he commented. "You look pale. Marge, have a seat."

He pulled up a folding chair for her to sit down in. "Are you okay? Jeez, I didn't think you'd get so worked up over this." He apologized. "I'm sorry, Marge. I guess I tend to detach myself from all this gruesomeness. You know, when you've done this for so long."

"No, Jim. It's not that. It's just—" Margie stopped herself.

"What?" Jim paused also. Then his eyes widened, as if a light bulb just went off in his head. "Hey, don't tell me you *knew* this guy?" Jim shook his head in almost a panic.

"Uh..." Marge tried to stall for time, while she searched the recesses of her mind for a believable lie.

"Oh, shit! Marge, tell me what's going on!" Jim demanded. He held her by the shoulders, as he glared at her.

"I can't..." she stated weakly.

He started to shake her forcefully. "Margie, tell me! Do you know this guy, or don't you?"

"Yes!" she blurted. "He's my brother-in-law, Stanley Peters! My little sister Ellen killed him." She burst into tears.

Jim was enraged. He angrily slammed his hand down on the autopsy table, then reflexively shook it in pain. "Goddammit! Why didn't you tell me, Marge? I can't be seeing you! Don't you know this is a conflict of interest right here? Shit!"

Margie sat wailing, as Jim continued his ranting. "You were just using me this whole time! You picked me up at The Peacock, knowing that you were gonna use me to get information about this case, weren't you?" Then he slammed his hand down on the table once more and yelled, "Fuck!"

She quickly gathered her wits about her. She rose to her feet and grabbed *him* by the shoulders. "Jim, listen to me. You've gotta change your report! You've gotta help me! My sister is a good woman. You ask anybody in the town—even the Sheriff—and they'll tell you *Stanley deserved to die*. He was a mean, despicable excuse for a human being. He was a drunk, and he abused Ellen and her son for twenty-seven years! If she killed him, he drove her to it!"

He pushed her away. "Don't touch me!"

Marge again approached him, pleading. "Please, Jim. She's my sister. She's lost her mind. She's the only thing I have. I can't lose her, too! Yes, Jim. I did use you, but you've gotta know that I did it for my little sister."

Jim was almost hysterical. "What the hell do you want from me?"

"You've gotta make up something. Falsify the report. Say Stanley was crushed accidentally, end of story. Nobody'll know. Nobody'll care. Nobody even liked Stanley! Please, Jim. I can't see my baby sister get sent to jail!" Marge's face was wet with tears as she pleaded her case.

Jim finally calmed himself, as he disappointedly shook his head. "No, Marge. I can't do that. I would lose my job. I could go to jail. This is all I have. My career is my life."

It was now Marge's turn to be enraged. *How can he be so damned selfish?* "What about me? Don't you care about me? I just lost my husband. Now you want me to lose my sister, too?"

"I simply can't do that, Marge. I can't file a false report for you. You can't ask me to do that. Then, *I* would lose everything."

Now Marge was furious. She picked up her purse and struck Jim on the head. "Well," she cried, "You've definitely lost me! You can go screw yourself, Doctor James McDaniel the third, MD/PhD! 'cause you certainly aren't going to get any more screwing from me!"

Chapter 20

Marge's drive from Bismarck back to Himmel was a blur. She was engrossed in thought. Her sister had murdered Stanley. *Ellen can't go to jail,* she thought to herself over and over. *She wouldn't make it there. Stanley brought all this upon himself. And now, who was going to suffer? Ellen. Hadn't Ellen suffered enough already? She doesn't deserve this.*

She had difficulty watching the road, because she was blinded by her endless flood of tears. Margie was angry. She was angry at Stanley for being so hateful all his life and provoking Ellen to kill him. She was angry at God for robbing her of her happy life with John. She was angry at Ellen for not having divorced Stanley early in their marriage. Finally, she was most angry at Jim. What made her—for even just a brief moment—think that Jim even cared for her? If he loved her, he would've done whatever she asked, whatever the cost. *John* would have done that for her. But John *loved* Marge. What made her think that Jim or any other man could ever love her the way John did?

"Oh my God!" Marge hollered to herself, snorting back her snot-filled nose. "I'm going to be a lonely old lady with twenty cats!" she blubbered. "I don't wanna be a cat lady..." She cried some more. Finally, she resolved she was going to attempt to—inasmuch as possible—cheer herself up.

She turned on the radio, determined to overcome her woes. *Maybe I just need some happy music to cheer me up*, she thought to herself. She tuned the radio to a bluegrass station, which played a lively, upbeat version of a newly released Alison Krauss song. *Oh good*, she thought to herself. *Maybe **this** will cheer me up*. The song was entitled *Every Time You Say Goodbye*. "What the hell?" Margie asked herself. As the singer sang cheerily about "tears in her eyes," she decided it was too much. *How ironic*, she thought. *How can this girl be joyfully stroking her fiddle about something so sad?*

Frustrated, she was determined to find a better station. She turned the dial, tuning through the static. She finally arrived at a '50s station. *Good*, she thought. *We can sing some sock hop music. This brings back some old memories.* The song was *Bye, Bye Love* by the Everly Brothers. *Now, **this** is upbeat.* Don and Phil Everly strummed their guitars, singing in harmony: "Bye, bye love. Hello loneliness. Hello emptiness. I think I'm gonna cry..."

"For Chrissakes!" Marge cried. Disgusted, she flipped off the radio. "How can you sing such friggin' happy songs about being dumped? I'd rather listen to myself sit here and bawl."

When she arrived back to town, it was 10 P.M. All the stores were closed, but the Trading Post was still open. She turned into the bar and slammed on her brakes. She marched in. She looked like a wreck. She had been crying nonstop during her entire trip home in the car. Her face was swollen, and her hair was a mess. Her waterproof mascara had finally run, and she had two black smears of eye makeup beneath her puffy, reddened eyes. She flopped down at the bar, next to William Knutson.

Doris stood at the bar, looking surprised. "Hello, Margie. You need something?"

"Yes, Doris," Marge replied. "Give me a Jim Beam and keep it comin' 'til the bottle's gone."

"Are you sure, Marge?"

"Oh, Doris. I've never been so sure of anything in my life."

William attempted to strike up a conversation with Marge. "Hard day, eh, Marge?"

"You can say that again," she responded.

"Doris, this one's on me," William stated.

Doris nodded.

"Would ya like ta talk abote it, Marge?" William inquired. "Ya know, I'm quite a good listener."

"No thanks, William. I think I just want to sit here and wallow in my own self-pity. That seems like the fitting thing to do at the moment."

"Sure, Marge. Doris, just keep it comin'. My treat, Marge."

"Thanks, William. I owe you." Marge lifted her glass.

Thirty minutes had passed, and in her silence, Marge had downed four glasses of Jim Beam.

William tried, once again, to distract Marge with small talk. "Say, I don't mean ta pry or anything, but how's Miss Ellie doin'?"

"Good. She's living in her own little loony world," Marge answered cynically.

"I see she's let her hair down, so ta speak. She's lookin' awfully pretty these days. But I haven't seen her around in a week er so."

"Oh, she's been on a trip. My son Joseph took her over to the Mall of America in Minneapolis." Marge was slurring her words.

"I bet she likes that, eh? Say, have ya heard from Stanley these days?" William inquired.

"Not exactly heard from him. More like smelled his putrefied, rotting corpse," Marge replied.

William looked shocked. "Ya mean, Stanley's dead?"

"Deader than a doornail. Stan Junior and I found him buried under a whole pile of tools in his barn last week."

"Say, that's what the auction is all abote?" William asked.

"Yep. We're getting rid of all of Stanley's shit."

William frowned sympathetically. "Oh, I'll bet Miss Ellie's devastated." He looked up at Doris, "Did ya know abote this, Doris?"

"Sure, William. After all, I'm married to Paul. He doesn't keep secrets from me," Doris replied. She turned to Marge. "Marge, are you okay? I don't think you're in any condition to drive home. You've had quite a few drinks there. Maybe you can get William to take you home."

"Be glad to," William offered. He politely helped Margie off her stool, and set a $20 bill on the bar for Doris. Then he escorted Marge out to his car.

Marge reclined in the passenger's seat of William's car, in a drunken stupor.

"Are ya okay, Miss Marge? Let me know if I need ta pull over for ya," he offered.

Clearly inebriated, Marge sang the words to *Bye Bye Love* as she laughed loudly. "Ha! Isn't that hysterical, William?"

"What, Miss Marge?"

"'Hello loneliness. I think I'm gonna die.' And he's singin' all happy and shit. Ha! It's a scream!" Margie joked.

"Oh, Marge. Yer goin' ta have ta sleep this one off. Don't worry, I'll get ya home," he stated assuredly.

When they arrived at Marge's farmhouse, William carried Marge to bed. He removed her shoes, and tucked her under her blankets. Marge patted him on the head. "You're such a sweet boy, William. You know what I think?" she asked.

"What, Miss Marge?"

"I think you should so totally pork my sister. She likes you, William. And you know—she's single now!" Margie chortled and patted William's cheek adoringly.

"Aw, shucks, Marge. Ya get some rest now, eh? Ya got a big day ahead with the auction in the mornin'."

"Ya," Margie stated mockingly. "Big day, eh? Don't cha know." Almost immediately Margie drifted off to sleep, snoring loudly.

William Knutson quietly let himself out.

Chapter 21

Marge rose early the next morning, again hungover. Stan and Rosa were already awake, preparing for the big auction to be held at the barn. The plan was for Rosa to tend to the 900 line, while Marge and Stan did some last minute setting up for the sale. It was scheduled to begin promptly at 10 A.M.

"Morning, Aunt Marge," Stan cheerfully greeted.

Marge stumbled into the kitchen. Her eyes were puffy from crying the night before and were red and swollen. She seemed distracted and started searching through the kitchen drawers. She pulled out Ellie's lefse pin. She pulled out a paper grocery sack, stuffing the pin into the bag.

"What's going on, Aunt Marge?" Stan Junior asked.

"I'm gonna confess," Marge declared.

Stan Junior looked shaken. "Confess to what, Aunt Marge?"

"Murder. Your father was murdered, and I killed him," she stated, defiantly. "I just need to figure out where I hid the murder weapon."

"Wait a minute, Aunt Marge. *You* didn't kill Dad. You couldn't have."

She answered her nephew matter-of-factly. She was distracted by her search. "What do you know about it? You just showed up last week. This has been going on for months." She pilfered through a few more drawers.

She reached up to clumsily search through the kitchen cabinets. She carelessly and noisily pulled all the pots and pans off their shelves, tossing them on the floor one by one. "Ellie? Where'd you put it?" She pulled down a stack of clean plates and cast them to the floor, breaking several of them.

Stan Junior tried to stop her. "Now, Aunt Marge. Let's not be hasty. Maybe there's another way out of this."

"I don't think so, Stan baby. Somebody killed your father. Somebody's gonna have to fry, and I don't want it to be your crazy mother," she declared.

After Margie emptied the upper cabinets, she leaned down to the cabinet below the kitchen sink. She removed the box of trash bags. She removed the old box of rat poison. "This box must be thirty friggin' years old! Do they even make this crap anymore?" She set it aside. She leaned her head into see what still lay under the sink. She pulled out a can of Drano, some SOS pads, and a large box of Arm and Hammer baking soda.

"Wait, I see something there..." she leaned her ear against the cabinet, reaching as far as she could into the darkness. She grappled for it—whatever it was that lay on the floor, strategically hidden behind everything else.

"Bingo," she whispered to herself. Marge retrieved the object and examined it. She opened her palm to discover there, in her right hand, was a yellow-handled Phillips-head screwdriver with a twelve-inch shaft. And conveniently, still on its metal shaft—was the dried blood of her slain brother-in-law, Stanley Peters Senior.

Fifteen minutes later, Marge Carter marched into Sheriff Baker's office unannounced. She carried a rolled-up paper sack.

"Hi, Marge. What brings ya here this time of day? Aren't ya abote ta get ready fer the auction?" Paul Baker inquired.

Marge ignored his attempts at small talk. "I'm here to make a confession, Sheriff," she declared.

"A confession?" The Sheriff looked puzzled. "Fer what?"

She dropped the paper sack on the Sheriff's desk. She drew in one deep breath and exhaled her entire confession. "Sheriff, I killed Stanley Peters. I piled all his shit in the barn. Then, I lured him into the barn and pushed the entire pile of shit on top of him. As he lay helpless, trapped beneath his pile of shit, I whacked him upside the head repeatedly with a lefse pin, knocking him unconscious. Then I stabbed him in the heart with a screwdriver. It's all in this bag, Sheriff—the murder weapon and the lefse pin!" Spent, Marge drew in another breath and flopped herself down on the chair behind her.

"Well!" Paul Baker stated thoughtfully, "I'm not sure how ta respond ta that, Marge. Ya seem ta have thought this thing through quite well." He scratched his chin. "Tell me, what makes ya think I believe ya, eh?"

"What d'ya mean, Paul? I'm telling you. I did it. I killed Stanley. He deserved to die. Nobody else was gonna do it. He had been abusing my sister for years in this town, and nobody did a friggin' thing about it. Somebody had to, so I did it," Marge stated, emphatically.

"Nope." Paul seemed resolutely unconvinced by her confession.

She was clearly taken off-guard. "What d'ya mean, 'Nope?'"

"Marge, I don't believe ya killed Stanley. There's simply not enough evidence."

Margie shook her head in disbelief. She stood and leaned over in Paul's face, as she spoke slowly. "I'm telling you that I killed Stanley Peters! I just told you exactly how I committed the crime, and I even brought you a bag with the murder weapon inside! And you have the nerve to tell me that you don't have enough evidence?" Marge was flabbergasted.

"Ya, that's what I'm sayin', Marge. Anyways, how did ya know that's how Stanley was killed in the first place?" he interrogated.

"Because I did it! Don't you get it? I wanted to protect my sister, so I did it!" she demanded. She pounded her fist down on his desk to emphasize her point.

"No, ya didn't," Paul restated.

"Yes, I did!" Marge argued.

"Look, Marge. We could go on fer days like this, arguing." He paused and then suspiciously lifted his brow. "Say, this wouldn't have anything ta do with the Medical Examiner from Bismarck, would it?"

"What does that matter?" she asked, defensively.

"Well, it seems that I spoke ta Jim McDaniel early this mornin'."

"You did?"

"Yep. Needless ta say, he was a tad bit upset. He stated that ya—and I quote—'tried ta seduce him fer infermation abote the case.'" Paul snickered a bit.

"Well, yes," she bragged, "I *did* seduce him…"

"And he gave ya some confidential infermation abote the report he intended ta file, eh?" Paul asked.

"He did. But that doesn't change the fact that I killed Stanley Peters. I had both the means and the motive."

"Well, if it's any consolation, Marge, I talked Doctor McDaniel inta postponin' the final release of his report. That is, 'til we can gather some more infermation," Paul stated.

"More information?" Marge asked.

"Ya. I don't know if ya realize this, Miss Marge, but ya seemed ta have done a number on Jim's poor heart. I've never seen him as upset abote any woman since his ex-wife dumped him. He's a wreck."

She grinned bashfully. "Really, Sheriff?"

"Oh, ya. He seems ta have it somethin' awful fer ya. And I'd hate ta see ya get carted off ta jail right now. Ya know, with the auction and all. And who knows? Maybe ya might find that ya weren't usin' him, so much as maybe ya like him, too."

"Well, I can honestly say that I do like him," she confessed. "He's dreamy. A little stubborn and pompous, but he's still nice."

"Anyways, I think now's not the time fer a confession. Maybe wait a few days, 'til Miss Ellie gets back, and we'll continue our investigation then, eh?" He pushed the paper sack back toward Marge. "In the meantime, the Coroner is goin' ta release Stan's body fer a funeral."

"Funeral? You mean we're going to have to bury him?" Marge asked resentfully.

"Ya. And somebody's goin' ta have ta break the news ta poor Ellie, when she gets back."

"Really, Sheriff. Don't you think she might already know?" Marge queried.

"I'm not sure, Marge. I still don't quite believe that Miss Ellie has it in her ta kill her husband. Ya, I know it was a long time comin' fer him. But I just can't believe that abote her.

"But somethin' ya don't know abote me and Jim, Miss Marge, is that we go way back—almost ta when he first came here. He's a lot like me. He knows that the law doesn't always work in favor of the good or the innocent. Sometimes ya have ta bend the rules a little ta let the good guy go free. Maybe what we need ta do is ta convince Doctor McDaniel that, if he changes his report, the good guy—or gal—*will* go free. If we show him how bad an egg old Stanley was, maybe he can figger somethin' ote, eh?"

"I don't think I was very convincing." Marge commented.

"Well, we've still got some time here. His report won't be due for another four weeks. Let's see what happens. In the meantime, I'll see ya at the auction. I'm interested in seeing what ya might fetch fer those guns of Stanley's. He's got a set of antique pistols I'm just dyin' ta bid on."

Marge quietly picked up her sack of evidence and turned to leave. "Yes, Paul. Maybe you'll get lucky on those guns. Maybe you'll get really lucky."

After Marge left the jailhouse, Paul Baker opened his manila file folder, which contained the details of Stanley's case. He picked up a yellow flyer—the advertisement for Marge and Ellie's 900 number. He studied the boudoir photo of Margie, as he smiled.

"Miss Marge," he whispered. "Yer still one handsome lady." He thoughtfully gazed out across his desk, as he crumpled the advertisement into a compact ball. Then he dropped his yellow wad of paper into his trash bin.

Chapter 22

There's nothing flamboyant about a North Dakota farm auction. There is also nothing *like* a North Dakota farm auction—or any rural auction, for that matter. When one considers the auction process, film clips of Sotheby's or Christie's auctions come to mind. Of course, these auctions are conducted with the utmost dignity and decorum. A particular item of value is displayed for auction. The item presented for auction is usually a highly esteemed antique, and the auctioneer adds to this impression by creating an air of sophistication. He is often a polished, attractive individual, tastefully and formally dressed. Even the auction attendees appear to be refined and well-educated. As they demurely bid for their expensive, highly sought after prize, every move is calculated. Every action is plotted. No words are wasted, and every nod is purposeful.

That being said, a rural farm auction differs tremendously from its city cousin. If one has never been raised on or near a farm, one might ever be denied the satisfaction of such a circus. A North Dakota farm—or any Midwest farm auction—is much like an estate carnival. If the seller is fortunate to still be among the living, he or she may choose to hold an auction in order to retire, liquidate the farm, buy a Winnebago and travel. If the seller has been reduced to auction because of rotten luck, death, or other tragedy, buyers clamor in from miles away to capitalize on the seller's misfortune, just the same. It makes no difference what the purpose of the sale is. What matters are the items being sold, their perceived value to the buyer, and how much the buyer is willing to pay for the privilege of taking them off the seller's hands.

During a rural auction, nothing is overblown. Nothing comes with a warranty. Every item is sold as is. And remarkably, buyers may perceive value in the seemingly worthless. This was the case with the auction of the estate of Stanley Peters Senior, who had recently met his untimely demise in the barn of his North Dakota farm.

Unlike its city cousin counterpart, the country auction's setting is almost always the site of the estate being liquidated. There are no luxuriously upholstered chairs in which to recline. Bidders stand uncomfortably all day long, often arriving hours earlier to inspect the desired merchandise. One has the opportunity to "kick the tires", so to speak, since it is clearly understood that every item is sold "as is". As in any auction, the phrase of the day is "Buyer beware." If one has purchased a lemon, one is stuck with a lemon. There are no refunds of any kind for an unsatisfied consumer of auctioned goods.

Finally, the demeanor of the auctioneer for a farm auction is significantly different from that of a Sotheby's auction. One can rely on the former auctioneer to always be comically entertaining. He and his runners work very hard for their keep, which consists entirely of an agreed upon percentage of the auction's profits. Therefore, it is in the auctioneer's best interest to fetch the highest price for the item. A skilled farm auctioneer can fly by the seat of his pants, making even the most unfavorable items seem more attractive to the potential buyer. The key for the successful auctioneer is to strike a fine balance between offering the deal of a lifetime and a giving the show of a lifetime.

Even the mere sing-songy refrain of the auctioneer's voice hypnotically lulls any potential buyers into bidding on an otherwise ordinary and commonplace piece of crap. As he entertains bids from the crowd, he interjects a cacophony of nonverbal sounds. Buyers are invited to ask pointed questions about the product and inspect it one last time, before they fancy a bid. All the while, appointed runners weave through the standing crowd, displaying boxes of items small enough to carry for any last-minute inspection.

After Stanley married Ellen and moved to the Severtsen farm, he brought with him all his belongings from Texas. During his subsequent twenty-seven year marriage to Ellie, he attended every local auction held within a one-hundred mile radius of their farm in Himmel. After each said auction, Stanley inevitably returned home with at least ten or twelve newly acquired items. These purchases were collectibles, ranging from small knickknacks to monstrosities such as old car frames and farm equipment he never used. In addition, some of the tools formerly belonged to Anders before he died. Most of these more archaic farm utensils were hand operated. And all of Anders' rare automated machinery had fallen into an inoperable state of disrepair under Stanley's supervision.

The auction of Stanley Peters' estate began promptly at 10 A.M. Some of the more anxious townspeople of Himmel showed up at the old Severtsen farm as early as 8 A.M, with the sole intent to inventory the items being offered up for sale. Some might have considered the assembly of this congregation somewhat disrespectful to the memory of the recently deceased. To an outsider, it might have seemed as though the entire town of Himmel had anticipated Stanley's inevitable demise for quite some time—much like a group of vultures circling a dying elephant on the Serengeti. Perhaps, if Stanley were someone *other than* Stanley Peters, Sr. (a more respected citizen of the town, for example), the citizens of Himmel might be more reluctant to so quickly lay claim to his numerous possessions. They might have at least granted Stanley's family a decent period of mourning before swooping down on their prey in search of fresh meat.

Even though most Himmelians graciously ignored Stanley Peters' cantankerousness throughout the last twenty-seven years, no one in town ever claimed to like him. He had wronged, insulted, abused, or owed money to nearly every member of the Himmel community at some point during his career as the town drunk. No one suffered from the loss of Stanley Peters. And a few outspoken individuals in the town (Margie included) openly admitted that Stanley and his family were better off, now that he was finally dead.

Ultimately, the nature of auctions in North Dakota—as with all estate sales—has always been more of a practical resignation to the cyclicality of life. As man turns to dust, so too do his prized possessions change hands of ownership. Life moves on, and so do the everyday things from which life's pleasures are ultimately derived.

The auction of Stanley's estate began with the smaller, more incidental items being offered for bid first. As the day progressed and the two flatbed trailers were emptied of their wares, the crowd migrated toward the larger farm tools and equipment, which surrounded the periphery of the barn. The old car skeletons and frames littering the estate were the next to go. Finally, the guns and higher ticket items were the last to be sold. In this way, the auctioneer could guarantee crowd participation until the finale, after the last bid for the most desirable item was accepted.

The first item up for bid was a large box of Stanley's books. These were clearly books that Stanley never read, which he mainly kept stacked on his bookshelf in the living room farmhouse. These were also the books that Ellie had relocated to the barn the previous November, just before Stanley's death. Most of the books were works of fiction—true crime, romance novels, and murder mysteries—whose spines were still as crisp as if they had never been opened. An occasional book in the collection was well-worn by an avid reader, but these were obviously gleaned from a reader/seller at another auction. But by and large, almost all the books contained in Stanley's collection were in near-mint condition.

"Twenty-five, five, twenty-five... Beededteeded. Can I get it? Five, ten, badatadat, twenty? Habdtadud...Twenty? The auctioneer chanted his multisyllabic gibberish, interspersed with scant information about the current high bid. He pointed to an interested bidder, who nodded plainly, as he exhibited an interest in the books. The bidding soon climaxed and then waned, as the bid price climbed until all but one bidder withdrew his interest. Soon, the auctioneer pointed to Doris Baker and announced, "Sold! To the young lady in the back!"

Doris smiled, as the auctioneer held up yet another box of books to auction. This box contained books of a different variety. Most were hunting and fishing manuals. Also included in this stack were several collectors catalogs for guns and rifles. The auctioneer tried to entice potential buyers for the antique guns being sold later that day. "Want to know how much those guns are goin' ta be worth? Right here. It's all right here. Can I get twenty for an opening bid?"

Doris stood by later, as the opening bid was placed for one of Stanley's bookshelves. Paul bid eleven dollars. Befuddled, Doris quizzed Paul as to why he would even bid on a bookcase. He thoughtfully responded, "Yer goin' ta need somethin' ta put yer new books in."

The stacks of *National Enquirer Magazine* were the next to go. It was easy to see how the auctioneer was so successful at his craft. He had a knack for making even the most hum drum of collections seem fascinating. "Here's a little bit o' history right here! Be a part o' the celebrity lifestyle, right here in Himmel! Can I have five dollars for an opening bid?" Sure enough, the stacks of worn scandal magazines fetched the sum of five dollars from bidder Elmer Gietzen.

As the auction of the smaller items progressed, Marge and Stan assisted the runners by displaying the boxes of items throughout the buying crowd. In addition, if a potential buyer hollered out a question about the merchandise, Stan quickly blurted out what scant information he had regarding the condition or age of the item. Of course, all this information was provided solely to aid the potential buyer in making a wisely informed purchase.

The crowd moved to the larger items. Stan stood by, juiced with adrenaline and ready to answer any additional questions about the products being sold. But at this point, Marge soon found herself largely obsolete. As a result, she treated herself to some cotton candy and a large glass of lemonade at a vendor's food trailer. As the spectators' level of engagement grew in intensity, Marge had also become so engrossed in the auction that she quickly forgot about her dramatic confession at Sheriff Baker's office, just hours earlier.

Soon the final bid was complete, and the long day of auctioning had ended. Both the attendees and auctioneers were exhausted. The last of the bills had been settled up, and the crowd had dissipated. If the purchased items were sufficiently small enough to be hauled away in a box, the victor left carrying his spoils home.

Otherwise, the purchasers made arrangements to tow the larger items at a future date. Mr. Olstad had purchased Stanley's 1955 Willys Jeep. He planned to show up the next morning with a trailer to haul all the spare car parts and frame away.

Sheriff Baker picked up Doris's box of books and handed them to his eldest son. He also handed him the Winchester 1200 rifle, which he acquired for $50. He handed the bookcase to his youngest son. "Take these ote to the truck. Would ya, boys?"

His obedient sons did as they were instructed. Paul then turned to Marge. "Looks like ya did pretty well selling yer goods, Marge," he commented. "Had a pretty good turnote of townsfolk here, eh? I think we cleaned ya ote."

"I'm amazed that anybody would even buy this shit," Marge answered. "Of course, *your* stuff's not shit, Paul. But it was hard to see anybody taking an interest in any of that other junk. I can't believe that half-filled boxed of empty spray paint cans sold! What're people thinking?"

"I'm not sure I woulda paid one buck fer that myself. But Ed Gunderson will probably find a use fer it. One thing abote

Stanley Peters. He sure didn't like ta part with anything." Paul snickered, while Doris seemed clearly amused.

"That's putting it mildly, Sheriff. I hope that Stan Junior decides that all his profits have been worth his effort," Marge added.

"I was disappointed ta see that ya took the pistols off the auction block," Paul commented sadly.

"I guess Stan Junior decided to keep them as a memento of his dad. Everything else got sold, and he plans on giving all the proceeds to Ellie," Margie stated.

"Ya know, Miss Marge. It's always been hard ta see how Stanley Peters could have sired such a decent young man," Paul commented. "I suppose it has more ta do with his mother's influence than anything else. Miss Severtsen's a good woman."

Marge agreed with the Sheriff. "I've always wondered how Stanley could have spawned such a great kid, myself. Stan Junior doesn't have a mean bone in his entire body. Ellie sure did something right."

Although Marge had been distracted by the auction, both Paul and Doris sensed her growing look of distress. She seemed both preoccupied with Stanley's pending murder investigation and concerned for her little sister.

"Miss Severtsen's fortunate to have her son and sister around ta help," Paul complimented.

Doris patted Marge assuringly on the shoulder. "It'll all work out, Marge. Just wait and see."

"Hope so, Doris. At this point, all I *can* do is wait and see," Margie responded blankly.

Early the following afternoon, Joseph drove Ellen home to North Dakota. They left Minneapolis before sunrise, making only a few brief stops during their trip. Joseph wanted to make good time, because he needed to return to Minnesota shortly after midnight and be to work early the next morning.

Marge greeted the travelers in the driveway, as they approached the farmhouse. She had just finished cleaning the barn. Stan Junior was in town to get his final check from the auction proceeds. Marge wore a pair of Stanley's old overalls, which were clearly about twenty inches too large in the waist. The excess fabric hung in flaps and puckers around her waist and thighs. She comically resembled a pregnant woman in denim riding chaps.

She opened the door for Ellie, greeting her sister with her customary cheek-to-cheek embrace. "How are ya, lass?"

"Oh, we're just peachy, hon'," Ellen answered. "My nephew was a wonderful host. I had a good visit with Lars and Gunnar," she added.

"How are the little imps?" Marge inquired sarcastically.

"Well, hon'. They're not quite so little anymore. But they're still ornery as ever," Ellie joked.

Little Robert let out a whine, reminding Ellen that he was patiently awaiting rescue from the back seat. "Okay, hon'. I'm comin'," she assured. She unlatched his car seat and handed the infant to Marge.

Marge hid her face behind the baby, as she whispered to Joseph. "How'd Ellie do?" she asked, careful not to let her sister hear.

"Fine, Ma," Joseph whispered, not moving his lips. "She's nuts, but she's harmless."

"I wouldn't be so sure about that," his mother commented under her breath.

After a considerable bit of struggling, Ellen finally managed to free Robert's carrier from the back seat. Margie invited Joseph into the house for grub. "Are you hungry?"

"No," Joseph replied. "Gotta get back to work. Uncle Lars needs me in the morning."

"Are you sure?" Marge asked. "I could threaten to rough him up a little again…"

"Don't be ridiculous, Ma. I actually *need* my job." Joseph kissed Marge and Ellen farewell. "Bye, Ma. Bye, Aunt Ellie. Thanks for coming to visit." He turned to shake Little Robert's slobbery hand. "So long, little man. Come see us again."

They each waved goodbye to Joseph, as he boarded his car and drove out of sight.

Ellen noted the farm's newly barren landscape. "Where are all Stanley's cars?" she asked, puzzled.

Marge reluctantly began her explanation of the prior week's events. "Sister, you and I need to talk."

"Margie," Ellen asked suspiciously. "What did ya do?"

"I should probably show you what I did," Margie stated cautiously. "But just in case, I'm just gonna hold Little Robert." She directed her sister out to the opened barn doors.

The two sisters approached the barn. Ellie stood dumbstruck. She gazed into the empty barn, which had once been piled floor-to-ceiling with all of Stanley's possessions. All that remained in the barn now were a few hand tools and 50 feet of heavy-duty rope. Everything else had been auctioned off or hauled away. Even the straw from the floor had been swept away and burned.

"Oh my gosh, Marge! What happened?" Ellie exclaimed in a tone of sheer panic.

Marge held Little Robert in front of her face defensively. "Don't hurt me, Ellie! Remember, I'm holding your grandchild!" Little Robert babbled and sucked on his fist. He was completely oblivious to the fact that his great aunt was now using him as a human shield. Marge blurted, "We auctioned off all of Stanley's shit!"

Shocked, Ellen surveyed the empty barn. "Oh, my heavens…" she uttered weakly. Then her face transitioned to a look of sheer horror, as she recalled her husband's final threats of retaliation for anyone who tampered with his belongings. "Stanley will be furious when he comes home!" Overwhelmed, she collapsed on the inverted paint bucket. "Oh, Marge—what am I goin' ta tell Stanley?"

Marge watched Ellen in a state of disbelief. She had been so sure that Ellie had murdered Stanley, yet she still anticipated his return. *Ellie is obviously in denial about this whole thing. Doesn't she remember leaving his corpse to rot in the barn?*

Margie stuttered as she squatted down to speak to her sister. She perched Robert on her hip and focused intently on her sister's face. "Wait a minute, Ellie. You mean—you really don't remember what happened to Stanley?"

Ellen responded, "No, Margie. Why? What happened ta him?"

Margie astonishedly contemplated her sister's response. Perhaps she truly has blocked this entire traumatic episode from her mind. *Surely, she would admit to me—her trusted sister—if she remembered killing him. What does she have to hide from **me**?*

Ellen repeated her question for her older sister. "Tell me, Margie. Where's Stanley?"

Margie's mind was instantly flooded with feelings of extreme guilt. If Ellie had murdered Stanley as she suspected, and she obliterated the entire episode from her memory, why should Marge accuse her of being a murderess now? She had gone to such great lengths to protect her youngest sister thus far. Yes, Paul Baker had stifled her previous efforts to confess to the murder, but he had only postponed the inevitable. Eventually, Marge would have to falsely confess to the crime, brandishing both the murder weapon and Ellie's lefse pin. But still, there was absolutely no way Marge was going to let her little sister go to jail.

How would reminding Ellie that she was Stanley's killer ultimately help her now? Marge considered her response to Ellie. She finally determined that it would not be helpful to disclose the truth to Ellen. *Better to lie to Ellie and tell her that Stanley simply died in the barn, buried under a pile of his own tools. Farm accidents happen every day in North Dakota. That explanation wouldn't be too far-fetched. It won't do anyone any good to lay the blame on my already traumatized, half-senile sister. When it comes time for me to confess to the crime, Ellen might hate **me**, but she wouldn't have to hate **herself**.* No, she thought to herself resolutely, *there's no way that I can accuse the sweetest person alive of murdering a man who was quite possibly the most hateful, despicable human being to ever walk the face of the earth!*

As she considered these things, Margie resolved that she would never disclose the truth about Stanley's death to her youngest sister. She decided that she would simply tell Ellen exactly what Ellie needed to hear. And what Ellen needed to hear was nothing but a calculated and deliberate, boldfaced lie.

Margie looked Ellen squarely in the eye. "Sister," she began earnestly, "I don't know how to tell you this, so I'm gonna come right out and say it. Stanley's not coming back for his things. As a matter of fact, Stanley's not coming back—*ever.*"

Chapter 23

"Den, you pick up yer special lefse stick, and scoop up yer bread under de middle. Flip it onto de griddle, and cook until it starts to bubble like a pancake. Just a few seconds. Den you pick it up de same way—under de middle wit' yer stick—and flip it over. See? Some brown spots, but it's not cooked so long dat it's crispy. Ya, dat's it. Perfectly cooked."
SIGRID SEVERTSEN

Ellie Severtsen stood solemnly cuddling her young grandson in the kitchen of her North Dakota farmhouse. She had just learned, minutes before, that her elderly husband had been discovered dead in her old barn. His lifeless corpse had probably been preserved in her barn most of the winter, frozen into one very large "Stanley popsicle", and buried under a heap of his rusty tools and equipment.

Ellen was certainly moved by the news of her husband's death, but she had come to accept the fact that Stanley was advanced in years. He was twenty-one years older than she. In addition, he was an alcoholic, who had cheated death on many occasions during his lifetime. There was no question in anyone's mind that Stanley would soon meet his maker. The real question was *how* he would ultimately "kick the can".

Her older sister had finally broken the sad news to her. Both Marge and Ellie's son had discovered Stanley's decomposing body in the barn almost two weeks ago, while they cleaned the barn to prepare for an auction. Ellie was overcome by guilt in the knowledge that her closest sister and her only son were the unfortunate ones to have come across Stanley's remains. How horrible it must have been for Stan Junior to see his father dead in such a fashion. Stan had always been a devoted son to Stanley.

The curious thing about Margie's revelation to Ellen was that Stanley's passing seemed like news to Ellen. Margie was sure that Ellen not only *knew* that Stanley lay dead in the barn, but she was 99% positive that Ellen was the one who had *killed* Stanley. Not that Margie blamed Ellen for ever being driven to murder her crotchety spouse. What terrified Marge more was her younger sister's surprised response to the news. She concluded that Ellie had most certainly blotted out the entire episode from her already fading memory.

Ellen sat soberly hugging her young grandson at the kitchen table. She expected to be greeted by her young daughter-in-law, Rosa, when she entered the farmhouse. But Rosa seemed to be indisposed at the moment. Ellie thought she detected the faint sounds of Rosa vomiting in the nearby bathroom.

Just then, Margie's 900 number rang. Ellen looked around and called for Rosa. The cordless phone rang several times. She started to panic. *What'll I do? I don't know how to answer Margie's line! Maybe I'll just answer as Elsa Dietrich and tell them to call back later.*

She picked up the phone and stammered. "1…1-900-H..HOT-MAMA. Uh, Th..This is Elsa Dietrich speaking. Can ya call back later?" she asked.

The caller was undeterred. It was Jack, Marge's habitual caller. He was looking for the "Old Gabrielle."

"Oh ya, Jack. I'm sorry. She's not here right now. If ya call back in another twenty minutes, ya can speak ta the other Gabrielle," she assured him.

Jack seemed desperate. Ellie could tell that he had been crying. He needed to speak to the *other Gabrielle*—the older one. *The girl in the ad.* He told Ellie that only *that Gabrielle* knew him and understood him. If only he knew her real name. If only he could find out where she lived. If only he could speak to her and see her, he could confide in her his most intimate secrets. *She* would understand.

Ellie sympathized with the caller. "Oh my gosh, ya sound so derned unhappy. I really feel fer ya. No," she added decisively. "I can't give that kinda infermation ote."

He pleaded ever more desperately with Ellen for some shred of information about Margie. He was at the end of his rope. He had lost his job. They were about to shut his phone off. He could no longer afford to keep calling, and his own mother was about to kick him out of her house. He just needed someone to talk to.

"Well, ya can talk ta me, if ya'd like." Ellie volunteered. "I just found ote that my poor husband has died. I know what yer goin' through, hon.' I'd be glad ta listen."

Jack sobbed frantically. He asserted that, although Ellie seemed nice enough, he needed to talk to the *other Gabrielle*. Only *she* understood his innermost thoughts and feelings. As he continued to explain the futility of his current life's

240

situation, Ellen suddenly recalled her conversation with Margie about the doctor who had been calling on the 900 line.

"Well, I know that she said she had someone callin' fer her on this line. I guess it won't hurt ta tell ya a little abote her. Ya, okay. But ya have ta promise not ta tell a livin' soul abote this. She's my sister, Margie Carter. We live up here in Himmel, North Dakota."

The caller seemed surprise. Marge had him convinced all along that she lived in sunny Florida.

"Oh no, hon.' She hasn't lived there since last summer, when the hurricane blew everything away. She lives up here with me on the farm. Her husband John died late last year, and we're up here all alone. This number's the only thing we have ta sustain ourselves. Nope, there aren't any men around ta care for us, now. We're all by ourselves. Just me and Margie." Ellen seemed a little aloof, as she spoke about being alone with no man to protect her. In truth, Stanley had *never* been there to protect her. But Jack didn't need to know that.

Jack was relieved that Ellie had given him this vital information about Marge's identity and whereabouts. He thanked her for the information.

"Yer welcome, Jack. If yer ever in North Dakota, come see us anytime," Ellie stated. "Oh, and ya can always call her here. Just give her a few more days, and I'm sure she'll be back ta take yer call. Bye, hon.'" Ellen hung up the phone.

Rosa entered the room as Ellen hung up the phone. "Hi Mom," she greeted, as she excitedly grabbed Little Robert from his grandmother's arms. Ellen kissed her daughter-in-law on the cheek.

"Hi, hon.' I had ta answer Marge's line, because ya weren't here," Ellie stated.

"I haven't been feeling well lately," Rosa admitted.

"Ya, I see that." Ellie grinned shrewdly. "Mornin' sickness, eh?"

Ellen had keenly perceived Rosa's current predicament. It seemed her recent activity answering the 900 line had not only enhanced Rosa's sex life, it boosted her apparent fertility. "Don' tell Stan. He might be upset. I just have to figure out how to gently break the news to him."

Ellie bounced excitedly. "Oh, I'm goin' ta be a grandma again!" She kissed her daughter-in-law once more. "I'm so happy fer ya, hon.'"

"Please don't say anything, Mom. I have to figure out the right time to tell Stan."

Ellie crossed her heart and placed her finger over her mouth. "My lips are sealed, dear."

"Who was that on the phone just now?" Rosa inquired.

"Oh, nobody hon.' Just somebody callin' fer Margie," she replied matter-of-factly. She joyfully turned her attention to her young grandson. "Oh, Little Robert! Yer goin' ta have a little brother or sister soon. Aren't ya excited??"

John Jacob Harvey rested his mother's phone receiver back into its cradle. His cheeks were wet with tears. He had borne his soul to a strange woman on the 900 line, while he sat on his mother's plastic-covered sofa. He wore a white t-shirt and white pair of painter's jeans. Both his jeans and t-shirt were coated with dried spatters of various shades of interior house paint. He wore a pair of worn work boots.

John Jacob lived with his mother in her clean but modest Pineville, North Carolina home. He was thirty-five years old and single. He had a very strong, rural deep-South accent. He had struggled to find regular work his entire life. This was due mostly to the fact that he wasn't very bright, he wasn't very skilled, and he had never been very dependable.

He had a curious receding hairline and a bald spot which extended around the back of his head in a horseshoe pattern. This left a small tuft of dark brown hair just over his frontal lobe. In a mistaken effort to preserve his youthful appearance, he kept this tuft of hair uncut. It hung down in front of his forehead, where he combed it into a wicked point. He possessed dark brown, almost soulless eyes and sunken cheekbones, which made him appear gaunt.

In rare moments, John Jacob would grin, revealing his oversized incisors and his fifty cent grin. That is to say, he had a sufficiently large enough gap between his two front teeth that one could squeeze two quarters side-by-side into the space. His body frame was small and wiry. During his childhood, he was very self-conscious of his small stature. As a result, he constantly bullied weaker students at least two grades younger than he.

John Jacob was a regular caller to the sex chat line, 1-900-HOT-MAMA. He had racked up a bill of over $3,000, which neither he nor his mother could afford to pay. His mother was retired, and he was now jobless, so the phone company had since threatened to cut off their phone service.

Only his mother called him John Jacob. His few friends and the rest of his estranged family called him Jack. His mother had threatened to kick him out of her house if she ever found out that he had been calling Marge's number. Jack waited until his mother left the house before secretly making his calls. But it was simply a matter of time before the next phone bill arrived—or the phone was shut off completely.

He had scratched down Marge's name, along with the name of the town where she lived onto a memo pad which sat next to the phone. He tore off the top sheet, folded it, and stuffed it in his jeans pocket.

His mother was a short, stocky woman of 5'3". She was sufficiently overweight and suffered from arthritis, which meant that she hobbled everywhere she went. As a result, she wore Naturalizers with knee-high pantyhose for more comfortable walking. Even though she always wore long skirts, the rolled-down tops of her pantyhose were still visible under her skirt hem. She had long gray hair, which she kept tied up in a French twist. If it were not for the sour expression which was permanently carved on her old wrinkled face, one might have perceived her as a wrinkled old grandma. But she, in fact, had no grandchildren. John Jacob was her only son.

Jack's mother walked through the front door, returning home with a bag of groceries. She was livid. "Did yew call that number agin'?" She set down her bag of groceries. As she peeled each food item out of her paper bag, she droned on about John Jacob's uselessness, his laziness, his selfishness, and the exorbitantly large phone bill he had racked up in recent months.

"Is this the way I raised ya?" she continued with her back to her son. "I cain't believe y'all are this irresponsible! What the hail is wrong wit' ya that ya cain't git off'n yer dead ass and git' a goddam jawb???" She was furious. "I want cha outta hare 'fore nahtfawl. Ya hare me??? And don' cha dare traw ta tawk mae inta lettin' yew stay, yew sorrah som' bitch!"

It really hadn't dawned on John Jacob's mother that, by calling him a son of a bitch, she was indirectly insulting herself. A better insult might have been to simply call him a bastard. Although he was legitimate, his mother never really wanted him to begin with. After her husband walked out on them when John Jacob was nine, she blamed her son for her estranged husband's departure. In fact, from the time he was a small child, John Jacob's mother believed *all* her miseries were attributable to John Jacob.

It hadn't always been like that. When he was a toddler, he tried to be good. But it seemed as though, when he was good, he was almost transparent. He soon discovered that he could gain more attention—albeit *bad* attention—by misbehaving. As he grew older, the nature of his transgressions grew more severe—so severe, only a few unlucky dead people and God himself knew the truth about his crimes.

Eventually, John Jacob's deviousness became part of his self-fulfilling prophecy. He realized that his mother derived her own sense of self-worth by belittling her son. Consequently, he decided early on that he would give her as many reasons as he could to blame him for all her woes. In a twisted way, he was being the *good* son by being willing to be the *bad* son.

But Jack was now thirty-five, jobless, and completely unfulfilled. Aside from his dysfunctional relationship with his mother, the only other romantic relationships he could carry on were at strip clubs and with women who answered his numerous 900 calls. Even then, these women were *paid* to talk to him. When they ridiculed him for being unemployed, impotent, and living with his mother, they were essentially treating him just like his mother treated him.

He decided that he had been the whipping boy long enough. He had been the subject of mockery for every woman whose life he had ever touched. He no longer wished to be ridiculed, and he was tired of shouldering the blame for his mother's misfortunes and her failed marriage.

John Jacob quietly unplugged both ends of the long, coiled phone cable. He blankly studied his hands, as he wrapped each end of the cord through his palms several times. He turned to his mother, who still had her back to him while she stocked the kitchen pantry. As she continued her speech regarding her son's numerous inadequacies, he snuck up behind her with the telephone cord wound around his hands. Mrs. Harvey's final diatribe was not the usual critical put-down of her inadequate son. Her last speech was the subtle sounds of barely audible gasps, as her frustrated and humiliated son choked the life out of her.

It was over in just moments. He stood over his dead mother and relished the deafening silence. He attained an almost blissful state of tranquility, as he kneeled over his mother's corpse. He quizzically cocked his head and waited for her to open her eyes. Realizing that she would not wake from her slumber, he frowned and shrugged his shoulders.

During his entire exchange with his mother and his subsequent murder of her, John Jacob Harvey uttered not a single word. He eventually rose and calmly stepped over the lifeless body of Mrs. Harvey. He snatched the green duffel bag which he had previously packed, and he immediately moved out of his mother's home.

After all, that *was* what his mother had asked John Jacob to do all along.

Paul Baker rested at the edge of his bed, as he readied himself for sleep. His wife, Doris, rummaged through the box of books she had previously purchased at Stanley Peters' estate auction. She studied each of the titles as she stood in her floor-length night gown. She loved to read anything she could get her hands on, and she had incorporated reading books into her bedtime ritual.

"Hmm. Now what do I want to read?" she asked herself, glancing into the box. "I think I want something that looks well read. I guess, if somebody else liked it enough to read it, I should find it interesting." She picked up a Harlequin romance novel. "Maybe this." She read the synopsis on the back of the book, then placed it back in the box. "Naw, not in the mood for that." She glanced over at her husband. "Paul looks like he needs some rest." She chuckled to herself and studied the contents of the box a bit more. Then she noticed a particularly worn copy of *The Pale Horse* by Agatha Christie. "Yes, this'll do." She repeated the title aloud as she examined the cover. "A compelling mystery by Agatha Christerie—hmm, that rhymes…" She joked to herself as she fluffed up her pillow and nestled herself under the covers on her side of their queen-sized bed.

Paul also wriggled himself under the comforter on his side of the bed. He switched off his bed lamp and kissed Doris goodnight. He turned on his side facing his wife as she sat upright reading. He closed his eyes and drifted off into peaceful oblivion.

"Hmmf," Doris grunted, bewildered. She studied the pages of the book in her hands, scanning each one. She tapped her drowsy husband on the shoulder. "Paul? Are you awake?"

He sleepily opened one eye. "Hmm? What is it?"

"Something very curious about this book, Paul."

"What's that?" he asked.

"This book is underlined, like someone has studied it. Every occurrence of the word "thallium" is underlined. All references to the symptoms of thallium poisoning are underlined—like fever and hair falling out by the roots."

She opened the inside back cover, pointing to it. "And here, Paul. Someone has scrawled something."

"What does it say?" Paul inquired, now fully awake and interested.

"It says: "Yum Yum Rat Vittles, Lootafish, kills a Norway rat.""

"Yum Yum Rat Vittles? That old-timey rat poison?" Paul asked.

"Yeah, my dad used to use that stuff for rats in the barn. You know, before they took it off the market twenty years ago," Doris answered.

"Lootafish? What do you think that is?"

"Maybe they mean '*lutefisk*'. Perhaps whoever wrote this wasn't a Norwegian." Doris suggested.

Paul sat upright on his side of the queen-sized bed. Doris handed him the book, as he examined the pages.

"You know what I think, Paul?" Doris inquired of her husband.

Paul nodded affirmingly to his wife. "I know what yer thinkin', Doris. Looks ta me like someone tried ta use this book less fer entertainment and more as a recipe fer murder."

Chapter 24

The turnout for the funeral of Stanley Peters was not nearly as big as the turnout for the auction of Stanley Peters' belongings. Surprisingly, many Himmel townsfolk did show up for the memorial service to offer support for Stanley's grieving widow, Ellen. She had been a respected member of the town all her life. For over a quarter of a century, she had served as a beloved elementary school teacher.

Since Stanley Peters hadn't the interest in making pre-arranged funeral plans, Stan Junior took it upon himself to use a portion of the proceeds from the auction to purchase a casket and plot for his father's body. The memorial service was held at the local funeral home. Although Stan Junior tried to talk Pastor Anderson of Himmel Lutheran into performing the memorial service, the Pastor believed it might be somewhat offensive to the longstanding members of the church to hold Stanley's funeral there. True, Ellie and Stan were members of the church, but Stanley himself had never attended a service there. In fact, Pastor Anderson was concerned that some of the Lutheran parishioners might consider the simple act of carting Stanley Peters' dead body into the sanctuary a bit sacrilegious.

That being said, the Himmel Funeral Home reluctantly held the funeral service for Stanley. Because he could find no other willing participant to eulogize his father, Stan Junior decided to say a few words in his father's memory. He stood at the podium, gazing down at Stanley's closed casket, which was draped in flowers.

"No one here would ever dare to say that my father, Stanley Peters Senior, was a good and decent man. He was hard to live with. He was hard on everyone who loved him. He was stubborn. And sometimes, he could be downright mean.

"Mom had told me once that Dad came to town twenty-seven years ago, after his first son, Robert, had been killed in Vietnam. Here in Himmel, he met Mom. He married her, and he made Himmel and Grandpa Anders' farm his home. I'm glad for that. I grew up here, knowing the people of this town, working with them, and loving them.

"Even though my dad was hard on people, I never felt judged by others here because of him. I once asked Mom what she might have seen in Dad when she married him. He seemed mad all the time—especially at her.

"And you know what she told me? She said she had dated his first son, Robert, for many years. He was a very good man. I would have liked him. Then she said that *I* was a good young man. And she said, "If Stanley could father two such wonderful young men, there has to be something good about his character—something wonderful that nobody else could see.

"I'm standing here today, because I just wanted to say: Dad, I hope that you and Robert are together and happy. And I hope that the 'good part of your character' is enough good to gain you access to the Pearly Gates of Heaven. Maybe one day I'll see you both there. You and my big brother, Robert.

"Goodbye, Dad. I love you."

Stan Junior walked softly beside his father's casket and gently rested his hand on the coffin. Ellen sobbed weakly.

In contrast, Marge sat beside her, practically wailing. "I don't know why I'm bawling," she cried as she blew her nose into a handful of tissue. "I *hated* Stanley!"

Ellie patted her sister supportively on the back. "Thanks fer being here, hon'. I can't tell ya how much it means ta me and Stan."

As was customary, the Director of the Himmel Funeral Home entreated volunteers to share testimony regarding the deceased. "Anybody? Feel free to stand and share your memories of Stanley with us." Of course, about four minutes of complete silence ensued, since no one had anything nice to say about Stanley.

Finally, William Knutson came forward. He nervously cleared his throat as he addressed the mourners. "Hi. My name is William Knutson. I've lived in Himmel all my life. As a matter o' fact, I went ta school with Miss Ellie here, who was Stanley's wife."

"There's not a whole lot ta say abote Stanley. Mostly I just sat next ta him at the Trading Post. Doris brought him drinks." He nodded and waved at Doris. "He loved his Jack Daniels bourbon. And he loved his two sons, Robert and Stan Junior. He bragged abote 'em all the time."

"When Stanley got ta drinkin', he'd sometimes lay inta me abote Miss Ellie. I think he musta loved her somethin' fierce, if he could get so worked up in tryin' ta slug me. He did that a couple o' times. He wasn't a sure shot, but he seemed to throw those punches at the wind somethin' wild."

The mourners chuckled quietly, as William seemed to have run out of steam.

"Well, I guess I'll just finish by saying, So long, Stanley. See ya in the big bar up in the sky, eh?"

William Knutson returned to his seat as the service closed. The majority of the attendees gathered in the funeral home lobby, while immediate family members and close friends marched two blocks down to the Himmel Cemetery. Stan Junior had managed to extend the Severtsen family plot to include two extra plots next to his great-grandmother Sigrid's grave. One plot was intended for Stanley, and the plot next to Stanley's had been purchased for Ellie, whenever she passed away.

Ellie took Stan Junior's arm during the short journey behind the Hearse, which contained Stanley's coffin. "That was a fine thing ya said abote yer father, Stan. I'm so proud of ya."

Stan Junior seemed miffed at his mother. "I don't understand why you're not more upset, Mom."

Ellen was baffled. "I don't understand what ya mean, Son. How am I supposed ta act?"

"More upset than you are," he answered smartly. He was still clearly shaken. He handed her a check for the remainder of the auction proceeds.

"What's this?" Ellie asked.

"It's the money from the auction. Now you and Aunt Marge don't have to do that 900 number nonsense anymore." Robert pleaded with his mother sincerely while he handed her the check.

Ellen glanced down at sum on the check. "Oh my heavens!" she exclaimed. She gratefully kissed Stan on the cheek. "Thank ya so much, Son." Then she wiped her lipstick off his cheek with her thumb. "Ya were always such a good boy."

He pleaded with her again. "So, you're gonna shut down the 900 numbers and retire?" Stan Junior was almost demanding her compliance now.

"Oh, heavens no!" Ellie replied. "I have no intention of giving up now."

Stan was perplexed. "No, Mom," he commanded, "I won't have you doing that anymore. You're too good for that. I won't stand for it!"

"Well, Son," Ellen answered defiantly. "I'm not sure that's *yer* decision ta make!"

"I'm just saying, Mom. I don't think you should be doing that. I worry about you."

"I know ya do, Stan, hon'. But there's a lot ya don't know abote me. Really, Son. I can take care of myself. I'll be fine," she assured him.

Marge was ten steps behind Ellie and Stan, walking beside Paul and Doris Baker. Paul had pulled Stanley's copy of *The Pale Horse* out of his suit pocket, careful not to let Ellie see.

"Marge, I know this really isn't the time nor the place, but I got ta ask ya somethin'," Paul began.

"Sure, Paul. What is it?"

"See this book here?" He showed her the Agatha Christie book.

"Sure. That was Stanley's book. We packed it in the box for the auction."

"Well, does yer sister still eat lutefisk?" Paul inquired.

"Naw. We hated that crap. Grandmother and Father were the only people in the family who ate that stuff. None of us kids ever liked it," Marge stated. She stuck out her tongue and shivered in disgust. "Sorry, Paul. Just the mere thought of eating that gelatinous, stinky fish crap makes we want to throw up!"

"Well here's the thing. We've been tryin' ta figger ote whose writin' this is." He opened the inside back cover etched with misspelled scrawls.

"I'm pretty sure it's Stanley's handwriting." She took the book from him, as she examined the inside cover more closely. "Definitely. Who else's writing would it be? I know it's not Ellie's." She read the scrawls more carefully. "Wait— Yum Yum Rat Vittles? Ellie still has a half-used box of that crap under her sink!"

When the funeral party arrived at the cemetery, little additional tribute was paid to Stanley. Pastor Anderson read a few passages from the New Testament, and the consecration of the grave was complete. The majority of the crowd had retreated. Ellen, Stan, Rosa, Sheriff Baker, and Doris were left standing at the grave site.

Ellen tossed a handful of dirt onto Stanley's grave, as the coffin was lowered into the soil. "So long, Stanley. I hope ya find peace here." She glanced over at Sigrid's grave marker. "It was nice of Stan Junior ta find a plot right next ta Grandmother." As she turned back to her spouse's coffin, she added, "Now ya can take care of her in heaven, Stanley."

Paul, Marge, and Doris stood a few feet behind Ellen, as she quietly said her goodbyes to her late husband. But upon hearing Ellen's comments about her deceased grandmother,

Margie stepped forward. She placed her arm around her younger sister.

"Ellie, dear. Didn't you say that Grandmother *hated* Stanley?"

"Why yes, Margie. I told ya. After Stan Junior was born, she tried ta talk me inta divorcing poor Stanley. 'He's just a drone bee, now,' she would say. 'The queen has laid de egg. Winter's come. Time to send him away from de hive!' She really hated Stanley."

Marge glanced suspiciously behind her shoulder toward Paul. She quizzed her little sister some more. "But you said that Stanley *loved* Grandmother Sigrid."

"Well, ya hon'. I'm pretty sure he knew she didn't like him. I think he even overheard her say that we didn't need him around anymore. But he never once said a cross word ta her," Ellen informed her.

Marge was clearly in interrogation mode now. "And Stanley took care of Grandmother, just before she died?"

"Oh, ya. I had ta teach school, ya know. So Stanley stayed home and took care of the baby and Grandmother." Ellen smiled. "He was so good ta her. He even had Mrs. Olstad make lutefisk special, just fer her. She ate that right up 'til the very end. 'Til she couldn't even keep *that* down anymore," Ellen stated innocently.

Paul stepped up to Ellen, as he spoke. "What did yer grandma die of again, Miss Severtsen?"

"Don't know fer sure. She died suddenly, in just a few days. She had a terribly high fever. It was awful. And she complained that her feet hurt her."

"Her feet?" Paul inquired, puzzled.

"Ya. She said that she <u>felt like there were a thousand little needles, pokin' inta the soles of her feet</u>. And I remember sitting at her bedside, readin' ta her. One night, I leaned over ta kiss her goodnight, and <u>her hair came off in a tuft in my hand</u>. Oh my gosh. I was horrified. I started ta scream.

"Well, Stanley came in and calmed me down. He really was good ta her. Anyways, she died shortly after that. Don't cha know, Marge, I tried a couple 'o times ta get her ta see a doctor, but she never would have it." Ellen looked horrified, as she recounted the gruesome story of her grandmother's sudden death.

"I kept that lock of her hair in the box under my bed. Ya know, the box with all Robert's letters?"

Margie nodded. She was uncharacteristically speechless, as she struggled to assemble the details of Sigrid's passing. She stood, largely motionless and dazed.

"Well, hon'. I guess I'm goin' ta go over and brush off Robert's grave while I'm here," she stated. Stan Junior followed closely behind his mother, as the pair left for Robert's family plot on the far side of the cemetery.

After Ellen excused herself, Margie frowned at Paul Baker. "Sheriff?"

"Yes, Miss Marge?"

"Are you thinking what I'm thinking?"

"I think I am," Paul acknowledged.

Doris interjected, "I think we are *all* thinking what you're thinking, Marge."

Marge scowled at Stanley's coffin, now seated in its freshly dug hole, six feet below. She hatefully kicked more dirt into the grave and shouted, "You burn in hell, Stanley Peters!"

Ellen Severtsen attentively brushed dirt off the modest gravestone of Robert Peters, as she knelt down in the grass. She hung her head and sobbed quietly to herself.

Stan Junior stood behind her. "Mom?"

She failed to hear him. She was too entrenched in her own grief and self-pity to hear anyone.

He spoke louder, this time almost yelling. "Mom! I'm talking to you!"

She glanced up at her son, clearly in distress. "Oh, heavens. I'm sorry, Robert. I didn't mean ta ignore ya."

Stan Junior was outraged. Not only was his grief-stricken mother ignoring his pleas for attention, she had called him by the wrong name once again. "Mom! I'm *Stan Junior!*"

"What, Son?"

"You called me *Robert* again, Mom!" Stan Junior was overwrought.

"Oh, dear. I'm sorry, Son."

"You're sorry? Really, Mom. You're *sorry?*" He shook his head in disbelief. "I just don't get it. I mean, *I just do not get it!*"

Ellen swabbed her wet nose with her handkerchief and rose to her feet. "What, Son? What don't ya get?"

"I don't get how you're more worked up over Robert being dead than my own father. How does that happen?" he inquired impatiently.

"What? Ya mean Stanley?"

"Yes, Mom—Stanley! Remember Stanley? You had a child by him. You lived with him for twenty-seven friggin' years? You clubbed him over the head with a lefse pin? Yeah!

That Stanley!" Stan yelled disrespectfully at his mother now. "What's *wrong* with you, Mom?"

"Well, Son. Fer starters, Stanley isn't yer real father," she stated calmly.

"Huh?" Stan Junior glared at his mother, speechless.

Ellen shook her head, as she mumbled. "I know I shoulda told ya a long time ago, Son. I really meant ta tell ya, but things didn't seem ta turn ote the way we had planned."

"The way *who* planned?" Stan was clearly tormented now. He didn't know if Ellie was telling him the truth or leading him into some crazy fantasy of hers.

"The way yer great-grandmother and I planned," Ellen stated.

"What're you talking about, Mom? Have you completely lost it?"

"No dear, I'm very sane," Ellen assured him. She seemed suddenly concerned by the look of anguish in her son's weary face. "Oh goodness, Son. Have a seat. Ya look white as a sheet." She motioned for Stan Junior to be seated on a nearby bench while she sat next to him.

"I've got ta tell ya a story, now. And—I know ya might get mad at me—but I'm goin' ta tell ya the truth anyways. It's time fer me ta just come clean, once and fer all."

Chapter 25

Stanley Peters, Jr. sat next to his mother in the old Himmel Cemetery. He was in shock—confounded by her revelation that the man he had called "Dad" for the last twenty-six years was not his father at all, but his grandfather.

"What d'ya mean Stanley Peters is not my father? How could that be? Mom! You even named me after him!" Stan shook while he screamed at Ellie.

"Well, naming ya Stan Junior was really Stanley's idea. He insisted on it," his mother answered.

"So, Mom. Tell me—who *is* my father?" he inquired.

"Why, *Robert*, of course."

"But wasn't Robert killed in '65 in Vietnam? He probably hadn't been to Himmel since he enlisted in '64, right? I was born in April of '66," Stan commented.

"Didn't it occur ta ya that yer birthday was a little early?" Ellen asked her son. "Stanley and I were married in November of '65. You were born in April of '66. I think ya might have been a tad early ta be considered conceived in wedlock," his mother stated.

"Okay, but—help me out—I don't get how Stanley is not my father, but Robert is…"

And so, to explain the mystery of Stan Junior's paternity, Ellen recounted the story of her rendezvous with her son's true father, Robert Peters.

Although Ellie Severtsen and Robert Peters had known each other since they were eighteen and fifteen, respectively, they didn't officially date until three years later, when Robert turned eighteen. By that time, Ellen's father, Anders, had passed away. And Sigrid sent Ellie off to Dickinson College for two years to become a teacher.

Shortly thereafter, Robert's grandfather also passed away, leaving him with a sufficient inheritance to pay for a four-year college education at North Dakota State University. He went to college and qualified for an educational deferment from the draft until he graduated in the spring of '64.

As U.S. activity in the East seemed to be again heightening, Robert—now equipped with a college degree—knew it would be inevitable that troops would eventually be sent to war. He also felt, if he enlisted in the Armed forces early enough, he could serve his tour of duty before the war in Vietnam escalated and the United States committed more troops to the war effort. Conscription would most certainly be more aggressively enforced, if the U.S. became more involved in East Asia.

Robert was, by no means, a coward. But he fully understood the ramifications of military decisions being made by removed politicians in Washington. He had no interest in dying in vain, but he also had no intention of skirting what he felt was his national duty. And perhaps, if he was permitted to use his education and military training to effect change, he might have felt as though he had made a difference in the battlefield.

Ellie was completely against Robert's enlistment from day one. They argued extensively about it. She believed that he should simply wait to see if his number in the lottery ever came up. If it did, he could go. If it didn't, he could stay in Himmel, marry her, and make a life for himself there.

After a considerable amount of debate, Robert won out. He enlisted in the Army almost immediately after his graduation. "I'll do this first," he promised Ellie. "Then, I'll come back to you, marry you, and we can start a family together. There is no honor in dodging the draft, even if you have dodged it with a little good luck. There will be men dying out there soon, and who am I to say that I am any better than they are?"

She realized that it was Robert's tremendous sense of commitment and honor that had attracted her to him in the first place. True, Robert was a very physically attractive man. His brilliant blue eyes seemed to pierce her soul when he spoke to her. The sound of his voice calmed her. And his warm and inviting kisses made her heart flutter. But even after six years of steady dating, he never made an inappropriate move on Ellen. Yes, Robert was an honorable man, and that was why Ellie loved him.

In July of '64, Robert was sent to Fort Benning, Georgia, to serve in the 1st Battalion, 7th Cavalry, as Infantryman in the new Airmobile Division of the Special Forces. It was a very stressful and harrowing time for him. Everything seemed so tentative. The political system was crumbling. President Johnson fumbled to secure his governmental stronghold on communism and steady the reigns of democracy. The nature of the draft had changed, and the commitment of troops to Vietnam seemed inevitable.

Despite his intense training, Robert still found time to write Ellen letters, which she kept in a box under her bed. His carefully penned letters told of the horrors of war and death and spoke of the political and racial tensions prevalent in the South. He even spoke of meeting his father on several occasions, while Stanley still lived in Texas. Robert stated that, after serving in the military, he gained a more insightful understanding of his father, who served in the Army during World War II.

In one of his later letters to Ellie, Robert wrote:

"You cannot grow up a good man and be a good soldier, without losing a little of yourself in the field. It's just not possible to wrong someone in war—friend or foe—if you remind yourself of sins you have committed there. You cannot survive, if you do not relinquish the human side of yourself to combat. Even if you return home alive, your conscience, your innocence, and your virtue are most certainly left behind, slain on the battlefield."

During the Christmas of '64, Robert was granted a short leave. He traveled from Fort Benning to Bismarck by train. Ellie and Robert's mother picked him up at the station. He stayed at his grandfather's farm for the holidays, but he and Ellen were almost inseparable during that time. Finally, after six years of abstinence, Robert and Ellie consummated their relationship. Ellie was a virgin of twenty-seven. Robert was twenty-four.

As she recalled that very special Christmas, Ellen thought of all the countless stories from her college schoolmates about their sexual prowess. These were young Midwestern girls who were well-educated. Many had embraced a coming of age— the sexual revolution. With the advent of oral contraceptives, even the Catholic girls considered sex for recreation. Nobody believed that holding out for one's true love was something that a smart girl needed to do.

But Ellie was different. She never seemed to mind if people ridiculed her for upholding traditional values. She embraced the idea of being considered old-fashioned. She loved feeling connected to her past, her home, and her Norwegian family heritage.

Most of all, both Ellie and Robert were hopeless romantics. Yes, they were both well-educated, articulate, and practical. But they were also hopelessly in love. They clung to the hope that, as soon as Robert could return to Himmel, he had every intention of making Ellen his wife.

When he returned to Fort Benning after Christmas leave, Ellie was distraught. Again, they wrote every day, without remission. Ellen cherished Robert's letters. He was so articulate and strong. She was so enamored with him. After their last Christmas together, she could say without a doubt—that he was a passionate and considerate lover.

She melted like sand through his fingers, when he lovingly caressed her cheek. She swooned at the mere sound of his voice, when he called her by name. She lay naked in the loft of the barn, as he made passionate love to her. How she yearned to be held in his strong arms. How she desired to catch a glimpse of his nude silhouette against the sunlight once more.

All Ellie's hopes crashed to the ground on July 28, when President Johnson announced that he would be deploying Robert's Division to Vietnam. *He is surely as good as dead*, she thought to herself. *I can't live without Robert. I couldn't possibly survive without him.*

Robert's next letter to Ellen confirmed that he was being sent to East Asia. But he also added that he had to meet Ellie one last time before being shipped out. School was then out for summer vacation. He could take a train to Minneapolis, if she would drive to meet him. There they could spend a few precious days together, before he was deployed to 'Nam. So Ellie announced to her grandmother that she would be going on a trip for several days. Not to worry. She would return home in time to ready herself for the next school year.

Ellen's drive to Minnesota was the first time she had ever left the state. No one in the family even knew that she had taken this trip to Minneapolis. She was, after all, having a clandestine rendezvous with her soldier lover. She was an unmarried teacher in a small town of predominantly Catholic and Lutheran Norwegians and Germans. If word ever got out about Ellie's indiscretions with Robert—however virtuous her ultimate intentions—she would lose both her career and her reputation. After all, it hadn't been long since rural North Dakota teachers were threatened with firing, if they even loitered at the ice cream shop or didn't wear at least two petticoats. True, the rules of conduct for teachers had relaxed since 1923, but the moral standards for teachers during that time were still quite strict.

They met at the Chrome Motel in Minneapolis and pretended to be on their honeymoon. During their five-day stay during the first week of August, they rarely left their hotel room. They spent every possible moment with each other, lying naked in each other's arms, conversing, and making love. *If I could only stop time right here,* Ellen thought to herself, *I could die right in this moment. I could never love anyone the way that I have loved Robert.*

When Ellie reluctantly returned to Himmel after her rendezvous with Robert, she had hell to pay with her Grandmother. "I know dat you were out dere wit' Robert," Sigrid perceptibly concluded. "I'm not a fool, Ellie."

"I know, Grandmother. But I love him, and there's nothin' ya can say that'll change things now. I've given myself ta him, and he's goin' ta marry me, when he comes home," Ellie confidently declared.

Robert's ship left Charleston, South Carolina on August 14th, 1965. It took his unit almost an entire month to reach his base camp in An Khe, a village 42 miles west of Qui Non.

As Ellie struggled with launching the new school year, dealing with her overwhelming feelings of loneliness, and the realization that she was now one month pregnant with Robert's child, she vacillated between feelings of abandonment and hopefulness. *Perhaps this will soon be over, and Robert can return to me. We can carry on our lives as husband and wife.*

After the second full month of Ellie's pregnancy had progressed, it became increasingly harder to hide her state from her Grandmother. She finally admitted the truth to Sigrid. "What are you goin' ta do, now? Der is no husband ta support you."

Ellie considered the possibility of moving away for a short while. This way, she wouldn't have to risk losing her career, if she returned. She was faced with a dilemma. She was a single schoolteacher in a small town. And now she was two months pregnant. She needed her $400 a month checks to support her aging Grandmother. How could she manage?

Ellie finally penned her final letter to Robert during the first week of November, 1965. This was the letter informing her that she was, indeed, pregnant. She needed his help to get her out of this mess. She needed him to do the right thing and marry her now. Her unborn child needed legitimacy, and he needed a father. She could no longer wait for him, as they originally planned. Now was the time.

Unfortunately, *that* was the letter Robert never received. He was killed on November 14st , in the battle of Ia Drang Valley. Ellen was three months pregnant and visibly showing. She would no longer be able to hide her pregnancy in the sleepy little town of Himmel.

She was devastated. The only love of her life had been barbarically attacked and murdered half a world away. He had abandoned her and her unborn child. What's worse, she now desperately needed her job in Himmel. Her Grandmother relied on her small paychecks to support them. If news of her pending pregnancy were to slip out now, she would most certainly lose her job and her standing in the Himmel community.

As she struggled to make sense of her seemingly directionless life, she sank into an abysmal depression. For the first week, she ate almost nothing and walked through life in a fog. After the Army brought Robert's body back and his funeral was held, Ellie had the misfortune to meet Robert's despicable father, Stanley Peters.

And that is when Sigrid put her master plan into action.

Grandmother's plan was simple. It was a well-known fact that Stanley Peters was an opportunistic drunk. He would attend Robert's memorial service, making every effort to weasel his way into the Himmel community. Most likely, as the mourners met at Robert's mother's farm, Stanley would be left to wallow away his misery at the local tavern. He would have to stay in the small two-room motel in the center of town. This motel was conveniently close to the tavern. Ellen could meet Stanley at the bar, get Stanley drunk, and seduce him in his motel room. She could later convince Stanley that he had fathered her baby. He would be required to do the only respectable thing he could do, which was to marry her.

It was a simple plan, and Ellen carried out her grandmother's plan to the letter. She *did* meet him at the local bar, while he sobbed over his sixth glass of bourbon. And she also escorted him, half-conscious, to his hotel room. But what Ellie did not count on was the fact that Stanley's war injury had rendered him completely impotent. He could no longer perform sexually.

She was, in fact, pleasantly surprised that Stanley could not perform at all in the bedroom. She was prepared to seduce him, despite the fact that she found him repulsive. As a result, she did what any young and desperate, pregnant, young female in her position would do. She waited for Stanley to pass out on the bed and stripped him of all his clothing. Then she stripped down to her naked body, and slept next to him in his bed. When he awoke, hungover and devoid of any memory of the previous evening, she deceived him into believing that he had made passionate and unforgettable love to her. Two weeks later, she convinced him that he had impregnated her, and he quickly married her.

Those events preceded Ellen and Stanley's twenty-seven year marriage made in hell.

Now, of course, Ellie knew the *entire* truth. She was originally riddled with guilt over the thought that she had deceived Stanley into thinking that Stan Junior was his son.

In reality, he had read her letter to Robert even before they wed. He knew full well that Ellie had tried to pull the wool over his eyes—and over the eyes of the citizens of Himmel. But he played along with her charade. He was certain that his first wife had spread word of his impotency to all her trusted friends and family. Boasting that he had sired Ellen's son— his grandson—made him appear potent and virile. And despite Stanley's repeated denials that he ever cared what the people of Himmel thought of him, he—at the very least— wanted them to perceive him as masculine.

□□□□□□

"I'm sorry, Son. I wanted ta tell ya the truth sooner. I suppose, as time wore on and Grandmother Sigrid passed away, I worried more abote what people might've thought abote *yer* reputation than *mine*. Most 'o the time, it just seemed easier ta stay with Stan, even after yer great-grandmother tried ta convince me ta kick him ote.

"Ya probably know this now that ya have a little one, but ya try ta do right by yer kids. Ya try ta set a good example fer them. Truth is, they grow up however they're goin' ta grow up. Ya really haven't got much ta do with how they come ote. They are who they are. Ya just keep 'em fed and clothed and make 'em brush their teeth once in a while. Other than that, ya can only hope that they come back ta ya and don't hate ya fer makin' 'em do that stuff."

Stan sat completely silent, as he listened to his mother recount the story of his conception and the true identity of his father. After hearing Ellen's confession and her newly modified philosophy on child-rearing, all his pent-up anger over the events of the previous few weeks seemed to dissipate.

Ellie continued. "I hope ya don't hate me fer this, Son. Ya know I love ya. I want ya ta be happy."

"No, Mom," Stan assured her. "I don't hate you. I could never hate you." He paused thoughtfully. "Deep down I had always hoped that Stanley wasn't my real father. I think I secretly hoped that Robert—or someone like him—was my real father. I think that's why I named my own son after him."

He continued. "I'm kinda glad that Stanley is only my grandfather. Maybe that means the bad genes have been diluted out two generations." He chuckled, as he presented his theory to Ellen.

Ellie chuckled also. "Maybe so, Son. On the bright side, now that Stanley's dead, ya could change yer name ta whatever else ya want. Whatever ya decide is okee dokee by me." She smiled again, and patted her son on the cheek.

"Oh, and Son?"

"Yes, Mom."

"I want ya ta come live with me here in North Dakota. With Rosa and my two grandbabies." Ellie smiled.

"Grand*babies*?" Stan asked pointedly.

Ellen cringed, after she suddenly realized she had revealed Rosa's latest secret. "Ooops! I think I let the cat ote 'o the bag. Rosa's goin' ta kill me!"

Chapter 26

Marge Carter hurriedly whizzed past the reception counter of the Himmel County jailhouse. She dressed in a pair of jeans, a t-shirt, and flip flops. She wore no makeup, and her hair was scrunched up with a banana clip. She carried a plastic Ziploc baggie in her hand.

"I have urgent business with the Sheriff," she quickly informed the dispatcher. "I've only got a couple of minutes before Ellie gets back."

She made her way to Paul Baker's office. Paul stood to greet her.

"Hi, Marge. What brings ya here taday?"

"I haven't got time for small talk, Paul. I only have a few minutes before Ellie gets back. I have to stop by Larson's Grocer on the way home and pick up some cough drops," Margie snapped.

"In that case, what can I do fer ya taday?" the Sheriff inquired.

"Here's that disgusting lock of Grandmother's hair." She handed him the clear Ziploc bag with Ellie's recovered tuft of Sigrid's locks. "Do you have any idea how hard it is to sneak around in Ellie's room with that woman still in the house? My sister watches me like a friggin' hawk!

Paul examined the item, which Marge had delivered to him. "I can't thank ya enough, Marge. I'm much obliged."

"Sure, Paul. So now what?" Margie asked, resting her hands on her hips.

"I send this ta the crime lab, and we wait," he answered.

"Wait? Are you serious? How long will *that* take?"

"Two, maybe four weeks, tops."

"Four weeks??? I haven't got four weeks!" Marge was clearly upset.

Paul lifted his hand to quiet Marge. His deliberate manner seemed to have a calming effect on her. "Relax, Marge." He sat down at his desk. "Jim McDaniel has agreed ta delay his report until this toxicology report comes back. In the meantime, I will try ta expedite matters."

"I get it. Then what?" Marge asked.

"If the hair analysis shows that Sigrid was poisoned, we have probable cause ta search the house and exhume the body. Then we send it off ta Jim. But ya need ta make sure that ya don't get rid of that box of rat poison," Paul stated.

"But Grandmother's been dead for twenty-five years. Isn't it a bit late to be digging her up? What's left of her?"

"Skeletal remains, hair, teeth, and nails. People have been known ta dig up corpses a hundred years old ta see if they've been arsenic poisoned. There's no statute of limitations fer murder in North Dakota. As a matter of fact, I'm surprised that the Himmel Sheriff didn't do this back in '67. I suppose Stanley wasn't a suspect back then. Anyways, we wait. That's all we can do."

"And if you don't find anything?" Marge asked worriedly.

"We'll cross that bridge if we get there. Ya needn't fret over that now, Marge. Why don't ya head on over ta Larson's real quick? Ya do sound a bit hoarse. Are ya comin' down with somethin'? Paul probed.

"No, Paul. Just a lot of talking on the phone," she stated ambiguously.

"I'll bet." The Sheriff winked at Marge mischievously. "A lot of people lookin' ta make lefse these days, eh?"

"Yes, Paul. A lot of hungry, lonely, creepy guys."

Margie stood at the checkout counter of Larson's Grocer and Drug. She pushed ten boxes of Chloraseptic Throat Lozenges over to Agnes.

Agnes frowned. "Sore throat?"

Marge responded sarcastically. "How'd you guess?" Then she added apologetically. "Sorry, Agnes. I didn't mean to be fresh, but my throat is sore. I've been talking non-stop, and now I'm hoarse."

"Ya mean on the 900 line?"

"Yeah. Everybody wants a piece—of Ellie's lefse recipe."

"Oh," Agnes stated surprised. "I thought you and Ellie had a sexy chat line."

Now, *Margie* was surprised. She thought she and Ellie had done a good job of keeping the nature of the 900 line a secret. "Well, it is," she affirmed. "But Ellie doesn't want people in the town to know that."

"Oh. Too late fer than, hon.' Everybody in town knows abote it. Not too many secrets around here.'"

"Really?"

"Oh ya, sure. If it weren't fer gossip in Himmel, people wouldn't have anything ta talk abote."

"I see," Margie stated curiously.

Agnes's face lit up as she tried to change the subject. "Say, Bill has this fabulous cough syrup ya might be able ta use. Let's see if he can fix ya up."

Marge followed Agnes to Bill's pharmacy window, located in the rear of the grocery store. The pharmacy appeared empty. Agnes called for her husband, who popped his head out from behind a supply shelf in the back.

"Hon! Margie needs some of yer miracle throat cure."

"Oh sure. Too much talkin' on the phone, Marge?" He pointed to his throat.

Marge nodded. "Agnes seems to think you can fix me up."

Bill answered, "Oh, you betcha. Usually it's prescription only, but fer Ellie's sister, I can make an exception." He assembled the necessary tools to compound Marge's cough syrup as he spoke. "One spoonful of this elixir, and it'll knock that laryngitis right on its backside. Just give me a sec."

He pulled an empty glass cough syrup bottle off the shelf. Agnes stood in front of the druggist's window to keep Margie company while she waited for Bill to prepare his concoction. Sales were slow this time of day. There wasn't anyone in the store except for Marge, Agnes, and Bill.

"So, Agnes," Marge inquired curiously, "What else do you know?"

"What d'ya mean, Marge?"

"Well, I suppose—you owning a drug store and all—that you knew Stan's wife Rosa is pregnant?"

Bill stopped his stirring for a moment and raised his head. "We're not supposed ta talk abote that stuff, Marge. Patient confidentiality."

Agnes chimed in. "We sorta suspected, when she came in last week ta buy the EPT test."

"Hmmm," Margie responded thoughtfully. "—And I suppose you knew that Stanley was not Stan Junior's father?"

273

"Oh ya. We suspected that from the beginnin'. Stan Junior was born the same time my oldest son Andrew was born," Agnes answered. "Well, naturally we just assumed he might belong ta Robert," Agnes replied.

Marge found herself amused by the fact that Agnes seemed to know more about Marge's family than Marge seemed to. She decided to test Agnes.

"So, tell me, Agnes. Did you think that Stanley poisoned Grandmother?"

"Oh no, hon.' That took us by surprise. If *that's* true, Mrs. Olstad will be glad ta know that."

"Why would Mrs. Olstad be glad about Stanley poisoning Grandmother?" Marge asked, a bit puzzled.

"Now everyone can start eating her lutefisk again. Nobody ate it after yer grandmother died. Poor Mrs. Olstad. She really loved ta make lutefisk. She got a bad rap fer that one, don't cha know."

"I'm sure she did. Now tell me, Agnes. Did you hear that Ellie probably killed Stanley?"

Bill chimed in, as he affixed a label to Marge's brown syrup bottle. "I don't see why she didn't do him in sooner!"

Agnes scolded Bill. "Now, Bill!" She turned to Marge. "It's just that everybody loves Ellie, Marge. Ya certainly can't fault her fer takin' matters inta her own hands."

Marge agreed with Agnes, as she dug for more information. "Nope. Can't blame my sister a bit. You're right. But did you know he was frozen out in the barn all winter?"

"No. The auction was the first time we'd heard abote that," Agnes replied.

Margie paused a moment. She thoughtfully furrowed her brow. "So what about *me*, Agnes?"

"What abote ya, Marge?" Agnes looked a little puzzled.

"You know. What have you heard about *me*? Anything?"

In a perverted way, Marge relished the idea of being the subject of small town gossip. It was much better than being a forgotten nobody. She would much prefer being hated by every green-eyed woman in the town than to be invisible. Margie reasoned that, if she were the subject of town gossip, that would mean that at least *someone* in the town perceived her as interesting enough to spread rumors about.

But Marge was discovering during her cross-examination of Agnes Larson, that all Agnes's gossip was, indeed—true.

Agnes squirmed around uncomfortably, as Margie posed the question to her again. "I'm serious, Agnes. What have you heard about *me*? You can say it. You know I'm not embarrassed by anything. I don't care what people think of me."

Agnes blushed. "Ya mean the bit abote you and Jim McDaniel, the Medical Examiner in Bismarck? Oh gosh, Marge. Ya can't believe everything ya hear."

"Sure you can. What did you hear?" she probed.

"Oh, that ya slept with him ta tell ya abote Stanley's autopsy?"

"Yeah, that one. You don't think I might do some fool thing like that?" Marge asked amusedly.

Bill stepped out in front of the window and handed Marge her cough syrup. "Here ya go. Special fer Marge Carter."

"Oh, I get it," Marge commented. "You're just dancing around the topic, because you don't think Jim McDaniel would pick me up at a bar and make wild, passionate love to me."

"Nonsense, Marge. I didn't say that," Agnes shook her head.

"Ya could pick *me* up at a bar any day, Marge!" Bill remarked.

Agnes slapped Bill on the arm. She again scolded him. "Ya need ta watch yerself, Bill Larson! I'll not have ya harassin' the customers!"

Bill rubbed his sore arm. "I'm just sayin'. Marge is an attractive woman. Why wouldn't I pick her up at a bar?" He backpedaled a bit. "I mean….if I didn't have a sweet wonderful woman already waitin' fer me at home….."

Agnes glared at her husband, as he responded defensively, "What? I'm old, but I'm not dead, woman!"

Margie smiled, waving her newly made bottle of miracle elixir. "Thanks, Bill." She kissed him affectionately on the cheek. "Really, Bill. I mean it. Thanks a lot. I needed that." She winked at him flirtatiously, as she turned to leave. Agnes again glared at her spouse.

Marge exited Larson's Grocer and was encouraged by the sound of Agnes and Bill Larson arguing about her. Bill tried unsuccessfully to defend himself from his jealous wife's wrath.

"Don't ya be encouragin' Marge, now!" she snapped.

"What, I can't look? I said I'm sorry…"

"Ya better be sorry. Be careful, Bill Larson. Ya might lose that wanderin' eye!"

Marge closed the shop door behind her, as she whispered to herself, "I may be an old lady, but I still got it…"

It had been two weeks since Marge Carter delivered her Grandmother's lock of hair to Sheriff Baker's office. Marge sat at the kitchen table of the old farmhouse, speaking to a caller on the 900 line. When she heard a knock on the kitchen door, she called to Ellie. She held her palm over the receiver.

"Answer the door, would you, Ellie? And don't let them in. I'm on the phone!"

Ellie did as she was instructed. But when she answered the door, Sheriff Paul Baker and three police officers stood on the porch.

"Good morning, Miss Severtsen," Paul greeted. "May we come in?"

Ellie hesitantly let them in. "Sure, Paul. What brings ya here? Gosh, this looks like official business." She started to look worried.

He removed his hat, stepped in, and pulled out a folded piece of paper. "I'm afraid it is, Miss Severtsen. I have a search warrant fer yer property," he announced.

Marge spoke into the phone receiver. "I'm gonna have to call you back. Somebody's here. Okay, then. *You* call *me* back. I said that I can't talk right now!" She abruptly hung up the phone.

Paul looked over at Marge. "Marge, ya don't have ta hang up on *my* account. I won't be long."

"Can I ask you what you're looking for?" Marge inquired.

"Miss Severtsen, Marge—we have reason ta believe that yer grandmother was poisoned," Paul stated.

"Ya mean Grandmother Sigrid?" Ellie asked.

"Yes, ma'am," Paul replied. "We have reason ta believe that yer late husband Stanley may have poisoned her ta death."

He nodded to his two deputies, who each donned latex gloves and started searching the kitchen cupboards. He nodded to the third deputy. "Brad, search the upstairs."

Ellen was shaken. Marge put her arm around her sister's shoulder to offer her support. "I don't think I understand, Paul. What makes ya think Stanley poisoned Grandmother?" inquired Ellen.

Paul retrieve Stanley's book, *The Pale Horse*, from his vest pocket and offered his explanation. "Doris purchased this book, belonging ta Stanley at the auction three weeks ago. Do ya recognize this book?"

"Ya. It's one of Stanley's books," she replied.

He opened the book to reveal the writing scrawled on the back inside cover.

"And do ya recognize this handwritin'?"

"Oh, ya. It's Stanley's fer sure, Paul."

"Can ya read what it says, Miss Severtsen?"

"It looks like it says, 'Yum Yum Rat Vittles, Lootafish'—oh goodness, Stanley never was a good speller—'Kills a Norway Rat.'" Ellen looked at Paul, puzzled.

One of the Himmel deputies opened the cabinet beneath the kitchen sink. He knelt down and retrieved the box of rat poison. He called out to Paul, "Sheriff! Found it!"

Paul Baker took the box from his deputy. He read the box aloud. "*Yum Yum Rat Vittles*. Hmmm." He studied the package of rat poison. The packaging and the name seemed ironically harmless. Depicted on the front of the box were two cuddly and loveable rats, seated at a meal, with knife and fork in hand and napkins tied around their necks. To the right of the dining rodents was one dead rodent, sprawled out, with his eyes X'ed out.

Paul read the chemical ingredients of the box of twenty-five year old rodenticide. "Active ingredient: thallium." He held the box up to Ellie. "Miss Severtsen, how long ago did ya purchase this box of rat poison?"

Ellen stared at the box blankly. "Why, I didn't purchase it, Paul. Stanley bought that box years ago, when we were first married," she replied. "He said he had ta kill a Norway rat, hiding ote here—in the kitchen."

"And did ya ever see this rat?" Paul inquired.

"Why no."

"Do ya know what this reference ta 'lootafish' is all abote, Miss Severtsen?" Paul asked.

"I don't know, Paul. He did have Mrs. Olstad make lutefisk fer my grandmother. He took care of her, when she died."

"I see. Have ya had any since yer grandmother passed?"

"Oh, no. He threw all the pots and pans away and forbade it from bein' in the house." Ellen responded.

"One final question, Miss Severtsen. Did Stanley have reason ta kill yer grandmother?"

"She never really *did* like Stanley. She wanted me ta divorce him after Stan Junior was born. But Stanley was always so good ta her. I'm not sure why he'd want ta kill her, if he liked her so much."

"What woulda happened ta Stanley, if ya divorced him all those years ago like yer grandmother wanted?" Paul asked.

"I don't think Stanley woulda had anywhere ta go. He had no home and no job. He was disabled because of his war injury. Robert's mother had divorced him years before. I suppose he woulda been ote on his ear."

Just then, the deputy rummaging under the sink pulled out another item of interest—Ellie's bloody screwdriver. "Sheriff!" he yelled.

Paul shook his head at the deputy and motioned for him to put the screwdriver back under the sink. Perplexed, the deputy shrugged his shoulders and did as he was instructed.

"Well, Miss Severtsen, yer sister was kind enough ta be concerned abote yer Grandmother, when I showed her this book. She gave me yer Grandmother's lock of hair. I'm sorry ta say that we tested it, and it came up positive fer thallium poisoning."

Ellen turned pale. "Oh, my goodness..."

"Yes, ma'am. I'm afraid we have enough evidence here ta start an official investigation inta the death of yer grandmother. I suspect that yer late husband may have poisoned yer grandmother's lutefisk with this box of rat poison, and we need ta have the Coroner confirm whether or not that's true. We're goin' ta have ta get permission ta exhume her body. Will ya sign fer that?"

Marge nodded to her sister. "Yes, Paul. We'll sign whatever you need us to sign." She hugged her younger sister, who was clearly in shock about the whole ordeal.

Paul patted Ellie on the shoulder. "I'm sorry ta have ta break this sad news ta ya abote yer grandmother, ladies. I'll get Margie ta come down ta the station ta sign the papers."

Marge agreed. "Just let me know when." She suspiciously bit her lip. "Actually, the sooner the better. I seem to be running out of time."

He lifted his hat to the Severtsen sisters. "I want ta thank ya fer yer time, ladies. Feel free ta get back ta yer 900 chattin'."

After the Sheriff and his deputies left, Ellen stood in the kitchen, shaking. Marge again tried to comfort her.

"Goodness, Marge. I can't believe that Stanley would kill Grandmother," Ellie stated in disbelief.

Marge hugged her sister once more. "I know it's hard to believe, Ellie. But think about it. Have you ever known Stanley to be nice to *anyone*? Right there, you gotta know. If he was nice to Grandmother, he had to have *something* up his sleeve!"

YUM YUM RAT VITTLES ™

Kills Norway Rats

Active Ingredient: Thallium

Chapter 27

The Severtsen sisters had, once again, gathered around the kitchen table to engage in their lucrative business of answering their 900 numbers. Unlike other days, Ellie's line—1-900-OLD-LADYs—seemed to be ringing off the hook. Ironically, Margie's line seemed to be dead. She picked up the cordless handset to make sure that she still had a dial tone.

"Yep. I guess the phone's working," Margie remarked to herself. "Must just be the season for masochistic freaks. The average perverted schmoe doesn't seem to be calling today."

Ellie hung up her call. "Cheer up, hon.' Business'll pick up soon fer ya. They're probably just takin' a break."

Ellie's line rang again. She answered the line. Margie rose and walked to the fridge. She retrieved a roll of lefse and smeared a few slices with butter, while she eavesdropped on Ellie's call.

"Ooooh. Somebody's been a very naughty boy! I'm sure that if I told yer mother how ya had been behaving, she would be very disappointed in ya. Do ya want me to tell yer mommy how bad yah've been, or should I just take care of matters myself? ...That's right. Unzip yer pants and show me yer bare bottom. I'm givin' ya the spankin' of a lifetime fer that!" She started to relentlessly whack her lefse stick against the wooden table. As a matter of fact, Ellie's lefse stick had become more abused and worn than her pin.

She seems to be doing quite well with those calls, Margie thought to herself, as she stuffed her mouth with the delicious potato flatbread. *Actually, Ellie might be enjoying this **more** than her callers.*

She thought about Ellie' past relationship with Stanley. She then pondered the fact that Ellie was still the most likely murder suspect for his death. *I'm so glad the Sherriff isn't here to see her take this call. There would be little doubt in anyone's mind that she had killed Stanley, if they could see how much she seems to **like** pretending to be Elsa Dietrich.*

It was now the first week in July, exactly two months to the day that she and Stan Junior discovered Stanley's corpse in the barn. Stan Junior and his family had returned to Tucson over a month ago, despite Ellie's repeated pleas for him to stay.

And it had been three weeks since Paul Baker presented Ellie with the warrant to search the house. The following day, Margie granted the Medical Examiner permission to exhume the remains of her grandmother. Aside from the imminent results of the autopsy, Margie was still unsure about what Jim McDaniel's actual conclusion would be. She considered the thought that perhaps she had hampered justice by tampering with it. Maybe Jim would make things difficult for her out of spite for having been duped by her.

Margie wondered more about Jim McDaniel. She hadn't heard from him since she left the Medical Examiner's office, upset at his refusal to falsify the report. *Why did he have to be so stubborn? If I could've only persuaded him to help me out. If I could've only convinced him of what a horrible excuse for a human being Stanley Peters was.* As she contemplated her nonexistent relationship with Jim compounded by the sudden scarcity of 900 calls, she determined that perhaps her feminine wiles weren't what they used to be.

Even though she never admitted it to anyone, Margie considered the idea that maybe she *missed* Jim. She wouldn't go so far as to say she *loved* him, but she rarely admitted that to John—even though they had been married forty years. If Jim hadn't been so stubborn and hurt, they could've had something more. *Well,* she thought, *Maybe Paul can use his wiles to convince him to get both me and Ellie off the hook.*

Ellie concluded her call with one forceful snap of the lefse stick to the table. She practically screamed into the phone. "Now, I hope yer satisfied with yerself! Ya need to think abote what you've done. Don't call me, unless yer ready ta apologize!" She hung up the line, smiling almost evilly. This disturbed Marge a bit. Her jaw dropped, revealing the chewed up bits of flatbread still in her mouth.

Ellie looked up at her sister. "What, hon'. Somethin' wrong?"

Margie shook her head in disbelief. "No, Ellie dear. Nothing at all."

Just then, Margie's 900 line started to ring. She enthusiastically picked up the call, even before the second ring had finished.

"1-900-HOT-MAMA. This is Gabrielle. Tell me about your intimate fantasies."

Margie grinned from ear to ear, as she listened to the caller identify himself.

Ellie watched her sister intently, while Margie became suddenly perky. "Who is it, hon'? Is it *him*?" She now listened quietly to Marge's end of the phone conversation. She acknowledged that the caller on the line was, indeed—her estranged lover, Dr. Jim McDaniel.

Ellen had no clue what Margie's lover was actually saying to her. But she seemed to enjoy living vicariously through her older sister as Marge fielded her call. Ellie cheered her sister on and joyfully whispered. "Oh! I'm so glad fer ya, hon'!"

Jim McDaniel called Marge to inform her that he was about to issue his final report on the death of her grandmother. He concluded that Sigrid had been poisoned by thallium. This was supported by the trace metal hair analysis on the lock of hair Marge provided as well as the hair samples taken from her grandmother's exhumed body. He had concluded that the box of Yum Yum Rat Vittles, recovered from the Severtsen kitchen, was consistent with the exorbitantly high levels of thallium found in the hair shaft of Sigrid Severtsen. She was most likely poisoned by Stanley. He theorized that Stanley methodically tampered with the lutefisk Mrs. Olstad so thoughtfully prepared for his wife's dying grandmother, before serving it to her in bed.

Jim also stated that—in his expert opinion—Stanley must not have been too bright a criminal. Although he seemed to evade suspicion from members of the Himmel community by "killing Sigrid with kindness," he never once felt compelled to hide the murder weapon (the box of old rat poison) or his recipe for murder (his marked up copy of *The Pale Horse*). Jim also added that, prior to the EPA ban on thallium-laced rat poison in 1972, people were dropping like flies. In fact, thallium and its predecessor metal, arsenic, were sometimes facetiously known as "inheritance powder." He commented that, unless the killer's family and friends started mysteriously dropping dead, one after another, officials were not necessarily clued into anything suspicious. Often, the victim was dead before being reduced to seeking medical attention. And the murderer was usually in charge of the final disposition of the corpse. They would make every attempt to expedite burial as quickly as possible, before arousing suspicion about the true nature of the deceased's death.

Marge listened intently as Jim talked about Stanley's case. Then he spoke about Stanley's murder. He had also determined that, since Stanley had unquestionably murdered Sigrid, and since Stanley himself was now dead, the best thing for all parties involved would be to conclude that Stanley died in the barn "of accidental means". He hadn't derived the exact details of Stanley's "official death", but Jim stated adamantly that he would not mention the beatings with the lefse pin or the final death blow to the chest with the screwdriver. Ultimately, if there was no mention of foul play in the final report, there would be no murder investigation.

Upon hearing this, Marge heaved a great sigh of relief. Her little sister was no longer the prime suspect in Stanley's death, because officially Stanley wasn't killed. And Margie would no longer be faced with the dilemma of a false confession. "I don't know how to thank you enough, Jim. If it's worth anything, I'm sorry that I underestimated you. I'm truly grateful—for *everything*."

There was a short pause, as Jim changed the subject. He explained that he called Margie on the 900 line, because he still didn't know how to get in touch with her. He could have gotten her information from Paul, but he felt it less intrusive if he asked her personally. He wanted to see her again, and he wanted to come by to visit.

Marge immediately switched into flirtation mode. "Oh, and you're tired of paying $5.99 for the first five minutes and $.99 thereafter? ...So you want me to give you my home number? And my address?...Hmm, how do I know I can trust you?"

She teased Jim, but she finally consented to giving him her private home number and the farm address. He stated that he would be leaving his apartment shortly to come up and see her. In the meantime, she needed to "get rid of her kid sister," so they could engage in some (as he put it) "long-overdue naked wrestling."

"Okay, Jim. I'll see you in an hour. Drive fast!"

As she hung up the line, Ellen clapped for her sister once again. "Oh, Marge. He's comin' ta see ya now?" she inquired.

"He'll be here in about an hour," Marge answered. "Say, Ellie..."

Ellie interrupted, giddy with excitement for her sister. "—Say no more, hon.' I'm goin' ta town." As she walked to the door, she turned to Margie and hugged her. "Really, hon', I'm so happy fer ya!"

Although she was unaware of the details which eventually reunited Margie and Jim, Ellen was happy for her sister. She thought to herself. *Margie has finally found someone who will make her happy. She had been so lonely after John died.* She borrowed the Lincoln to make her trip to town. *Margie doesn't need me in her hair,* she thought. *She needs time alone with her new beau.*

She turned from the entrance to the driveway onto the main road and noticed an abandoned pickup on the side of the highway. She also noted that the pickup had North Carolina plates, with the slogan "first in flight." It looked as though the owner left his truck there and walked back to town. Ellen kept her eye out in the distance for any wandering hitchhikers.

She considered the North Carolina plates on the car. She had never seen North Carolina plates and pondered the "first in flight" slogan. For a moment, she reminisced about her students at Himmel Elementary. Ellen had often read them stories about the first flight of Wilbur and Orville Wright. *It's nice that an entire state would be able to take ownership of the accomplishments of two such creative boys*, she thought. She continued her diversion to town, as her thoughts turned again to Margie and her lover. *I would certainly love to meet this doctor, if Margie ever introduces me.*

An hour later, Margie waited anxiously for Jim McDaniel to meet her at the farm. She dressed casually in her blue jeans and t-shirt, but she powdered her face and put on a fresh coat of makeup. *After all, I don't want to appear too desperate. Pretty but casual is the best look for now*, she thought. She also tried not to gaze out the window too impatiently. She had determined that she would go about her daily routine and wait for Jim to knock on the door when he arrived.

Fifteen more minutes passed, before Margie heard footsteps on the front porch. She waited a few more minutes, expecting to hear a knock on the kitchen door. A little while longer there was still no knock. *I was sure that I heard someone out on the front porch*, she thought. Marge began to feel a bit paranoid.

As a precaution, she grabbed up the first potential weapon she could find—Ellie's lefse pin. She finally ventured out the kitchen door to the porch. "Jim?" she called. "Are you playing with me? Jim? C'mon, Jim. I know you're out here! You know I'm much too old to be playing these games. I'm an elderly woman. What if I fall and break a hip?"

She decided to step off the porch and search around back. *He has to be hiding from me. I heard him just minutes before.*

The moment she stepped off the front porch, someone had grabbed her from behind. He had his arm wound tightly around her neck, pulling him close to her. In fact, his grip was so tight, she realized he was seriously trying to choke her.

"Let go, you moron!" she gasped. "Jim, this is not funny!" She uttered these words, as her assailant tightened his grip around her neck even more forcefully. He coldly whispered into Margie's ear, as he pulled her closer to his breast.

"Nice ta see y'all agin' Miss Gabrielle. 'Member mae?"

Marge's eyes widened in fear. This wasn't Jim McDaniel who held her in the chokehold. But she *did* recognize the man's voice. "Jack?" she asked, terrified.

He roughly yanked her hair, as he spoke to her from behind. "Oooh, yer good, Miss Mawrgie. That *is* yer name, raght? Mawrgie?" While Jack spoke to Marge, he yanked periodically on her ponytail to emphasize his point. "It seems y'all pulled the wool over mah eyes. I thote you was young lady. Come ta find owt, you was older than my mawmaw. Nice o' y'all's sister ta teyall me 'bout where'n y'all liahved…."

"Ellie," Marge stated weakly, all the while gasping for breath. She dropped Ellie's lefse pin on the ground beside her.

"That har name? I thote it war Miss Dahtrick, er somethin'. Nice ta knaow. I guess she'n is gownna be neahxt." He yanked on her hair once more.

Marge had always suspected during her phone conversations with Jack that he had the makings of a serial killer. Her only consolation was that Jack had no idea where she lived. And now she knew that her little sister had unknowingly sold her out to this guy, who most certainly intended to kill both her *and* Ellie.

But Margie hadn't lived for thirty-five years in Florida without being a little crafty to the ways of the average serial killer. Jack had called her, because he found her sympathetic. She determined to talk her way out of this predicament. *Get 'em to sympathize with you. Make them understand there's a human being behind the face, and it'll be harder for them to kill you.*

"Okay, okay," Marge acquiesced. "I admit. I lied to you. If you just let me go, I can explain, Jack."

"Oh, no. Ah weyall nawt let y'all take advantage o' me like thaht. I kin see raght trhough y'all."

"No, Jack," Margie assured. "You don't know anything. You don't know how *I* feel about *you*. I *made* Ellie tell you where I lived. I *wanted* you to come see me." Her face was beet red, as she struggled to speak and inhale small gasps of air. "Just let me go, Jack. I'll show you what I mean." He had held his grip for so tightly so long, her consciousness was beginning to fade to black.

"Yew prahmise? No funny stuhff?"

Margie nodded. She was no longer able to speak.

"Ah meyan it. If y'all try somethin'. Ah'll fuckin' kihll ya!"

Margie nodded again.

He slowly released his grip and stepped back. Marge heaved in a desperate gulp of air, taking in several deep, wheezing breaths. She leaned against the porch rail, while she slowly regained her senses.

She struggled to reoxygenate her brain, while she surveyed her current situation. She could not lose her sense of reason. She had to remain calm. Ellen had taken the Lincoln. It seemed hopeless. There was no means for Margie to escape. The only tool she had at her disposal was Ellie's lefse pin, which lay on the ground beneath her feet.

However, it was apparent that her assailant also had no vehicle nearby. Therefore, he had no immediate means of escape. She figured that he must have parked his car somewhere remotely. She clearly had two choices: she could sweet talk Jack into letting her go, or she could render him physically unable to make chase. She would try the former, relying on the latter option as a Plan B.

Margie stood for several minutes, while she tried to stall Jack and assess her options. Then she turned to him.

"You know, Jack. I have a *lot* of callers call me. All kinds of guys. But there is *nobody* like you." She moved toward him and caressed his cheek. "You're special." She tried to seem believably infatuated with him. But in reality, it was more than Margie could do to keep from puking in his homely face.

"I mean, you're so *handsome*. I can't believe you don't have a girlfriend. Why is that? Your momma probably doesn't think the kind of girls you bring home are good enough for you?"

John Jacob pushed Marge's hand away, disgustedly. "Mah mawmma don't like nothin' nowadays. That's rahgtly 'cause she's deahd."

"Oh, you poor baby," Marge stated sympathetically. "She passed away?"

"Ah kihll'd her—just lahk Ah'm gonna kihll yew!"

As Jack approached Marge once more, she bent down to quickly scoop up Ellie's lefse pin. She grabbed it by its red wooden handle and wound it behind her head, striking John Jacob forcefully on his forehead. He reeled in pain, holding his noggin in his hand. Then she whacked him again, seven or eight times. All the while, he shielded himself defensively from her relentless blows. As she furiously wailed on his skull and forearms, he screamed in wild pain. She thought to herself. *This must be what Ellie felt like when she whacked off ole' Stanley.* Finally, she swung the pin behind her underhandedly, so she could lay one hard and desperate shot to the groin.

Unfortunately, John Jacob had anticipated this move and managed to grab the pin away from Marge. She was now without a weapon. The lefse pin was her only approximate means of self-defense. She fled out toward the barn, as fast as her legs could carry her. Perhaps if she equipped herself with one of the old rusty tools left there, she could disable Jack.

Regrettably for Margie, her flight to the barn wasn't really much of a chase at all. Despite a bruised noggin, the wiry and spry John Jacob caught up with her within fifty feet. He dropped the lefse pin, and grabbed her around the neck once more. Then he tightly wound her ponytail around his hand and dragged her another hundred feet out to the barn.

Once again, Marge tried to plead for her life. "Please, Jack! Don't do this! I know you didn't mean to kill your mother. And you don't want to kill me."

Furious, John Jacob struck Margie with a closed fist to the side of her skull. "Shuht up, bihtch! Don't sahy another wohrd! Ah'm gonna fuckin' kihll yew!"

He said nothing more, but brutally dragged her off to the open doors of the empty barn. He threw her prostrate on the ground. She pleaded again with her face in the dirt. "Please, Jack. I don't wanna die."

He grabbed the fifty foot spool of heavy-duty rope and threw the entire weight of his body onto Marge's back. John Jacob was only 145 pounds, but he pounced on her so savagely that the force completely knocked the breath from her.

He ruthlessly tied her hands behind her. Then he hoisted her weak, but still conscious body up by a beam of the loft and secured the opposite end of the rope by a hook on the barn door. She whimpered and pleaded for her life, but she was now bereft of energy. "I'm going to die here all by myself," she murmured to herself.

While she sat there, weak and hopeless, Marge heard the sound of a car pulling up. *Oh, my God, she thought. Ellie is here!* But then, when she considered the hopelessness of her situation and the potential danger to her sister, she screamed out as loudly as her lungs could manage. "Ellie! Go get the Sherriff! Don't come in here! He's gonna kill us!"

"Whah yew bihtch!" Again, John Jacob struck Marge with a closed fist. "Yew keehp yore fuckin' mouhth shuht!" He marched over to the far edge of the barn and grabbed a large, rusty shovel. He hid behind the open barn door, waiting for Marge's rescuer to approach.

Marge hung there, still suspended by her wrists and battling the blinding sunlight through the open barn doors. A figure appeared in the distance. It approached through the open barn doors. She struggled to make out the silhouette approaching from beyond the blinding sunlight. Tears and dirt also hampered her vision. Squinting, she realized it was Jim. He had finally arrived and heard her cries from the barn.

"Jim! Behind you!"

Before Jim could see who was behind him, John Jacob had struck him once on the back of the head with the rusty shovel and knocked him unconscious.

Twenty minutes later, Jim McDaniel regained consciousness. He found himself also suspended by his wrists from a beam in the loft of Marge's barn. Marge still hung a few feet down from him. She was desperate and hysterical and called to Jim to get him to wake up. She tried to persuade Jack not to hurt him. "Take *me*, Jack. You don't need him. He doesn't mean anything to me now. Let him go."

But her efforts were to no avail. John Jacob stood, coldly ignoring her, as he honed a rusty scythe blade with a whetstone. He methodically and rhythmically sharpened the blade, lost in his own bloodthirsty rumination.

Marge glanced over at her lover, as Jim slowly regained his wits. Her wrists were now raw, and she continually struggled to free herself of her bonds. Her face was bruised and bloody. Yet Jack stood, undeterred by her suffering and struggles, even as Jim regained consciousness.

John Jacob looked up at Jim, now aware that his second victim had come to his senses. "Look's lahk Miss Margie gowt a bowfrehnd," he stated calmly. He lifted the scythe blade to Jim's chin, smiling to reveal the fifty cent gap between his two front teeth. "Y'all look awful pertty. Come fer a dahte?

Hmmm." He studied his adversary in love. Then he studied the certain look of terror in Margie's eyes, as he smiled.

"Aw, Ah git it! She lahks yew." John Jacob nodded decisively and winked at Jim. "Then she's gownna luhv it when ah kihll yew fuhrst!" He held the scythe blade close to Jim's throat, grazing his flesh. He pursed his lips, as he studied the small drop of blood dripping down his victim's neck. Then he wiped Jim's blood off the tip of his blade with his index finger and licked his bloody fingertip. He examined the shimmer of the blade more intently.

"Naw, this is tew ruhsty." He picked up a ball peen hammer and a twelve-inch block of wood, holding the blade in his hands. John Jacob looked around the barn, shaking his head. Marge knew, from having watched Anders peen the scythe, that he was looking for something to sit on. The five gallon paint can wouldn't work for peening. Father had determined that the best peening stool for a rusty scythe blade was the old stump out back.

Margie spoke up, hoping that he would pay enough attention to hear. "There's a stump out back. You can sharpen that thing out there!"

John Jacob smiled at Margie. "Aw, ah git it! Mahybe yer tahred of this wuhn after awl? Er Mahybe yew jest don't wahnna prolongh his sufferin'? Tsk, tsk, tsk." He shook his head, as he sadistically snickered to himself. "Ah'll bae bahck. Don't yew trah nothin', ya hare?" He marched out the barn doors with tools in hand, as he headed for the old tree stump.

Jim had now fully regained his senses, as he glared at Marge in disbelief. "You trying to *help* him kill me better?" he asked sarcastically.

"Shut up!" Margie whispered urgently. "We gotta get each other loose before he gets back! Don't make any noise."

John Jacob had suspended both Marge and Jim by a beam of the loft. They were both tied by their wrists, at either end of one long length of rope. Marge propelled her body closer to Jim's by pushing her feet against a nearby beam. "This is all one rope. If you get me free, we'll both fall down."

"What am I supposed to use?" Jim asked skeptically.

"Try pushing yourself toward me. I will wrap my legs around your waist, and we can try to untie each other," she commanded.

As Marge once again pushed herself off, Jim swung his legs back and forth. "Wait," he stated. "We need to count, so we get together at the same time. Ready? One, two, three...."

Finally, they met at the center of the beam, from which they were suspended. Margie wrapped her legs around Jim's waist to hold him in place. Still, their wrists were five feet apart, suspended above them on the beam. Their hands would not reach.

"That's definitely not gonna work for us," Jim quipped. "Although I do like the sensation of having your legs wrapped around my waist again. This is a pretty good way to go. I mean—if you're gonna get cut open wide by a serial killer."

"Shut up, idiot. I'm not about to give up yet," Margie snapped. She countered more humbly. "I'll bet you're sorry you showed up here."

"Hey, if you're gonna die, you might as well die with the woman you love." Despite the desperateness of their current situation, Jim said this all matter-of-factly.

"Wait a minute. Did you say that you *loved* me?" Margie asked.

"Sure," said Jim. "You could say I was about to fall to pieces about the whole break up. Well—maybe *cut* to pieces is a better choice of words." He chuckled inappropriately.

For fifteen more minutes, Marge and Jim exhaustively tried to maneuver themselves free of their bondage. In fact, they had become completely oblivious to the whereabouts of Jack. While they made one last heated attempt to free their wrists of the rope, they plummeted five feet to the ground below.

They looked up to see that John Jacob stood above them, with a fully peened and sharpened scythe. He had used his sharpened blade to cut the rope free. He now stood with a demented and murderous expression. "Ah jest give y'all a lihtlle hand thehr," he stated, menacingly.

Marge had fallen face first onto the ground below, as the wind had once again been knocked from her lungs. But Jim had fallen on his backside and was still reeling from the painful impact to his lower spine. His wrists were still bound in front of him.

John Jacob lifted the scythe above his head, as Marge screamed. Knowing that he would soon be sliced to bits, Jim lifted his bound hands to reflexively shield himself from the blow. Jack flung the scythe blade at his stomach, leaving a one-half inch deep gash across the width of his abdomen. He had sliced through Jim's white cotton shirt, which was quickly becoming soaked with blood.

"Heh. Thawght ah was gohnna kihll y'all raght then, huh? Naw. That was jest prahctice!" Jack laughed demonically, reveling in his perversion.

Once more, John Jacob raised the scythe above his head. Jim cringed. Marge lifted her face up and screamed as she watched John Jacob's expression. His once cold, lifeless eyes had transformed into those of a bloodthirsty predator. Still helplessly bound, she could only watch as he raised the blade in the air and laughed.

The moment John Jacob started to bring his weapon down on Jim for one final blow, they heard a gunshot blast. John Jacob bolted backward, dropping the scythe behind him, as he fell to the ground. His eyes were still wide open, frozen with a look of pure evil. And between his eyes lay the entrance wound from a single gunshot.

Marge and Jim turned and squinted through the sunlight and the open barn doors. An image stood at the entrance, brandishing a firearm. It was Ellie. She had shot John Jacob between the eyes using Stanley's prized World War II rifle.

"Oh my God, it's you, Ellie!" Margie cried out in absolute relief.

Ellie marched into the barn, still charging with the rifle. She walked over to the lifeless body of John Jacob Harvey and kicked it hard in the ribs. She bent down to examine his face.

"That was Jack!" Margie cried hysterically. "He was so gonna kill us! Ellie! You saved our lives!"

Realizing that John Jacob Harvey was now dead, Ellie lowered her firearm. She studied his face and his frozen, evil expression. She sympathetically patted him on the cheek as she spoke to his lifeless corpse in an almost angelic voice.

"Looks like Jack has been a very naughty boy, eh?"

Chapter 28

> "Now, you just wait for it to cool and eat. Dat's all der is to it. I knew you could do it, Ellie. You were always my favorite. Some of de udders—Well, let's say dey don't have de Norwegian in dem. But you, Ellie, you are a Severtsen t'rough and t'rough. You can carry on Grandmodder's recipe and de Norwegian tradition." SIGRID SEVERTSEN

When news broke out that the town of Himmel had been visited by and delivered from the murderous grasp of serial killer John Jacob Harvey, the townsfolk were both panicked and relieved. Ellie had shot Margie's stalker and freed her sister and Dr. McDaniel, who immediately called the Sheriff out to investigate. Paul Baker noted John Jacob's deserted vehicle one mile down the highway and quickly traced the truck's plates back to North Carolina. One quick phone call to the Mecklenberg County Police Department revealed that John Jacob—or Jack, as he was commonly known—was at large in his home state. He had brutally slain his elderly mother three weeks prior, having mercilessly strangled her with a coiled telephone cable in her Pineville home. He was also suspected in several unsolved murders and missing persons cases in and around the city of Charlotte.

Ellen was quickly exonerated for having killed John Jacob Harvey. In fact, because she had rescued her older sister and the Medical Examiner (a State Official) from the clutches of a murderer, she was now regarded as a town celebrity.

Despite Ellie's previous attempts to hide the nature of her 900 business from the respectable people of Himmel, she decided it was no longer necessary to continue with her charade. During the events of recent months, Ellie realized that there really wasn't anything she had done to fool the crafty citizens of her hometown. They seemed to love her no matter what. Margie's influence had taught her one very important lesson: one should always be true to oneself. If one does that, happiness and love will follow.

Both Marge and Jim had witnessed Ellie's shooting of John Jacob Harvey. But there was still some shred of doubt about whether Ellen had truly murdered her late husband. Either she didn't recall killing Stanley, or perhaps she *did* remember but chose to lie about it. There was also the unlikely third possibility that someone *else* had murdered Stanley. It seemed no one in the town really knew for sure who killed Stanley Peters. But then, it was all too clear that no one in the town really cared.

In any event, all the authorities involved concluded that, since Stanley was a proven killer himself, justice would be better served if the case was reported as accidental and simply dropped. Jim McDaniel issued his final report. Paul Baker closed the case. There were no objections to this chosen course of action from the good people of Himmel. And there were definitely no objections from either Stanley's grandson (Stan Junior) or the Severtsen sisters. It was decided by all that the sooner people could move on with their boring lives and forget about Stanley Senior, the better. Once again, life was good in the sleepy little North Dakota town.

The following month of August, Stan Junior returned with his family to live with his mother in Himmel. He had secured employment with Mr. Heinle's Appliance Company, determined to keep the friendly folks of Himmel County warm throughout the blasting cold winters. More than likely, Rosa would see her first blizzard ever the coming winter. She was going to have to acclimate herself to this particularly cold climate. But she considered this a small price to pay for the luxury of having a satisfied husband and two willing babysitters close by to take care of her growing family.

In addition, Margie expanded the 900 business to include another line for Rosa—1-900-HOT-ROSA. Through her newly established line, Rosa catered to Hispanic callers, while she spoke to them in their native Spanish. Even though Stan Junior could not understand what she said to her callers, he no longer seemed to mind that she talked about sex all day. When she returned to the bedroom after a hard day at work, he happily realized that an entire day of phone calls made his wife pretty horny. Rosa could wake Stan up at any hour of the day or night, and he was perfectly content to cater to the needs of his young wife's increased libido.

After the dust settled from the events of the previous summer, Stan presented Sheriff Baker with his grandfather's set of Revolutionary War pistols. Although Paul was cautious that such an expensive gift might be perceived as a bribe, Stan argued that Paul had done a great deal for his mother as a citizen of Himmel—*not* as a law enforcement officer. His grandfather's and great-grandmother's murder cases had now been closed, and there was no way he should consider this gift a bribe. Paul and Doris had always looked out for Ellen. In addition, Stan explained that his recent discovery about his father's true identity rendered the need for keeping a memento of Stanley Senior obsolete.

After their near-death experience with serial killer John Jacob Harvey, Marge and Jim grew closer as a couple. Pretty soon, they spent every moment they could in each other's company. Jim usually visited Marge at the farm in the evening, while she answered her 900 line. He sat on the kitchen chair and Margie perched herself on his lap. As she carried on her conversation with her callers, she would simultaneously whisper her sexy words into Jim's ear. He could only stand about thirty minutes of this verbal foreplay. In between calls, he would whisk Margie off to the bedroom, where the entire household learned to ignore Marge's deafening screams of ecstasy which echoed throughout the old farmhouse.

Ellen Severtsen was blissfully happy to have her son, daughter-in-law, grandson, and favorite sister all living under her roof. True, she was a now a widow. But with her loved ones close by, she could face any obstacle. She had a successful business to keep her occupied, and she had the undying support of her fellow members of the Himmel community to sustain her. In addition, she continued to knit, assemble quilts, and—with her sister's assistance—make numerous batches of lefse for mass consumption.

One day in late August, the Severtsen sisters, Stan, Rosa, and Jim McDaniel gathered around the small kitchen table of their old farmhouse. The women answered their respective phone lines. As was the custom, Marge answered her line 1-900-HOT-MAMA, seated on Jim's lap. Little Robert clumsily hobbled his first infantile steps across the kitchen floor. Ellie brought a generous plate of lefse to the table, upon which they were about to feast.

She almost sat down, when she heard a knock on the kitchen door. She stepped over to the door to answer it. Recognizing the figure standing behind the screen, she smiled. It was William Knutson. He held a large bouquet of sunflowers in his arm. He stood in a Navy blue suit and was neatly groomed.

"Hello, Miss Ellie. I know I came by unannounced, but—well, I brought ya somethin'."

William handed Ellie the oversized bouquet of sunflowers, while they stood in the entryway. She studied the bouquet carefully. He had obviously picked the flowers from someone's farm. He had meticulously tied the arrangement up by lovingly winding twine all the way around the stems.

Touched, Ellie began to tear up. "Oh, goodness. This is sweetest thing anyone has ever given ta me," she remarked. "Thanks so much, William."

"I was tryin' ta decide what kind of flower ta get ya. 'What would Miss Ellie like?,' I asked myself. As I thought abote it, I thought ya kinda reminded me of a sunflower. It's a very happy flower. There are sunflowers all over the state. And it kinda seems like they're all the same. But really, every flower is very special. That's kind 'o how ya are ta me, Miss Ellie."

Ellie simply smiled and lifted the bouquet to her nose. "Ya look awfully nice, William. Are ya wearing yer church clothes?"

"Sure. I stopped hangin' ote at the Tradin' Post so much. I know how ya feel abote drinkin'. Ya know, because of Stanley and all."

William continued, "I wasn't sure if ya were ready fer gentleman callers. I know yer husband hasn't been dead very long. But—well, let's face it, Miss Ellie—I've wanted ta date ya my entire life. Ever since we were in school tagether. It's just ya were either too young or datin' Robert or married ta Stanley. And that wouldn't o' been right fer me ta try and date someone who was already spoken fer. But I'm fifty-five, Miss Ellie. And honestly, I'm running ote o' time."

"What are ya sayin', William?" Ellie was clearly flirting with William as he continued his romantic overtures.

"I'm sayin' I'd like ta court ya, if I can, Miss Ellie. I mean, if yer willin'."

Ellie paused thoughtfully. She placed her hand on William Knutson's shoulder and leaned over to kiss his cheek. "Well, ya—I'm ready as I'll ever be, William. But I gotta warn ya. We have this respectable business goin' in here, and I don't need any man tryin' ta get in the way of our success."

"'Course not, Miss Ellie. I would never stand in the way o' yer success." He peeked behind her at the family, gathered at the kitchen table. "Did I interrupt somethin'?"

"Not at all, William. We're sittin' down to a nice big plate of lefse. Would ya like ta join us?" Ellen invited.

"Ya don't need ta ask *me* twice, Miss Ellie!" William joyously exclaimed. "Everybody loves yer lefse!"

Author's Acknowledgements and Notes
Acknowledgements:

I would like to thank the following authors for providing me
with resources for the facts included in this work of fiction.
Their books gave me a great deal of insight into the daily life,
sacrifices, and hardships of both our soldiers and our teachers.

Gietzen, William Russell—   A *Dakota Boy Goes to War*
                              A *Dakota Boy at War*
Moore, Harold G. and Galloway, Joseph L.—*We Were*
                              Soldiers Once...And Young
Ziniel, Elfreda—   *The Little White School Houses*
                              on the Prairie

Notes to the Reader:
The town of *Himmel, North Dakota* is a complete fabrication.
Any attempt to find it on a map would be futile. The word
"himmel" translates from the Nordic and German words
meaning "heaven".
Bubba Q's and *Yum Yum Rat Vittles* are also completely
fictional. If you want great barbeque in Bismarck, try Famous
Dave's (but they weren't around in 1993). If you're trying to
find a thallium-laced rat poison, shame on you!

yum yum Rat vitties

roorefish

Kils A NORMy
RAT

L. Lee Starr is a multi-talented writer, publisher, and songwriter, who has lived in Saint Louis, Missouri for the past 14 years. She has earned bachelor's degrees in Psychology and Health Sciences. She currently works as Medical Laboratory Scientist for Barnes-Jewish Hospital in Saint Louis.

In 1994, she published a musical work entitled *No Secrets* under the pseudonym *A. Pariah*. In 2003, she recorded a CD of original Christian songs entitled *Metamorphosis* under her married name, Lois Prettyman. In addition to her musical interests, she performed in community theatre, informally studied art, designed works of stained glass, and ventured out into making hot glass beads in a profession known as lampwork.

Ms. Starr grew up in rural Connecticut, the daughter of an American father and her Korean mother, who immigrated to the U.S. in 1964. She moved to Avon Park, Florida in 1981 with her father and stepmother, where she met and married her current husband of 29 years, Joe Prettyman. She has one daughter, Ariel, who also lives in Saint Louis.

1-900-OLD-LADYs is her second book with Mystic Hippo Media Publishing. Her first release, entitled *Séance at the Lemp*, is also available on through Amazon, Smashwords, and www.mystichippo.com. She is currently working on an illustrated children's book entitled, *Huggily Buggily and the Magical Fart of Wind*, which is due for release at the end of 2012.

To find out more about her upcoming projects, please log on to www.mystichippo.com.